CW01633178

DEATH ON THE ELBE

KJ JULIAN

WOODBRIDGE
PUBLISHERS

Forest House, 3rd Floor 16-20
Clements Road Unit #2048
Ilford, IG1 1BA

Copyright © 2025 KJ Julian

ISBN (Paperback): 978-1-918130-34-8
ISBN (Hardback): 978-1-918130-33-1
ISBN (eBook): 978-1-918130-35-5

All rights reserved

This novel is entirely a work of fiction. The names, characters and incidents portrayed in it are the work of the author's own imagination. Any resemblance to actual persons, living or dead, locations or events is purely coincidental.

No part of this publication may be reproduced, stored in a retrieval system, copied in any form or by any means, electronic, mechanical, photocopying, recording or otherwise transmitted without written permission from the publisher. You must not circulate this book in any format.

Cover Design by Woodbridge Publishers.

To Pete and Steve, my Runes' readers.

Elegant Elbe and Berlin

Join Sovereign River Cruises as we sail along one of Europe's most unspoiled rivers. The Elbe is waiting to transport you on a magical journey from Berlin to Prague.*

Your journey begins with a two-night stay in a luxurious hotel in the centre of cosmopolitan Berlin, reunified and reborn after a decades-long postwar separation. Join our knowledgeable guides on excursions to the Brandenburg Gate, the Holocaust Memorial, Unter den Linden, Museum Island, the Reichstag, remnants of the wall which encircled West Berlin and Checkpoint Charlie.

As you bid 'auf Wiedersehen' to Berlin, you will travel by luxury coach to Potsdam to visit the beautiful Sanssouci Palace, a miniature Rococo masterpiece built as Frederick the Great's summer palace and Schloss Cecilienhoff, the former Hohenzollern family residence where Churchill, Truman and Stalin met to determine the political future of Europe in 1945.

From there, you will embark your ship, and the wonders of the Elbe will unfold as you cruise its elegant waters. Walk in Martin Luther's footsteps in Wittenberg, birthplace of the Protestant Reformation; be surprised with what you might see in the moat of Schloss Hartenfels in Torgau; watch as skilled artisans produce 'white gold' at the Meissen porcelain factory; be astonished by the majesty of Dresden, a phoenix risen from the ashes of war, before the spectacular sights of Saxon Switzerland – Bad Schandau and the Bastei – take your breath away.

All this within the regal splendour of your Floating Palace – the MV Baron von Habsburg. Fine dining, exquisite wines, spacious accommodation, attentive staff, sumptuously decorated public areas, we guarantee you the all-inclusive, ultra luxurious, six-star experience of a lifetime.

And, at the end of the cruise, you will travel to Prague, Czechia's atmospheric capital on the Vltava. A city of medieval, Romanesque, Baroque and Art Nouveau structures, such as the Astronomical Clock, the Old-New Synagogue, the iconic Charles Bridge and Prague Castle, with its rich tapestry of royal and ecclesiastical buildings, awaits your visit.

**Note on selected sailing dates, we will travel from Prague to Berlin.*

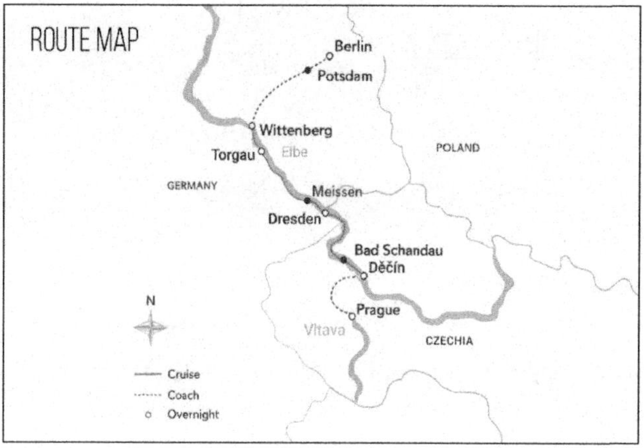

[Pages 42-44, Sovereign River Cruises – 2026 Brochure]

Baron von Habsburg
Built 2020
Length 108m
Cabins 46
Crew 34

<u>Top deck: Sun Deck</u>
From bow: open deck area with loungers/wheelhouse/Spa Pool/loungers and chairs (some under cover)/chess set/crew area in stern
stairways to/from Portcullis Lounge in bow on both sides and to/from Reception Area on both sides near Wheelhouse

<u>Buckingham Deck</u>
From bow: Portcullis Lounge (open 10 to late), including some seats outside and stairways to/from Sun Deck/coffee machine/reception area, inc. loos/external stairways to/from Sun Deck, and internal stairs down to Sandringham Deck
on port side – Royal Suite 201; Luxury Balcony Suites – odd numbers 203 to 235; Hotel Manager's cabin

on starboard side – Royal Suite 202; Luxury Balcony Suites – even numbers 204 to 236; Captain's cabin
in stern – small open area – smoking permitted

<u>Sandringham Deck</u>
From bow: Coronation Restaurant and galley/ internal stairs up to Buckingham Deck/Standard Staterooms with picture windows – 101 to 110/ Golden Crown Spa/ me and rest of crew in tiny little cabins/ storerooms/engine room

No locks – river very shallow
Staying at King Charles Hotel in Prague
90 minutes' drive to Děčín to board ship
Leave ship at Wittenberg, drive to Potsdam, and then to Grand Duchess Hotel Berlin
Memo from head office – call all suites and staterooms 'cabins', and 'guests', not 'passengers'

[Notes made by Mary Mead – June 2026]

1

Miss Mary Mead

Meet Miss Mary Mead, murder mystery aficionada. Anyone from Agatha Raisin to Agatha Christie and anything with 'Murder' or 'Paradise' in its title; she read them all and she watched them all. Usually more than once.

Mary was a native of Bury St Edmunds. She was born there, in the spring of 2001, she had been educated there from nursery school through to college, and she still lived with her parents in Cattishall.

Mary played netball, Wing Defence despite being only five feet four inches tall, for the Bury Barnstormers in the West Suffolk Netball League and was a regular attendee at the local Gym'll Fix It. And she supported Ipswich Town.

Mary also worked, for Sovereign River Cruises, and she had recently been promoted to the position of Cruise Director. Her first tour of duty in her new role was to start with the Elegant Elbe and Berlin cruise on the MV Baron von Habsburg, beginning in Prague on 12th June 2026 and ending in Berlin ten days later. She would then remain on board for a further six cruises. Mary was taking over from one of Sovereign's more experienced Cruise Directors, Max Hunt, but he would be staying on the ship for the cruise starting on 12th June.

She was off to the airport in the morning.

Her first ever cruise, as an Assistant Cruise Director on the Douro aboard the MV Duke of Sussex, had been the setting for two murders and an attempted murder, had seen the dismantling of a drug-smuggling ring and had led, directly or indirectly, amongst other things, to a suicide, two more murders, two divorces, two weddings, a ménage à trois and the public humiliation of a former Premier League footballer. It would be fair to say that Mary played a significant role in exposing the murderers and dismantling the drug-smuggling ring and could therefore probably be blamed for everything else which followed!

Returning from Portugal, Mary had feared the worst, needing to explain how she had left Porto with ninety guests and only eighty-four of them were on the flights back to the United Kingdom at the end of the cruise. But a laudatory letter to Sovereign River Cruises about Mary, and her sleuthing, from Superintendent Carlos Colombo of the Portuguese *Polícia Judiçiaria* ensured that her maiden voyage did not end with her career sinking like the Titanic.

Since then, Mary had only lost one more guest permanently – a spritely ninety-five-year-old gentleman from Christmassy Winterbottom in Cheshire named Freddie Botham who slipped on the ice in Rüdesheim during a Rhine Yuletide Markets cruise, after consuming a significant quantity of Rüdesheimer Kaffee, and sadly broke his neck. She had managed to end all her other cruises with a full complement of guests and, in addition to the Rhine Yuletide Markets, she had also been on the MV Prince of Orléans, sailing from Paris to Arromanches along the Seine, and on the Danube aboard the MV Empress Elisabeth. And she had successfully navigated four more cruises on the Douro.

Mary looked again at the notes she had made about the Baron von Habsburg and revisited the passenger manifest.

For her first Elbe cruise, she would be starting, and hopefully finishing, with eighty-eight guests – not passengers, manifest notwithstanding. Mary would be flying on EasyAir from Stansted to Prague with just twenty-seven of them; the majority had opted to fly from Heathrow with British Airways where it was possible to upgrade to Club Europe. The guests whom she would be meeting at Stansted included a Burrage-Hunt – the name rang a bell, the Dickies – old friends, the Waterstones, the Heffers, the Blackwells, the Smiths and the Eagles, and a Lord and Lady Hayter.

Those flying from Heathrow included a Mortimer – a King's Counsel, apparently, the Bearskin-Greens – Sir Claude and Lady Liz, the Harrows, two American couples, Mr and Mrs Nixon from Vermont and Mr and Mrs Harris from Florida, and a Mrs Jane Stanhope. Mary hoped that this would be her friend from her first Douro cruise, although she didn't recognise Jane's address from the manifest.

"What will they be like? Will they get on? Will they like me?" she asked herself. Tonight, they were, mostly, just names; tomorrow, they would be her guests.

"And what about Max? And the crew?"

She would soon find out.

Climbing into bed, she opened Google Translate on her work laptop – a Dell Inspiron 16 – but fell asleep before she managed to get anywhere close to pronouncing *strč prst skrz krk* in Czech.

It was, however, unlikely that she would need to tell anyone she met in Prague to "stick a finger through the neck."

2

Mrs Jane Stanhope

Jane Stanhope finished reading about Berliner Dom, put down her slightly out-of-date DK Eyewitness Travel – Berlin, borrowed from her great friend Vera Marple's daughter, and picked up her mobile phone. Although she was now seventy-six years old and did not own a personal computer of any description, she had become quite adept at using the technology afforded by her Samsung Galaxy S23, particularly when it came to taking photographs or sending messages on WhatsApp. Jane was short and well-padded and had silvery-white hair with a few blue streaks. She wore blue-framed glasses which matched the streaks in her hair.

Jane and Vera became travelling companions in the years after their husbands, Barnaby and Endeavour, succumbed to COVID-19 on the same day and on the same ward in Peterborough City Hospital. They particularly enjoyed river cruises and visiting cathedrals and churches.

The two friends had been guests on Mary Mead's maiden voyage on the Duke of Sussex. At the time, Jane was living alone in an eighteenth-century stone cottage in the village of Water Newton, just a few miles from the centre of Peterborough. Vera lived about ten miles away in a two-bedroom bungalow on the outskirts of Stilton.

Sadly, Vera had a nasty fall just a few weeks after their return from Portugal and, with restricted mobility the consequence of a broken hip, she had moved in with her daughter, Agatha, who was then living in Folkestone on the Kent coast.

Jane and Vera continued to talk to one another several times a week but they missed each other's company. Jane's children, Scarlett and Duke, both worked and lived in London, so she also saw very little of them, and there were no grandchildren for her to spoil. Accordingly, Jane decided to sell her property in Water Newton and she relocated to Mount Olympus Retirement Village, a little more than twenty minutes by bus from Folkestone. She now met up with Vera on a regular basis again.

The first person to introduce herself after Jane had moved into her two-bedroom apartment in Zeus

Court was Helen. Helen had, in her younger days, been a supermodel but, during the last ten years of her gainful employment, she had become the face of a company focussing on extended cruises to the Aegean.

Jane was not really sure that she could remember how Helen managed to extract the information but, once the fact of the murders on the Duke of Sussex had been inveigled out of her, she received an invitation from Helen to attend a meeting of what was apparently known as the TV Murder Club. Some of the residents of Mount Olympus had been inspired to form the club after reading the adventures of Elizabeth, Joyce, Ibrahim and Ron and their Thursday Murder Club.

The TV Murder Club didn't normally investigate real murders. Its members would watch a murder mystery on television but would pause the programme when the detective, professional or amateur, was about to unmask the murderer. They would then discuss the evidence and reach a consensus as to the identity of the killer. And then continue watching to the end of the programme. Jane had agreed to present the details of the Douro murders to the club.

Armed with a packet of Hobnobs and a bottle of Gonzales Byass Tio Pepe Fino sherry, both acquired from the newly-opened Tunbridge Wells Waitrose, Jane duly presented herself at 11.00 am on the following Wednesday in the Card Room. Helen introduced her to the other club members.

Cassandra used to be an actuary and although, seemingly without fail, she was able to identify the murderer, she was never able to convince the other club members. Troy was a retired detective chief inspector with the Thames Valley police and, over the course of his career, he claimed to have investigated nearly four hundred suspicious deaths.

Hector had been a professional footballer and, in his prime, he was considered to be the finest defender in the country. His playing career had been cut short by an Achilles problem. The final member of the club was Penelope. She had been a lady-in-waiting to a member of the Royal Family and, indeed, was a Lady. Penelope was something of an eccentric: she occupied her days making patchwork quilts and still drove a pink Rolls-Royce.

Jane took them through the events on the Duke of Sussex. She was very impressed with their analysis, although they didn't do as well as Mary. It was agreed that an ability to speak Romanian would undoubtedly have helped.

Jane accepted an invitation to join the club, but she would be the first to admit that her enjoyment of a good murder mystery had been somewhat tempered by her involvement in real-life murders. In any event, she turned up with her Hobnobs and her sherry each Wednesday and usually agreed with Cassandra's predictions. Over time, she became good friends with Lady Penelope in particular.

At Vera's prompting, Jane was persuaded to go on another cruise, travelling by herself. Vera's daughter had been in Berlin for work – hence the guidebook – and she had waxed lyrical about the city. A cruise from Berlin to Prague along the Elbe seemed promising. There were only a few cruise companies operating on the Elbe but Jane decided, in any event, that she was first going to see what Sovereign River Cruises had to offer.

A very nice lady named Ricki, who worked in the management office at Mount Olympus, arranged for a copy of the Sovereign River Cruises 2026 brochure to be sent to her and, once it had arrived and been assiduously perused, Jane called Vera and the pair of them discussed the many different ecclesiastical sights which awaited the would-be Elbe cruiser. Apart from Berliner Dom, there were cathedrals and churches to visit in Prague, Dresden, Meissen, Wittenberg and Torgau.

"Right, I'm going," she almost shouted down the phone to Vera.

Jane spoke to a most helpful young man named Osman at Sovereign River Cruises in Manchester. There were just a couple of single occupancy cabins on the Baron von Habsburg still available for the cruise which started in Prague on 12th June 2026.

By looking at the brochure, Jane already realised that the ship only had two decks for passengers. Whether this was because the bridges were lower, or the Elbe was shallower than the other rivers on which she had cruised, she wasn't sure. But, anyway, she took Standard Stateroom 101 and, somewhat hesitantly, provided her debit card details over the phone.

She was mightily relieved when her bank statement arrived a few days later with no unexpected debits and the same post brought formal confirmation from Sovereign River Cruises that her booking had been processed.

And Lady Penelope had offered to drive her to Heathrow in the morning.

"That would be fab!" Jane had replied.

Vera answered Jane's call on the first ring. They chatted for ten minutes before Vera had to go out, wishing Jane, "Bon voyage!"

3

Mrs Lucy Burrage and Mr Max Hunt

There had been a hen party of five twenty-something girls from Southend-on-Sea on Mary's maiden voyage, including Ali Burrage, the bride-to-be, and her younger sister, Ellie.

Mrs Lucy Burrage, Ali's and Ellie's aunt, had been married to their Uncle Ned. Lucy had been widowed when her husband had died of a heart attack after he realised that they had won £7,535,435 on the National Lottery. Auntie Lucy had provided £18,000 towards the cost of the hen cruise for the girls.

With her newly-won wealth, she had decided, amongst other things, to learn how to drive, although she could, of course, now afford a chauffeur-driven limousine. In any event, she booked a series of lessons with Drive Like a Hunt, sole proprietor Lando Hunt.

Lucy had already celebrated her forty-ninth birthday three times but she still retained a keen interest in fashion, although not necessarily age-appropriate fashion. However, she had always kept herself in good shape, so décolleté tops and tight-fitting skirts still complemented her figure. She made weekly visits to her hairdresser, Mario, at A Cut Above the Rest in Southend-on-Sea's The Royals Shopping Centre, and was currently strawberry blonde. Fingers and Toes, where her niece Ali used to work, had assumed responsibility for maintaining her well-trimmed and highly colourful nails.

As for her driving instructor, Lando Hunt had aspired to two things in life: to drive extremely fast and to seduce as many of his female clients as he possibly could. Sometimes simultaneously. Although already in his late fifties, good looks and well-toned pecs helped the achievement of the second of these aspirations. Lucy, as with many who had learnt about reverse parking, hand brakes and gear sticks before her, was smitten by Lando but, most definitely a first, seemingly so was Lando smitten by Lucy. Whether or not her wealth had anything to do with the process of Lando being smitten, they were married, after a high-speed, full-throttle romance, at Southend Registry Office on 2nd January 2026.

Sadly, not only did Lucy subsequently fail her driving test but, indulging his passion for fast cars and a pre-existing addiction to cocaine, both now affordable and financed through his matrimonially-acquired access to Lucy's millions, just two weeks after the wedding Lando managed to turn his green Porsche Taycan Turbo S into a raging inferno whilst leaving very little work for the crematorium oven.

Lando had been married once before, while still a teenager, and that union had produced a son. Lando was delighted when, after ten years of blissless marriage, his wife abandoned him and his son, filed for divorce, moved to Canada and re-married. He was even more delighted when his son left home at sixteen to join the Royal Navy as a Logistics and Personnel Rating. Signing the parental consent form had given him considerable pleasure.

Lando only disclosed the existence of the son to Lucy a week before the wedding – on Christmas Day to be precise – and, although this news had come as something of a shock to Lucy, and hardly the Christmas present which she was expecting, she nevertheless told Lando that she would like to meet him. So, once they were married but before Lando had self-immolated, she called her lawyer, Mr Tulkinghorn, the senior partner of Tulkinghorn and Tangle, to instruct a private detective to track him down. Ellie, her less-favourite niece, was employed as a legal assistant to the junior partner, Mr Tangle.

Within days after Lando's death – his remains were probably still warm – Mr Tulkinghorn's private detective, Mr Sid Shovell of DicksrUs Detective Agency, was able to unearth Lucy's newly-disclosed stepson.

Mr Shovell discovered that Max Hunt had left the Royal Navy after ten years of service and, with a background in catering, supplies and matters maritime, had joined Sovereign River Cruises. Max had now been with the cruise company for about thirteen years, ten of them as a Cruise Director.

Until he received a telephone call from Mr Tulkinghorn, Max was completely unaware that his father had remarried. Or died. With the regular Yuletide Markets cruises having come to an end, he had already flown back to England for a month's holiday when Lucy's lawyer rang. Max no longer owned a car, so he scrounged a lift down the A12 to attend the funeral service being held for his father at Southend Crematorium. And to meet his new stepmother.

Once Lando's earthly remains had been duly scattered off Southend Pier, Lucy made an appointment to see Mr Tulkinghorn. Her solicitor had written to her after the death of her first husband, strongly advising her that, as a multimillionaire, she should write a will. She had ignored his advice. Mr Tulkinghorn had contacted her again as soon as he had learnt that Mr Shovell had dug up Max and explained to Lucy the possible consequences of her dying intestate, particularly insofar as Max was concerned.

Lucy was not a 'charity' person, and Ali was really the only relative whom she had ever had time for. She had hardly spoken to her nieces' parents – her brother-in-law and his wife – for many years. Lucy was, however, beginning to warm to Ellie as she had been extremely helpful with all the funeral arrangements and, indeed, had been very supportive when Lucy needed a shoulder to cry on.

Once she had arrived for her appointment, Mr Tulkinghorn convinced her to make a will there and then. He needed two people to witness Lucy sign the document. Mr Tulkinghorn's secretary, Miss Penny Mooney, was told to be one of them but both Mr Tangle and his secretary were out of the office at the time. Ellie was there, but she was unable to act as a witness, so he asked a gentleman from Suffex Office Equipment Services which, as the name suggested, serviced office equipment throughout both Suffolk and Essex, to do the necessary.

Eddie Shearing had driven down from Ipswich that morning to unjam the paper from the office HP LaserJet Pro. Every time the secretaries wanted to make more than two copies of a document, the copy paper would get stuck in the machine. Mr Tulkinghorn asked Eddie to use Lucy's newly signed will as a test case to demonstrate that the photocopier had actually been restored to proper working order.

"I'll just go and make three copies, then," Eddie said, confident that he had fixed the problem.

Eddie had never seen a will before and so it was with passing interest that he glanced at each of the five pages as they entered the machine and reappeared in triplicate. Executors, discretionary trusts and personal chattels all flew over his head but something caught his eye – and he liked the idea of having a photocopy of his signature. So he made an extra copy of the will and, with the unauthorised copy in his jacket pocket, Eddie headed home to Suffolk. Ipswich Town were playing at Portman Road that evening and there was plenty of time for him to get back and have a couple of pints with his flatmates in The Black Horse Inn before they headed off to the football.

The newly-wed Burrage-Hunts had booked a honeymoon in the Caribbean before the incineration of the male half of the union, and £160,000 of engineering genius, had necessitated its cancellation. Stepmother and stepson had got on well at the funeral and they began to chat on the telephone from time to time. Max suddenly decided that he would try to persuade Lucy to book herself on a cruise with Sovereign to compensate for the cancelled Caribbean holiday. She was initially reluctant, reminding herself about the infamous Douro hen cruise, but she eventually relented on condition that he would also be on the ship.

Max was working at the time as the Cruise Director on a half-season of Elegant Elbe and Berlin cruises, travelling from Berlin to Prague and back from Prague to Berlin, but he was due to hand over to a new Cruise Director at the end of the cruise which started in Prague on 12th June. Lucy agreed to join him on this last cruise and left it to Max to arrange the booking. He secured Luxury Balcony Suite 234 near the stern of the ship on the starboard side for her.

Lucy checked her suitcase one last time. She decided that her black bikini should make the trip, given that it hardly took up any space or made any discernible dent in her luggage allowance. Or, indeed, covered very much of her ample assets. She had upgraded her flights with EasyAir which meant that she could drop off her suitcase at the Easier4U counters and carry an additional bag onto the plane. She had also booked herself into seat 1D.

Lucy arranged for a limousine to pick her up from Leigh-on-Sea at eight o'clock the next morning and deliver her to Stansted. One last look at her documents and then she settled down to an early night with ITV3 on the television in her bedroom. Death on the Nile, with David Suchet as Poirot, was showing yet again. She started to watch.

But then she started to think about the hen cruise as the body count mounted on the Nile.

She slept badly.

4

Horace Mortimer KC and Ms Phyllida Ballard

Horace Mortimer KC was undoubtedly one of the most successful criminal defence barristers ever to have appeared before the English courts. He was also one of the most notorious and least liked. Thanks to Horace's advocacy, at least one serial killer, two other murderers, five armed robbers and a veritable conspiracy of white-collar criminals still enjoyed unlimited, albeit in some cases closely monitored, freedom.

To say that Horace had a pleasant disposition would be some distance from the truth. Angela, his wife of more than twenty years, had recently decided that the benefits provided by his wealth and standing paled into insignificance when weighed against sharing her life with an arrogant, philandering and verbally abusive husband. She had, accordingly, removed herself and her dogs to the weekend cottage on the Norfolk coast which they had purchased in happier times. Now, watercolour painting, golf and a very attractive Italian waiter, Georgio, who served in an upmarket restaurant near Brancaster and was some fifteen years her junior, filled her days and filled her some nights.

Horace had a new girlfriend, Phyllida Ballard, a junior from his Chambers, Number 2 Equity Court, Queen's Bench Walk, Outer Temple. Phyllida was an attractive woman in her mid-thirties. She stood almost five feet ten inches tall and, notwithstanding late nights in Chambers and erratic eating habits, her weekly Pilates regime had managed to maintain her well-toned figure. She had shoulder-length, auburn-coloured hair which spent Phyllida's working days tied up in a bun but was allowed to swing free when socialising. When not enrobed and bewigged in barrister black and white, she liked to wear designer jeans and colourful blouses.

To celebrate the recent acquittal of a fraudulent cryptocurrency billionaire, and the appropriately extortionate fee paid by him, as well as his successful seduction of Ms Ballard, Horace was taking Phyllida on a river cruise.

Horace had recently finished reading a murder mystery set during a cruise on the Douro in Portugal. He was an avid reader of crime novels and watcher of detective programmes and would often imagine himself successfully defending the person charged with the relevant crime. He was rather taken by the idea of cruising.

He lived in an imposing, five-storey Regency house within a few yards of Sloane Square, now devoid of Angela's presence. Phyllida had not formally moved into the matrimonial home but her Oral-B IO toothbrush had taken up residence. Returning to Sloane Square after dinner at Lucky Cat 22 Bishopsgate one Friday evening in March, Horace pitched the cruise idea to Phyllida.

As Phyllida seemed enthusiastic, Horace fired up his HP Z Book Fury G11 and searched for European river cruises. There were plenty of rivers, the Seine, the Rhine, the Danube, the Rhône and so on, and quite a number of cruise companies like Viking, Scenic, Riviera and APT. He had never visited the eastern part of Germany and Dresden sounded interesting. Only a few companies organised Elbe cruises and Horace, an ardent royalist, was immediately attracted to Sovereign River Cruises.

"Here we go," he said, as he searched for availability on the Baron von Habsburg, "we could book this one, it leaves Prague on the twelfth of June and we should be back in the UK by the twenty-first." Horace had tickets for *Le Nozze di Figaro* at Glyndebourne on 24th June.

Phyllida was preparing for an important trial which was scheduled to start in the High Court just a few weeks after they would be returning from the cruise, so she was concerned to ensure that she would have internet access while she was away from Chambers. There were papers to read, research to be carried out, and a defence to be finalised. So she borrowed Horace's laptop and it only took a few moments before the screen was showing:

Wi-Fi on board

Wi-Fi is free and its use unlimited. MV Baron von Habsburg has been fitted with the most up-to-date communications equipment available, enabling our guests to access the benefits of superfast broadband in all the public areas of the ship. If you need privacy, a more limited broadband service is available in each cabin.

"OK, Horace, that looks perfect. Let's go!" she said excitedly.

5

Sir Claude and Lady Liz Bearskin-Green

Little did Horace realise when he was booking that, some six months prior to their dinner at Lucky Cat 22, Sir Claude Bearskin-Green had also booked the same cruise.

Sir Claude had been the Director of Public Prosecutions under a previous government until he had led the prosecution of a notorious gangster, Richard Soncreigh, the self-styled 'capo' of the Clapham Capulets. He had been charged with all manner of offences, including three counts of murder. Soncreigh had been filmed, for posterity, executing two members of a rival gang, the Morden Montagues, with a bullet to the back of the head of each of the kneeling gang members, and an unfortunate member of the public whose dog had strayed into the execution zone, rather more prosaically, with a single shot to the heart. 'Carrot Top' Butcher, the gang member who had been ordered to capture the graphic images on his smartphone, forwarded copies to his boss but, inadvertently, forgot to delete them from his own phone. This oversight proved exceptionally useful when an attempted, but unsuccessful, armed bank robbery had left Carrot Top needing something to trade with the Metropolitan Police in order to negotiate a shorter custodial sentence than might otherwise have been forthcoming.

With the photographs and Carrot Top's testimony, a guilty verdict, and a life sentence or three, seemed guaranteed. The Home Secretary of the day had already appeared on television to declare that his government had effectively delivered the end of the gang warfare which had blighted South London for more than ten years, announcing to the world the impending and inevitable incarceration of Richard Soncreigh. The Home Secretary of the day was soon to learn that he would only be Home Secretary for a few more of those days.

Richard Soncreigh was defended by Horace Mortimer KC (QC at the time). With a dazzling display of oratory, Horace had destroyed the prosecution's case. He was undoubtedly helped, however, by Carrot Top not providing the evidence which the prosecution had expected to hear. Carrot Top swore on oath in court that the police had paid him to doctor the photographs by substituting Richard Soncreigh's face for the face of an alleged hitman, another member of the Clapham Capulets who had himself been murdered in reprisal by the Morden Montagues shortly after the first murders. Carrot Top's unexpected testimony probably ensured the continued existence of his three sons, including his youngest, who seemed, much to his surprise, to have embarked on a career as a musician.

Soncreigh was acquitted. And, in securing Soncreigh's acquittal, Horace destroyed Sir Claude's career. At the end of the trial, photographs of a sneering Soncreigh being carried triumphantly on the shoulders of other, more loyal, members of the Clapham Capulets as he left the court, with a distraught Sir Claude looking on in despair in the background, had made the front pages of all the major daily newspapers other than the Star, which had led with 'Wife Ate My Hamster'.

Publicly humiliated, Sir Claude had little choice but to offer his resignation. The Prime Minister seemed only too happy to accept the offer and Sir Claude retired, with some ignominy, but with a generous government pension, to grow roses and play bridge in the village of Nettlebed.

Sadly, his wife, Lady Amelia Bearskin-Green, humiliated by her husband's fall from grace, became a recluse and essentially lost the will to live. She died within two years after Sir Claude's resignation. Sir Claude felt the loneliness of his widowhood and decided to enrol on a dating site for the over-fifties. Where, in short order, he met, wined, dined and married fifty-one-year-old Ms Liz Saunders-French.

His generous pension ensured that Sir Claude and his new wife could enjoy leisurely overseas holidays three or four times a year and they frequently chose to cruise the rivers of Europe with Sovereign River Cruises. They were, in fact, both members of the Royal Court – Sovereign's frequent travellers' club – with at least five cruises undertaken within a seven-year period. A Duke and a Duchess, to be precise.

It had been a few years since Sir Claude had been in Berlin. The last time he was there had been for a meeting of senior government lawyers from the European Union. He also owned a few valuable pieces of Meissen porcelain and Lady Liz had inherited some Bohemian glassware from her parents. Sir Claude had really enjoyed Berlin, so a chance to revisit the city and to go on a cruise holiday which would take in both Meissen and Prague seemed perfect. He was hoping that the cruise might provide him with the opportunity to complete a particular collection of porcelain figurines and, perhaps, a chance for Lady Liz to grow her collection of glassware. Accordingly, the Bearskin-Greens had booked themselves on the Elegant Elbe and Berlin cruise departing on 12th June 2026. They had secured Royal Suite 202 and an upgrade to Club Europe with British Airways.

As neither of them still drove a car, an Uber took them to Reading Station. They then caught an Elizabeth Line train to Heathrow before spending the night at the Sofitel London Hotel which was located adjacent to Terminal 5.

Had they arrived at the hotel thirty minutes later, they might have seen Horace and Phyllida arrive by taxi and check into their Prestige Suite. Had they decided to eat in La Belle Époque rather than Vivre, they might have found them sitting at the next table.

The following morning, Horace and Phyllida were still enjoying breakfast in the Club Millesime Lounge as Sir Claude and Lady Liz made their way into the terminal.

The reunion would have to wait.

6

Baron Hayter of Bedchester and Lady Gertrude Hayter

Lady Gertude Hayter was not a likeable person. Her unpopularity was more than amply demonstrated in 2025 when she failed to be elected to Rutshire County Council, notwithstanding that she was standing for Reform in the most pro-Brexit ward in the county. And lost to the Greens.

Gertrude was a large woman. She had been born large and she had become much larger over the years. But she also ate and drank to excess which, of course, had made her even larger still. She wore, almost invariably, a tweed suit with a white silk blouse, offset with a string of pearls and a heavily permed coiffure. Her Ladyship spoke with the plumiest of accents and her family, the Bedchester Cooper-Blacks, had farmed several thousand acres of Rutshire for almost six centuries.

Lady Hayter did not suffer fools – or at least those arguably more foolish than herself – gladly. She was, without a doubt, an egotistic, homophobic, racist bigot. And fat.

Her husband, Lord Hayter, on the other hand, was a very affable fellow. As plain Marmaduke Hayter, he had served for many years as the Member of Parliament for one of the rural Rutshire constituencies. As well as being a highly regarded constituency MP, Marmaduke held one or two lesser ministerial positions in a number of administrations. However, he began to find himself more and more at odds with the party line, not helped by his pro-European leanings. He did not seek re-election in 2024 but, much to the delight of the then Mrs Hayter, he was made a life peer and became Baron Hayter of Bedchester.

Lady Hayter idolised Donald Trump and was inspired by the thought of 'Making England Great Again'. She was not too bothered about Scotland, Wales or Northern Ireland. But, after her rejection in the county council elections, Lady Hayter felt that it was an appropriate moment to take a holiday and to rekindle relationships with some of her like-minded friends on the continent.

One of the many successful Reform candidates – a former cabinet minister – had once recommended river cruising to her and, with both assuaging disappointment and rekindling in mind, Royal Suite 201 aboard the Baron von Habsburg was duly commandeered for the Elegant Elbe and Berlin cruise starting in Prague on 12th June 2026.

The Hayters were in Clacton on the evening before they flew to Prague. They were attending a fund-raising event for the local Member of Parliament.

As they dressed for the evening – an informal event not requiring Lady Hayter to change out of her tweed two-piece and white silk blouse, although she did intend to upgrade the string of pearls to her second-best set – Lady Hayter was somewhat surprised by the paucity of clothing which she could now see had been packed into Lord Hayter's somewhat diminished suitcase.

"Why haven't you packed your dinner jacket, Marmaduke?" she demanded.

Lady Hayter's experience of river cruising was limited to a charity screening of Death on the Nile starring Peter Ustinov and she had therefore assumed a certain degree of formality would be de rigueur.

"Because, my dear, the information they sent to us states categorically that dress on board is informal.

It says we might want to consider a jacket on the formal evenings and there's only one of those," Lord Hayter riposted.

"Well, some of us still have standards," she snorted as she searched for the pearl upgrade within her significantly larger suitcase.

"Next year you'll be wanting to come back to Clacton to stay in a bed and breakfast and play bingo all day while you eat whelks," she continued.

"Well, dear," he countered, "I don't suppose I'll see your party leader here if I do."

Somewhat unusually, Lord Hayter realised, from the silence which followed, that he had managed to have the last word.

They departed for the fund-raiser without any further exchanges. The next time Lady Hayter spoke to her husband, it was to demand, somewhat ostentatiously, "Write Nigel a cheque for five thousand, dear.

"Guineas, of course."

7

Clarence and Marigold Harrow

Malo, real name Clarence Harrow, had been the frontman and lead vocalist for the Moss Gatherers. He had aspired to become the Prince of Darkness for the 1990s. But failed. His star was, however, briefly in the ascendancy when the five-piece quite heavy metal band from West London rose to fame as songs such as I am Satan, The Devil and Me, Beelzebub Baby and Highway to Hades all charted and earned the band several appearances on Top of the Pops and an appearance on Never Mind the Buzzcocks for Malo. Mephistopheles was in the album charts for more than thirty weeks.

They never made it in America or, indeed, to America as Malo insisted on ticking all the 'yes' boxes in the visa application form: 'Are you a terrorist?' 'Yes' and so on.

They did, however, make a number of successful forays into Europe.

Both Malo, and all the other original band members, were Old Hunstantonians, schoolmates from a small public school on the North Norfolk coast: Charles Bromley-Bow on lead guitar, Angus Croydon on bass, Russell 'Conway' Barnet on keyboards and Pontius Croydon, Angus's younger brother, on drums. Notwithstanding his public-school education, Malo felt that his POD aspirations would be better served if he affected a manner of speaking which sounded like Eliza Doolittle before her first lesson with Professor Henry Higgins. Although sometimes he forgot and spoke 'proper' English.

Pontius committed suicide on his twenty-seventh birthday, expressing the wish to join the pantheon of great musicians who had died at that age: Kurt Cobain, Brian Jones, Jim Morrison, Janis Joplin, Jimi Hendrix and Robert Johnson (and Amy Winehouse a few years later). It would be fair to say that, whenever someone tried to recall the names of the members of the '27-club', Pontius's name was more often than not, and possibly always, overlooked.

Pontius was replaced by Keith 'Red' Butcher in 1997 after Malo heard him playing a set at The Bull's

Head in Barnes. But for his unquestionable percussionist skills, Keith would almost certainly have followed in the footsteps of his father, his uncle and his two older brothers as a foot-soldier, and sometimes hit man, for a South London gang known as the Clapham Capulets.

As European tours became shorter, and venues in the United Kingdom grew ever smaller, the band decided to call it a day back in 2005 with a farewell tour of major European capitals.

Although Malo never used drugs, he was undoubtedly a heavy drinker – certainly heavier than the metal of his music. His first wife, Pansy, a backing singer, and his second wife, Daisy, a dancer, had each departed with a reasonably large chunk of his wealth, much of which was derived through inheritance rather than fees and royalties. Both cited his excessive drinking as the primary reason for their departure.

A meeting with his accountant to approve a particularly large transfer of funds to Daisy proved not only a sobering experience for Malo but also had the effect of going some way to sobering him up. Now almost sixty, Malo had a new wife, Marigold, his third, whom he had met online at u3a. Malo had been listening to Brian May on The One Show and became interested in astronomy. And Marigold, who had read astrophysics at university, led an Astronomy group on u3a which Malo joined. Love and planets, and the payments to Pansy and Daisy, had the effect of reducing his alcohol intake to more acceptable levels. That said, Malo still liked a drink, as did Marigold, and, between them, half a bottle of cognac could easily disappear over the course of an evening.

Marigold was an attractive woman in her late fifties. She stood almost five feet ten inches tall and, notwithstanding her drinking and, indeed, her smoking, her daily yoga exercises had managed to maintain her well-toned figure. She had shoulder-length, auburn-coloured hair which spent Marigold's teaching days tied up in a bun but was allowed to swing free at all other times. Whether teaching or not, she liked to wear colourful blouses and designer jeans.

Marigold also loved to travel and visit historical places and she finally managed to persuade Malo to go on a river cruise. As Malo had not been in Berlin or Prague since the Moss Gatherers' farewell tour, they agreed on the Sovereign River Cruises' Elegant Elbe and Berlin cruise on the Baron von Habsburg starting on 12th June 2026.

Malo checked again what the brochure said about drinks:

The Royal Drinks Package

From 10.00 am each day and throughout lunch and dinner, your all-inclusive Royal Drinks Package provides you with red, white, rosé, and sparkling wine, draught lagers and beers, soft drinks and juices. And from 5.00 pm until the bar closes, you can also enjoy our cocktails and mocktails, our house spirits – gin, vodka, whisky, brandy, and rum – and a wide range of liqueurs. Perhaps an ice-cold beer with your lunch, maybe a dry martini before dinner, enjoy some of Germany's finest wines with your gourmet dining experience, accompanied by a glass of port with our international cheese selection. And why not try a liqueur in the lounge as you enjoy the evening's entertainment?

"Didn't you say something about being able to purchase premium brands?" Malo asked Marigold, "I hope they've got me Remy Martin XO on board."

"Yes, you can," Marigold, who had actually read the entire brochure, confirmed, "and it says they will keep the minibar in our cabin filled up with whatever we want to order."

"So, I guess I'll be asking for a bottle of Remy a day. That should keep me old joints lubricated. That

OK with you, or would you prefer something else?" Malo asked almost solicitously.

"What I'd prefer is that you didn't plan to drink a bottle of cognac each day," is what she actually thought but she answered, "No thanks, lover. I'll be fine."

Marigold made contact with one of the companies which specialised in arranging cruising holidays. Her initial inquiry regarding the availability of Remy Martin XO cognac was positively answered with a call back in under half an hour. And, within little more time thereafter than it took to provide credit card details over the telephone and respond to an OTP, Mr and Mrs Clarence Harrow were booked into Luxury Balcony Suite 236 and on a British Airways flight from Heathrow with an upgrade to Club Europe. And with a regular supply of Remy Martin XO cognac.

The Moss Gatherers' farewell tour, specifically the concert in Prague, had ended in tragedy.

Ivana Pavlyuchelkova was only fifteen at the time. Martina, her older sister by three years, had persuaded their parents to let Ivana come with her to the concert. With some reluctance. Apart from Ivana's age and the fact that she had school the next day, neither of them could understand why anyone would want to watch, let alone listen to, the Moss

Gatherers. But Martina was a sensible girl – she was in her second year studying hospitality and tourism at a local college – and she had won the tickets in a college competition. The Velky Sal Lucerna, where the concert was being held, was within walking distance of the apartment where the girls lived with their parents.

It had become a tradition of Moss Gatherers' concerts, as the group indulged themselves with their final number, a frenzied rendition of Highway to Hades which had been known to last for upwards of ten minutes, for Charles to smash his guitar, for Red to snap his drumsticks in two and for Malo to rip up his now-sweat-sodden T-shirt. Pieces of guitar, drumstick and T-shirt would then be hurled, mostly by Malo, into the mosh pit.

On this particular occasion, the sharp end of a broken drumstick pierced Ivana's left eye and she died almost instantaneously.

With the general mayhem which always followed the end of a concert, Martina had become separated from her sister and it was only when the crowds had cleared that she could see Ivana lying motionless, no more than two metres from the front of the stage, with a small pool of blood forming around her head. Dead.

The Moss Gatherers were back in their tour bus and on the road to Berlin before an ambulance had even arrived at the stadium. The Czech authorities decided that there was little point in trying to take any action against Malo, or any of the other band members, particularly once Ivana's family was in receipt of a significant, but conditional, payment from the Moss Gatherers' management company. However, the Berlin concert was cancelled and the Moss Gatherers never performed again. But their income from royalties had remained healthy over the years, although no Moss Gatherers tribute band had ever emerged.

As for the other members of the band, Angus was now two years into a ten-year sentence in a Thai prison for offences involving underage boys. Charles had converted to Buddhism and was apparently living in Mayapur in West Bengal with his royalties helping to supplement the considerable sums of money donated by Alfred Ford, great-grandson of Henry himself, to finance the construction of the Hari Krishna Temple of the Vedic Planetarium.

Rather more prosaically, Conway died of a drug overdose and Red became, and still was, a baker.

8

Day 1 – Morning
Stansted Airport

Mary was out of bed, showered and dressed well before six o'clock. Not only was she excited about the cruise and her first outing as a Cruise Director – she took another look at her new 'Mary – Cruise Director' badges to make sure – but FIFA World Cup 26, taking place in three different countries, Mexico, the United States of America and Canada (she thought that Canada was still a country), had kicked-off overnight.

She was on the BBC News website even before she had checked the weather for Prague or the Stansted departures board. She read out the results for the opening games to herself: "Mexico 0 Niger 0. Italy 0 Iraq 0."

"Well," she thought, "I didn't miss much."

Mary travelled to Stansted by train. There were regular services from Bury St Edmunds to Cambridge, and from Cambridge to Stansted Airport, and she had managed so far to avoid any problems with striking train drivers and leaves on the line. She arrived too early, as usual, at 8.30 am.

Her twenty-seven guests had been instructed to look for Mary outside Costa Coffee from 9.30 am. EasyAir flight EA2261 was scheduled to depart at noon and arrive at Václav Havel Airport in Prague at 2.55 pm local time. Once she had arrived, she checked the flight information board. EA2261 was showing as ON TIME.

Mary then went to one of the bag drop counters and said, "au revoir" (hopefully not 'goodbye') to her pull-along. She then got herself a cappuccino from Costa Coffee, sat herself down on one of the nearby bench seats, checked for messages on her phone and read the match reports from the football.

The first two of her guests to put in an appearance were Lord and Lady Hayter at 9.25 am. His Lordship and Ladyship had spent the previous evening at the Chudleigh Hotel in Clacton and a limousine had picked them up from the hotel at 8.15 am. It was a beautiful, sunny morning and the journey westwards on the A12 had taken little more than an hour.

As they drove along, Lady Hayter started to read through the Sovereign River Cruises brochure again. She wanted to remind herself what had been promised so that she could be ready to complain whenever Sovereign failed to deliver. But she couldn't be bothered to check what was said about the Golden Crown Spa as she had no intention of visiting the place and it was certainly going to be off limits to Marmaduke.

Notwithstanding the temperature, Lady Hayter had inevitably chosen to travel in a matching tweed jacket and skirt with a white silk blouse and a set of pearls. And 'sensible' shoes. Lord Hayter was wearing somewhat more appropriate attire, mustard chinos, a much-worn blue linen jacket with a jaunty white handkerchief poking out of its breast pocket, a red and white checked shirt and, perhaps most surprisingly, a pair of Lululemon Cityverse sneakers.

His Lordship was soon to be seen pushing a luggage trolley on which their blue Samsonite suitcases were demonstrating a well-travelled appearance. Lady Hayter had booked Easier4U and reserved seats 1A and 1B as well as priority boarding. She had never flown with a budget airline before and was soon going to be disappointed.

Seeing what looked like potential guests, Mary raised her trusty clipboard on which her passenger manifest was indeed clipped. The non-clipped side bore the Sovereign River Cruises golden crown on a black background. She waved the clipboard and, as they still continued in her direction, she became confident about starting a conversation. She had accosted many an unsuspecting, non-Sovereign traveller in the past.

"Good morning, Mrs…?" Mary began.

"Lady Hayter, if you don't mind, young lady. I am surprised you didn't recognise me. Mind you, you young people never bother to read the newspapers or watch the news on television. Faces always stuck in your phones."

Swiftly hiding her mobile phone in the pocket of her trousers, Mary said, "Oh, I am very sorry, Lady Hayter. And you must be Lord Hayter."

"Guilty as charged," replied his Lordship, "and you must be Mary Mead, is that right?"

Before Mary could confirm her identity, her Ladyship interrupted, "Have we finished, young lady? I would like to find the lounge and have a stiff drink."

Mary doubted that she would find anything resembling an EasyAir lounge and she thought that it was, perhaps, a bit early for a stiff drink. But, to answer Lady Hayter's question, Mary answered, "First, your Ladyship, I need to check your passports and boarding passes. I see you are booked on

Easier4U so you can drop your cases off over there." She pointed to the Easier4U counters behind her which, fortunately, had no one queuing at the time.

"If you must," Lady Hayter begrudgingly replied. "You've got all the bumf, Marmaduke. Show them to your new friend, Mary."

Bumf duly checked, Mary's trusty green marker pen ruled through the names of Lord Marmaduke Hayter and Lady Gertrude Hayter on her manifest.

She thought that they were both about to head off in the direction of the Easier4U counters, so Mary was surprised when Lord Hayter turned round and asked her whether there was a smoking area inside the terminal. He took out a vape pen from his jacket pocket and held it up as if to validate his query.

"I think the only designated smoking areas are outside the terminal building. Once you've gone through security, that's probably it until you get to Prague," Mary replied, "but I'm not one hundred percent sure."

"There's an information desk over there," she added, pointing to the aforementioned desk which was in the opposite direction to the bag drop-off.

Lord Hayter gave a disappointed nod in acknowledgment. But, once their cases had been entrusted to the care of the airport's baggage handlers, Mary noticed that Lord Hayter abandoned his wife as she made her way towards security and took himself outside for a vape.

Although not witnessed by Mary, Lady Hayter managed to offend at least two members of the security staff. First, she complained to one of them about the necessity of removing her shoes and then insisted, as she stood with arms and legs akimbo, that a female handle the scanning of her body rather than the Asian gentleman who had been assigned to that task.

Lord Hayter, meanwhile, was able to spend an enjoyable ten minutes alone with his vaping before heading for a less-dramatic passage through security. He made no attempt to locate Lady Hayter and the couple were only reunited once he had boarded the plane.

The Waterstones, the Heffers, the Blackwells and the Smiths (there were always Smiths) arrived as an eightsome in a large people carrier taxi. They had spent the night in Cambridge in rooms in Porterhouse College. Four of the five ladies had graduated from the college twenty-five years previously and, every five years since their graduation, they had arranged to meet in Cambridge and then go away on holiday together. They were all still single for the five-year reunion in Malta but, by the time of the ten-year reunion in Paris, they were all engaged and were able to introduce their future husbands or, in the case of the Heffers, their future wife. By the time they got to the fifteenth year, they had all married, there were two small Blackwells and a baby Waterstone and the Heffers were working in Hong Kong – so Norfolk and no Heffers. They were all back in the United Kingdom for the twentieth (no new additions but Norfolk again). With children now old enough to be farmed out to grandparents, they were off to the Elbe for the twenty-fifth.

The Dickies from Billericay, whom she had previously met on the Douro, were also travelling with her. They both gave her a little hug when they arrived in front of Costa Coffee.

"Lovely to see you both. You're looking fantastic," said Mary, delighted to see some friendly faces after her encounter with her Ladyship.

"No more murders, please, Mary," Mr Dickie playfully demanded, "or they'll be putting the cost of my travel insurance up."

Max had messaged Mary the previous day to ask her to look out for his stepmother and he had predicted what she might be wearing. And there was really no mistaking the lady dressed in a Caine white leather biker jacket and extremely tight Polo Ralph Lauren boot jeans. She was tottering vertiginously on what appeared to be three-inch heels, courtesy of

Manolo Blahnik, and Mary felt that the trolley on which she was pushing her silver Rimowa Classic Check-In L suitcase was probably doubling up as a means of preventing her from toppling over.

Mary's dad was something of a cruciverbalist (his description, not Mary's) and he would delight in the discovery of new words. A recent addition to his vocabulary had been 'spathic' which, apparently, meant 'having an attractive cleavage'. Mary decided that Max's stepmother would definitely be considered spathic.

"Good morning, madam," said Mary as Lucy made a beeline towards Costa Coffee, "I think you must be Mrs Lucy Burrage-Hunt. You're Max's stepmother, aren't you?"

Lucy smiled and said, "And you must be Mary. Just call me Mrs Burrage – or Lucy, of course. I lost my husband before I could change the name in my passport, so I decided to keep my old name. Max made the booking for me and I don't think he realised. I know Max is a Hunt, but I'm sure he won't mind."

Mary was convinced that she recognised the name 'Burrage' but, before she could say anything to Lucy, Mr and Mrs Eagle from Eire, Mr and Mrs Rook from Avebury and Mr and Mrs Ali from Alexandra Palace all arrived at the same time and Lucy went to drop off her Rimowa. By 10.20 am, all twenty-seven guests were accounted for.

Mary put her green marker pen away and made her way through security. The information boards were still suggesting that EA2261 would be leaving ON TIME, the flight had acquired a gate number (17), and passengers were being instructed to GO TO GATE. So she headed towards the shuttle which would take her somewhat nearer to gate 17.

By the time Mary actually arrived at the departure gate, the information boards had changed their minds and were showing a twenty-minute delay.

As she chatted with her guests, while they waited patiently for the delayed EasyAir flight to board, Mary learnt, amongst other things, that Mrs Wendy Waterstone had a master's degree in European history and had been taught by Professor Clare Downing. Professor Downing had been a guest on her maiden cruise on the Douro. And Mrs Sally Smith was a natural scientist specialising in marine biology who liked to go for a run each morning.

Mary then chatted with Mrs Blackwell. She was a criminal lawyer, a partner in a small firm of solicitors in Battersea. Her husband was Professor of Toxicology at one of the London University colleges. Mrs Heffer (Cantab) taught A-level mathematics at a large academy school in Leicester and her wife, Mrs

Heffer (Oxon), was a consultant urologist and a Fellow of the Royal College of Surgeons of England. She worked primarily in private practice but spent two days a week at Leicester Royal Infirmary.

Mary also learnt that the Eagles were staunch Roman Catholics with very strong views about extra-marital and pre-marital relationships, divorce and abortion. They were, they informed her, very much in favour of disestablishmentarianism, not to replace the Church of England with a secular society, but with the re-establishment of the Roman Catholic Church.

Mary had to admit that she wasn't used to hearing twenty-four-letter words; she had counted up the letters on her fingers. She was pretty sure that the Eagles' views would not find universal acceptance on board and hoped that they were not planning to do anything untoward when they got to Wittenberg.

And then there was Lady Hayter.

"I wonder what they're like on the British Airways flight. Hopefully, no one quite so difficult," she thought to herself.

Hope springs eternal.

9

Day 1
BA852

At about the same time as the last of Mary's guests were arriving at Stansted, those guests flying from Terminal 5 at Heathrow began to board British Airways flight BA852 to Prague.

There were fifty-three passengers on the flight who were joining the Elegant Elbe and Berlin cruise, including four passengers who had arrived earlier that day from the United States. Five couples had paid an additional £280 per person to fly closer to the pilot in Club Europe.

Mr Horace Mortimer KC and Ms Phyllida Ballard had reserved seats 1A and 1C. Horace did not relish sitting in his seat sipping champagne while all the passengers destined for Economy Class inched their way past him along the aisle, overloaded with cabin bags and other paraphernalia, looking in expectation at their boarding passes and the seat numbers. "Do they really expect to find row 30 immediately behind row 1?" he used to mutter to himself. Accordingly, he remained in the lounge until LAST CALL appeared on the flight information boards and ignored the frequent pleas from Phyllida that they should go to the gate or they would miss the flight.

After some brisk walking, verging on intermediate sprinting, they boarded the Airbus A319 with the last few stragglers. Therefore, it was only then that Horace saw, in seats 2D and 2F, Sir Claude and Lady Liz Bearskin-Green.

"Well, well, well, if it isn't our learned King's Counsel!" chortled a somewhat surprised Sir Claude. "And who's your new lady friend? Oh, it must be your daughter. Is Angela all right? A little bird tells me that she is doing wonders for Anglo-Italian relations."

Horace chose to ignore him, took his seat by the window and accepted a glass of Castelnau Brut NV champagne. He had no carry-on luggage to worry about and he left Phyllida to find space for her cabin bag in the overhead lockers. At that point, Sir Claude noticed that her bag was sporting the unmistakable black and gold colours of a Sovereign River Cruises luggage tag.

"You're not on the Sovereign cruise to Berlin, are you?" he asked with a certain Machiavellian delight.

"Yes, we are," replied Phyllida. "It's Sir Claude, isn't it. My name is Phyllida."

"And you must be Lady Liz," she continued, addressing Sir Claude's wife.

"Sit down and shut up, for goodness's sake," said Horace, sounding annoyed, "the Captain wants to get going."

As their designated cabin steward began the thankless task of describing, to herself, the workings of the seat belts and the oxygen masks for the Club Europeans, and pointing out, to no one, their emergency exits, Sir Claude began to relish the prospect of ruining Horace's holiday in whatever way he could.

In front of him, in seats 1D and 1F, were Mr and Mrs Harrow – Malo and Marigold. Both of them had already finished their second glass of champagne.

In seats 3A and 3C were one of the couples from the United States. Bill Harris lived with his wife, Hillary, in Tampa Bay, Florida. Bill was a senior executive with Florida Uranium, Coal and Kerosene Union, a conglomerate which was steadily drilling, extracting and refining its way through Florida's natural resources, ensuring ever-increasing bonuses for Bill and ever-decreasing biodiversity for the state. Since the beginning of 2025, the permanent damage to Florida's fragile ecosystems, and the conglomerate's contribution to climate change, had both grown exponentially.

His wife, Hillary, 'Hill' to her friends, spent her days playing golf and tennis at Bradenton Links Golf and Country Club or attending fund-raisers for the local Republican party.

Bill and Hill were both wearing red baseball caps bearing the acronym 'MAGA' which sat somewhat incongruously with his blue blazer, button-down white shirt, grey chinos and brown loafers and her pale green trouser suit, buttercup-coloured silk blouse and white Gucci shoes.

Across the aisle, in seats 3D and 3F, were the other American couple, Donald and Sarah Nixon. They lived in Stowe in Vermont. Donald was a human rights lawyer but much of his time was spent assisting the senior state senator. Sarah hailed from Harlem and worked with a non-profit organisation based in Stowe which provided emergency assistance for homeless people. She had met her husband when he had accompanied the senator on a visit to her organisation. In her earlier years, she tended towards violent, angry outbursts and had spent a number of months as the guest of Vermont's Chittenden Regional Correctional Facility after being found guilty of stabbing – not fatally – one of her friends with a barbecue fork. While she was still living in New York, Sarah had once worked in the same bar as Alexandria Ocasio-Cortez and she had now become a fervent supporter of AOC.

Both Donald and Sarah were wearing denim jackets, jeans and trainers but Donald had 'Vote Bernie' on his T-shirt while Sarah's was emblazoned with AOC's face.

Fortunately, Bill and Sarah were in the two window seats, separated by spouses and the aisle, so their constant arguing was, at that stage, still a thing of the future. In any event, Sarah had other things on her mind. She hated flying and was already regretting her decision to give up vaping before she went on holiday. Sarah still had her vape pen and a bottle of her favourite nic salt vape juice in her handbag 'just in case', but there had been nowhere inside Heathrow for her to have a calming strawberry-flavoured nicotine fix before she boarded the flight.

Further back, in seat 22A, Jane Stanhope found herself sitting next to Mr and Mrs Triste from Tooting Common. Whenever someone mentioned Tooting Common in conversation, Jane was reminded of a news story about a Japanese tourist found wandering around the common looking for the Tutankhamun Exhibition.

For a couple going on holiday, Jane thought that they both seemed rather sad and, over the course of the next six hundred and forty-five airmiles, she learnt that their younger daughter had been murdered almost ten years ago. The daughter was still living at home with her parents at the time but she worked as an accountant in the City. Coming home late one night from the office, she was caught in the crossfire when she left Tooting Common underground station at the same time as two local gangs were setting out to decrease each other's membership numbers. She was hit by two bullets, one fired by a member of each gang, and died instantly. One of the perpetrators had, only days before, been acquitted on a murder charge after his barrister had successfully cast doubts about the integrity of the police evidence.

Her fiancé, who was German, had worked for an international bank in the City. Devastated, he returned to his home in Berlin. He had never married but had kept in touch with the Tristes over the years. The tenth anniversary of the murder was coming up at the end of June and he had asked them to come to Berlin for some form of celebration of their daughter's life. Their older daughter persuaded them that they should go and to take a holiday at the same time. They had been nowhere since the date of the shooting. She had suggested a river cruise, knew someone who had travelled with Sovereign River Cruises before and, after much prevarication, Luxury Balcony Suite 227 on the Baron von Habsburg departing from Prague on 12th June 2026 was booked.

Jane, however, had the impression that they would rather be avenging their daughter's death than celebrating her life.

BA852 was airborne within a few minutes of its scheduled departure time of 10.55 am.

10

Day 1
EA2261

The British Airways flight was already well on its way to Prague by the time all the passengers had boarded EasyAir flight EA2261 at Stansted.

The purchase of priority booking surprisingly ensured that Lady Hayter was the first to board and was firmly ensconced in seat 1A before anyone else had made it onto the plane. Lord Hayter only joined her after almost all the other passengers had taken their seats.

Lucy was the only other one of Mary's little lambs to have reserved a seat but she was the last person to board. Mary was just in front of her as she entered the aircraft and she thought that Lucy seemed apprehensive about the flight.

"Are you OK with flying?" she asked. "I'm sure the cabin crew can help you relax."

"It's not the flight I'm worried about," she replied as she stored her capacious cabin bag in the overhead locker and took her place in seat 1D, "it's the cruise!"

Mary was somewhat taken aback by her response but she didn't get a chance to ask Lucy what she meant as one of the members of the cabin crew suggested that she take her seat as soon as possible. And she still couldn't place the name.

As the doors closed and the plane began to reverse away from the airbridge, the Captain's voice demanded their attention. "Good afternoon, ladies and gentlemen, boys and girls. My name is Captain James Kirk and I will be flying this Airbus 320neo to a galaxy far, far away."

"Oh, no, it's Top Gun again," Mary thought to herself. This would be the third time that she had flown with him in less than twelve months.

"Just kidding," Top Gun continued. "I'm really Captain Peter Mitchell and with me on the flight deck today is First Officer Amelia Johnson. Apologies for the slight delay. We should be airborne within the next ten minutes and flying time to Prague will be one hour and fifty minutes. Weather on arrival is expected to be a very pleasant twenty-nine degrees centigrade.

If you've flown with me before, you will know that I have no idea what that is in Fahrenheit."

"Pathetic," emerged from Lady Hayter's lips. Whether this was a reference to her husband or a commentary on EasyAir's punctuality, the Captain's inability to provide a proper temperature, or life generally, is not known.

"The seat belt sign has been turned on," Captain Mitchell continued, "and EasyAir recommends that you keep your seat belt fastened at all times if you are not moving around the plane. We don't want to see you bouncing up and down like a yo-yo if we hit some unexpected turbulence."

Top Gun finished with, "In charge of your safety and pleasure in the cabin today is Purser Vickie Adams."

Vickie was a buxom lady of Caribbean descent who stretched the dark green skirt and pale green blouse of her EasyAir uniform to their maximum. She cheerfully introduced the four members of her cabin crew, Mel, Geraldine, Emma and Melanie, and they went through the usual safety briefing, which received the usual level of attention.

Mary found herself, not for the first time, near the back of the plane in seat 30D. Seats 30E and 30F were occupied by the Billericay Dickies. Both of them were asleep before the plane was airborne and slept all the way to Prague. So Mary checked her paperwork and then settled down to Julia Nevin's latest release, Death on the Rhône.

As usual, the combination of early starts and the monotonous tones of the Rolls-Royce Trent engines meant that those passengers, including Mary, who were not responsible for the behaviour of young children or the feeding of babies, soon dropped off to sleep. As a result, Mary missed the contretemps at the front of the plane when the passenger in seat 1A objected to having to pay for a gin and tonic on the basis that free drinks must have been part of flying Easier4U. She made a somewhat derogatory remark to Vickie which might well have been interpreted as having racial undertones. The passenger in seat 1D suggested that 1A was a disgrace and that she should apologise. 1A told her to mind her own business and Vickie told them both that she would ask the Captain to return to Stansted if they didn't settle down.

Seat 1B paid for 1A's drink.

The First Officer spoke. "Hello, this is your First Officer speaking. I hope you have enjoyed the flight. We will be starting our descent into Václav Havel Airport in about ten minutes' time and, if we don't get any issues with air traffic control, we should have you on the ground and at our gate at three o'clock, just five minutes behind schedule. We've managed to make up some time during the flight. Czechia is one hour ahead of the United Kingdom so you might want to set your watches. It's now 2.25 pm local time. It's a beautiful afternoon in Prague with the temperature around twenty-nine degrees. That's eighty-four degrees Fahrenheit. Cabin crew, prepare for landing."

Vickie took over from Amelia Johnson and issued dire warnings about the imminent closure of the toilets which led to lengthy queues forming at both ends of the plane. The reunion of feet with shoes which had been a tight fit when removed two hours previously proved, for many passengers, something of a challenge. Bags were stuffed under seats, tables were closed, rubbish was collected and, once the toilet queues had fully dissipated, all seat belts were fastened.

And a few minutes later, Mary Mead, Cruise Director, was on foreign soil again.

11

Day 1 – Afternoon and evening
Václav Havel Airport/King Charles Hotel

After a bit of stacking, BA852 landed twenty minutes behind schedule at Václav Havel Airport and deposited fifty-three Sovereign River Cruisers into the terminal. Fifty-three pieces of luggage duly appeared on the carousel and were collected by their owners. As instructed by Freda, the Sovereign River Cruises agent who had seen them off at Heathrow, they went through customs with their cases and looked for a young man named Ivan holding up a black board with the word 'Sovereign' written on it in gold letters.

Once he had placed a tick beside every name on his list of passengers, Ivan made a call to Viktor, the driver who would be taking them to the King Charles

Hotel in a bespoke Sovereign River Cruises coach (black with gold lettering and the crown logo emblazoned on each side). Viktor confirmed that he was in position and Ivan led cruisers and cases out of the terminal building and into the balmy late afternoon Prague sunshine. They were left in Viktor's capable hands as Ivan needed to be back in the terminal for the EasyAir flight which, he had noted, was due to land in a few minutes.

Mary and all her twenty-seven guests managed to clear immigration with a minimum degree of fuss, although Lady Hayter was outraged again because there was no fast-tracking for peers of the realm. As each of her guests recovered their case as it trundled round the luggage carousel, Mary directed them to go through customs and to look for Ivan and his sign.

In no time, they were all assembled, and Ivan summoned their transport. Viktor's wife, Viktoria, was driving a second, similarly-liveried coach, and she drew up outside the hotel just after 4.00 pm.

The King Charles Hotel in Prague occupied a prime site overlooking the Vltava River and was located no more than fifty metres from the start (or end) of Parizska, or Paris Street.

The King Charles was a large, modern hotel but it needed to be large with almost two hundred Sovereign River Cruises guests descending upon it, some at the end of their cruise from Berlin, while others were about to start their journey northwards.

Sovereign had been afforded exclusive use of the Ballroom on the lower ground floor and the hotel provided the company with dedicated check-in facilities for its guests as well as plenty of seating areas to accommodate them.

To the left of the Ballroom entrance there was a counter providing a resting place for a couple of laptops and a hotel phone. Hanging from the front of the counter was a black banner emblazoned with the word 'Sovereign' in gold letters and, of course, the ubiquitous three-pointed golden crown.

The Berlin guests arriving from Děčín at the end of their cruise had reached the hotel the previous afternoon, accompanied by Max and two local Sovereign employees, Tomáš and Pavel. Most of them had joined a Prague walking tour in the morning with Tomáš, Pavel and Ion, another local employee, acting as guides.

Max was now waiting for the coaches from the airport in his black polo shirt and black chinos, with his 'Max – Cruise Director' badge firmly pinned to his chest. Max enjoyed the same good looks and athletic build as his late father. Standing five feet nine inches tall, he wore his blonde hair short and his COVID-19 beard had long since disappeared. And, notwithstanding his ten years in the Royal Navy, he sported no obvious tattoos.

Once everyone from the British Airways contingent was inside in the air conditioning, and supplied with a cold towel and a welcoming drink, Max took to the microphone.

"Welcome, everyone, to Prague. Can I ask you all to get your keys from the reception desk behind me and then identify your luggage. The hotel staff will deliver it to your room as soon as possible. It's now twenty past three and the coach bringing our other guests who flew in from Stansted Airport should be arriving in less than an hour. Please could you all make your way back down by, say, four thirty and we can go through the arrangements for the next couple of days together."

Taxis had been booked for the remaining eight guests from the United States, including Mr and Mrs Streisand and Mr and Mrs Topol, who were arriving later on connecting flights from Frankfurt and Geneva, but none of them were expected until after 8.00 pm.

Forty minutes later, the Stansted coach pulled up outside the Ballroom entrance to the hotel. Mary was first off and, as she stepped down from the coach, she was greeted by Max with a perfunctory shake of the hand.

"Hi, Mary, great to meet you at last. I'll catch up with you in a minute."

Max moved past Mary to wait by the front door of the coach as the guests descended.

"Lucy, welcome," he enthused as Mrs Lucy Burrage disembarked, "so good to see you." He gave her an affectionate hug and asked, "How was your flight? I hope Mary has been looking after you."

"Slow down, Max," Lucy replied. "Yes, the flight was fine and Mary is an angel."

"OK, great. Let's have dinner tonight. Say eight o'clock down here. Now get inside the air-conditioning. They'll give you a cold drink and a towel."

Which she did, and they, being the hotel staff, also did.

Max turned his attention back to the hovering Mary Mead. "So, Mary, welcome to Prague. Let me introduce you to Tomáš and Pavel."

Tomáš and Pavel were also wearing standard Sovereign black polo shirts and black shorts.

Mary shook their proffered hands. And tried an "*Ahoj.*" Then a "*Nazdar.*" Her efforts seemed to go down well.

Max looked bemused and he readily admitted to Mary that he hadn't managed, or indeed tried, to pick up a single word of the Czech language. "You must excuse me, Mary," he then said, "I need to make some announcements. Let's have a drink later. Maybe seven thirty in the hotel bar. My shout."

Max went inside the hotel where the recent arrivals were enjoying their welcome drinks and the even more welcome air-conditioning.

He took the microphone and repeated, "Welcome, everyone, to Prague. Can I ask you all to get your room keys from the reception desk behind me and identify your luggage. The hotel staff will deliver it to your room as soon as possible." Their luggage had been seamlessly transferred from the pavement outside the airport terminal to the area to the side of the Sovereign counter.

"As soon as you have your keys, please take a seat as I need to give you all some information about your stay here in Prague."

By the time that the last of the Stansted passengers had their keys and taken their seats, the British Airways arrivals had drifted down from their rooms, many of them showing signs of a recent shower and change of clothes.

Max began, "So, ladies and gentlemen, welcome again to Prague.

"First of all, let me introduce you to the local members of our Sovereign team, Tomáš, Pavel and Ion." Ion had just returned from a tour of Prague

Castle with some of the guests who had arrived from Děčín the previous day. Each of them stepped forward and raised a hand as his name was called.

"All of them speak fluent English, Czech and German. Tomáš and Pavel will be travelling with us to Berlin but you will see all of them on the tours we have lined up in Prague.

"We've had some rain over the last week so there are absolutely no concerns about water levels. But the weather is set fair for the next ten days and you can expect temperatures around thirty degrees centigrade during the day."

"That's eighty-six degrees Fahrenheit," he added before Lady Hayter had a chance to say anything.

"Right, so tonight we are going to let you rest and recover from your travels. There are some excellent restaurants in the hotel but Ion and Pavel can give you some suggestions if you would like to go out. They will both be at the Sovereign counter behind me until ten o'clock.

"Well, tomorrow morning, we have a walking tour of Prague. You will need to meet down here by nine fifteen. We will split you into three groups. The tour will last three and a half hours and it will involve a fair amount of walking. Make sure that you wear a hat and take something to drink. You will find bottles of water in your room. They are free of charge. But be careful how you open them."

"How do we know what group we are in?" asked Sir Claude.

"Good point. Basically, you can choose whichever group you want to go with when you come down. But we'll make sure they all end up with about the same numbers. So, if you want to go with anyone in particular, it's probably better if you all arrive together and you don't leave it until the last minute. Clear?"

Sir Claude confirmed that it was. He had every intention of being in Horace Mortimer's group.

"Then, in the afternoon," Max continued, "there will be a tour to Hradčany Square and Prague Castle leaving at half past two. We will be taking a coach to cross the river and the tour will involve a lot less walking than the morning one. We should be back at the hotel by half past five.

"We have twenty-eight of you signed up for the folk evening tomorrow night and we can only accommodate another six guests so, if you do want to go on this excursion, I would suggest that you sign up before you go back to your room.

"For those staying in the city, anyone interested could go with Ion on a walking tour of Prague by night which will pay its respects to John Lennon Wall and end in a brewery. If you would like to join Ion, just turn up here at 8.00 pm.

"Finally, on Sunday morning, there is a two-hour tour of Jewish Prague leaving here at eight forty-five. There is very little walking involved. If you need any more information about any of these tours, speak to Ion or Pavel as soon as we've finished here.

"We will depart for the ship on Sunday, just after one o'clock. We will be travelling in two coaches. You will need either a red label or a yellow label to put on your luggage. These will be available from our counter from this evening. The yellow labels will leave in the first coach at about one fifteen and the red labels should leave by one thirty. Please write your cabin number on the label. We will get you to identify your luggage before you board your coach and the next time you see your cases they will be in your cabin on board the ship.

"You will need to check out of your hotel rooms by ten o'clock. Your luggage will be stored behind our counter.

"That's all from me. I am now going to hand you over to Tomáš."

Tomáš took the microphone from Max. "Good afternoon, ladies and gentlemen. Pavel and Ion are going to come round with whisper boxes. I'm sure you have all used these before but, if not, please ask any one of us to show you how they work. You will need these for all of our excursions in Prague apart from the folk evening.

"You will also be using these devices all the way through to Berlin and they have some additional functionality once we are on board the ship. There will, of course, be charging points in your cabins but please turn them off this evening and tomorrow night before you go to bed. There should then be more than enough charge to last you until we get to the ship.

"That's it. Have a lovely evening."

Once the announcements were over, Mary went up to her room and took a shower. She decided to keep wearing Sovereign black to meet Max as she thought it would be helpful if she were readily recognisable to any guests wandering around the hotel looking for information about the cruise.

At twenty-five past seven, she took a lift down to the Bridge Bar on the third floor. Max was already there, seated at a table. Much to Mary's surprise, Max was wearing an Ipswich Town replica shirt.

"Hi, Mary, have a seat," he said, beckoning a waiter to come over.

"Dry white wine, please, anything local," Mary ordered from the waiter as she sat down.

"You're a fan of the Tractor Boys?" she then asked Max.

"Man and boy," he replied.

"Me too," said Mary, "or woman and girl, I suppose, although I don't often manage to get to watch them. What about you, Max?"

"Well, obviously I'm away for quite a lot of the matches," Max answered, "but I share a flat with three other guys and we've got two season tickets between us. We work out how many matches we all go to and then we divi up the costs."

Mary was surprised to learn that Max still shared a flat. She had assumed that he would be married and, indeed, would have had a family.

"So do you think we can go back up again next season?" Max asked.

"I hope so but, even if we go up, I can see us coming straight down again," Mary responded. "What about you?"

"I guess you're probably right. Anyway, what about the World Cup? Who do you fancy?" Max continued.

"Well," said Mary, "you've got to be patriotic. I'm going to say England."

"I suppose you should be," Max replied, "but I've been studying the form books and the statistics.

And the weather forecasts. And the draw. My money is on Argentina."

When Max said that his money was on Argentina, his money really was on Argentina. Max subscribed to Betcha, an online betting site, and had a sizeable sum riding on the Argentinians. But there were many more games to play before the final and Max intended to have a fiver on each of them.

His Argentinian pronouncement seemed to have exhausted his capacity for conversation and he started to tap the screen on his smartphone.

"Sorry. Just checking the latest odds," he explained. And he tapped the screen a couple more times. Contemplated. And gave it one more tap.

Tapping done for the time being, Max then announced, "Look, I'm meeting my mum for dinner so I'm going to have to love you and leave you. I'll see you in the morning."

Mary was quite happy to forgo his loving but she was going to enjoy the rest of her glass of Thomas Losen Edition Riesling On Slate 2023, particularly once she had realised that he had left her with the bill for both their drinks. And that he had had two.

So much for his shout.

12

Days 1 and 2
Děčín

The cruise section of the tour from Berlin had ended at Děčín the previous day and the Baron von Habsburg had disgorged its ninety guests into the two bespoke Sovereign coaches, driven by Viktor and Viktoria, which had then headed to Prague accompanied by Max, Tomáš and Pavel. The coaches arrived at the King Charles Hotel shortly after 2.00 pm.

The ship's crew had over two and a half days before the next guests and, of course, Miss Mary Mead, would be arriving from Prague. They were all given some time off but with the new guests arriving on the Sunday, it was (mostly) all hands on, and below, deck on the Saturday.

Captain Suzanne Zimmermann was Sovereign River Cruises' only female captain. She had been steering the Baron von Habsburg for almost three years and was a native of Frankfurt. Her husband worked for Volkswagen at its so-called Transparent Factory in Dresden where the company manufactured the ID.3 electric vehicle. Dresden was now home for the Zimmermann family – four daughters aged between fourteen and ten and two cockapoo dogs called Russ and Conz.

Her First Officer was another German, Boris Stich, and the Second Officer, Mike Rosov, had been on the Duke of Sussex on Mary's first cruise on the Douro. Mike was from Ukraine and was in charge of all things IT. Leaving Boris in charge, Captain Zimmerman was in her car (naturally enough a Volkswagen ID.3), which she had left in Děčín, and was driving home to Dresden almost as soon as the Baron von Habsburg had moored. She wouldn't be back until Sunday lunchtime.

Mike Rosov had, in fact, only been on the ship for a week – the journey from Wittenberg to Děčín was his first on board the Baron von Habsburg. He had asked for a transfer from the Douro because he had fallen in love with, and had started to date, a member of the Duke of Sussex crew who herself had been transferred to the Elbe at the start of the 2026 cruising season.

The Chief Engineer, Ivor Trabant, was by far the oldest member of the crew, with more than forty years' experience of all those things mechanical and electrical which were required to keep the ship sailing and those on board happy. Ivor was from Slovenia but had lived in Germany for as long as he or anyone else could remember. With all pumps, dials and gauges checked, and nothing requiring his immediate attention, he indulged himself with some suntanning on the Sun Deck.

The ship had three sailors, all of them from Romania. Ilie and Marian had been with Sovereign for many years and were old hands but for Jan, who was no more than eighteen, this was his first gainful employment. The sailors did what sailors do, scrubbing the decks and washing the deck furniture, draining, cleaning and refilling the Spa Pool and attaching hoses which would fill the ship's diesel tanks and water tanks and empty its waste tank (a job for Jan). When the coaches arrived on Sunday, they would become porters for an hour or so. And after eleven o'clock each night, one of them would become the Night Duty Officer.

The Hotel Manager was Martina Pavlyucheklova. She was from Prague and had joined Sovereign River

Cruises when she was twenty years old as a cabin attendant after dropping out of college. Over the years, she had been promoted from cabin attendant to waiter, then to barman and then to Maître d'hôtel in the restaurant. She had now been in her current role for more than eight years. Martina had also worked on ships on the Rhine and the Danube but the Elbe, with its proximity to home, was her favourite river.

The Maître d'hôtel, Leiter Herberger, and the six waiters, Andreas, Bruno, Carl, Dietmar, Ernst and Franz, all came from what was once East Germany. When not serving in the Coronation Restaurant, the waiters also helped out in the Portcullis Lounge and on the Sun Deck. With no guests to wait upon, they could be seen folding napkins, polishing wine glasses and laying tables in preparation for the new arrivals. And playing cards.

The bartender, Pearl King, was originally from East Ham in London, and she had been with the Baron von 'absburg since its maiden voyage in 2020. She also had plenty of glasses to polish before restocking her bar from a delivery of supplies which had arrived in Děčín on the Saturday from Sovereign's central supply base in Amsterdam. She then needed to fill the minibars in each cabin with whatever favourite tipples had been requested. Any guests ordering premium labels would be charged but otherwise this service formed part of the Royal Drinks Package. Premium-wise, there was a bottle of Remy Martin XO cognac to go in Luxury Balcony Suite 236, to be replenished 'as and when', a bottle of Bollinger Rose Brut NV for Luxury Balcony Suite 234 (a special request from Max) and a bottle of Gordon's Special Dry London Gin for Royal Suite 201.

The Executive Chef, Marco-Peer Weiss, was a Hamburger. As was the case for almost the entire Sovereign fleet, the other galley crew members came from the Philippines: the 'boys' Alfredo, Benigno, Carmelo, Dario and Emil; and one 'girl', Francesca. The other 'girl' galley slave, Generosa, was flying home to Manila following a family bereavement. If it was in the galley and it moved, they cleaned it and, if it didn't move, they also cleaned it. Pantries, refrigerators and freezers were restocked as more local fresh produce arrived alongside the ship throughout the weekend to supplement the frozen, tinned, bagged and boxed supplies from the Netherlands.

The sommelier was another German, Wiener Pourra, known as 'Hot Dog' to the rest of the crew. He had already selected the wines to go with each of Herr Weiss's daily offerings in the Coronation

Restaurant and, once he had checked that his wine fridges had enough stocks to satisfy even the most bibulous of guests, he indulged in a bit of wine tasting.

The cabin attendants, Teresa, Kemi, Maggie and Liz, all hailed from England. Their families had emigrated to Europe during its membership of the European Union in anticipation of there being a future labour crisis in the United Kingdom with limited opportunities for women of their conservative values. They thoroughly cleaned the cabins, made up beds to order – twin or double – and satisfied specific requests for pillows – nine types were available. And, once the cabins were finished, they moved on to the Coronation Restaurant and the Portcullis Lounge.

There were two butlers. Rishi had only started working on the Duke of Sussex just before Mary's maiden voyage on that ship. He had suffered a midlife crisis in 2024 which had necessitated a career change. Rishi had been transferred to the Baron von Habsburg at the beginning of the 2026 cruising season on the Elbe. The other butler, Josh, found himself in a similar situation to Rishi at the beginning of 2025. The butlers were tasked with leaving welcoming cards, bowls of fruit and bottles of Moet & Chandon champagne in each of the Royal Suites and the thirty-four Luxury Balcony Suites on the Buckingham Deck but, otherwise, there was little buttling required until the new guests arrived from Prague.

There would be another familiar face for Mary – Barbie, the young laundry girl. Barbie, a Maltese, was known as 'Bruce' to all on board since she spent all of her time listening to heavy metal on her mobile phone – Iron Maiden/Bruce Dickinson. A new iPhone 15 Pro Max had recently been acquired to enhance her listening pleasure. Notwithstanding the lack of guests, Bruce was, as ever, surrounded by bedding, towels, tablecloths, napkins and uniforms, some dirty, some newly washed or in the dryer and some ready and waiting for the maiden's iron.

Blume, the receptionist, was from Berlin. In the absence of guests to receive, her job was to arrange the newly-delivered flowers, the largest display for the Portcullis Lounge, smaller displays for the Reception area and the Golden Crown Spa, even smaller displays for each table in the Coronation Restaurant and, finally, single stems for the Royal Suites and the Luxury Balcony Suites on Buckingham Deck.

Maggie was Blume's best friend and, whenever she had finished with her cleaning, she would come and help Blume with the flowers and, more importantly, gossip. They loved to gossip. To everyone. About everything. But mostly about everybody. There was a saying on the ship that, if you wanted everyone to know a secret, just tell Blume and Maggie to keep it a secret.

Rubee from Moldova worked in the Golden Crown Spa. The spa comprised no more than a treatment room for massages and a small salon where guests could have their fingernails manicured, their toenails pedicured and their hair washed, cut and permed. Once she had readied her domain for the anticipated flow of hair, hands, feet and bodies in need of dressing, creaming, painting or massaging, Rubee also helped out the cabin attendants with cleaning the general areas of the ship.

The final member of the crew was Bennie, the resident musician. Bennie was Swedish and, before joining Sovereign River Cruises, he had played keyboards in a group which had enjoyed some limited commercial success. His rendition of Dancing Queen was capable of getting even the most moribund of guests onto the small wooden area in front of the bar which passed as a dance floor. Bennie spent the weekend trying out some new material.

By the time Captain Zimmermann returned from satisfying her conjugal duties, the Baron von Habsburg was ready.

13

Day 2 – Morning
Prague

Mary's guests woke to a beautiful Prague morning. A few wispy clouds intruded into what was otherwise a clear blue sky and just the hint of a breeze would be sufficient to keep the temperature bearable as they saw the sights of Prague.

Max was already eating breakfast in the hotel coffee shop when Mary entered.

"Mind if I join you?" she asked.

"Of course, take a pew," Max replied.

Mary placed her mobile phone on the table and went in search of coffee and fruit. When she returned, laden with food and drink, she sat down and asked, "So how was your dinner last night?" Mary was hoping that the mention of dinner might jog his memory about the bar bill.

"Well," said Max, "I was expecting to have a nice quiet evening with my stepmother but she had hooked up with those people from that Cambridge college. She insisted on buying all eight of them dinner and we ended up in the hotel's Italian restaurant on the twentieth floor. It's called La Vista and it does have a great view. We had a very enjoyable meal discussing enlarged prostates, why drinking bleach is bad for your health and the morality of lying in court to ensure the acquittal of someone whom you believe to be innocent. So, the food was good and the wine was excellent, and I learned a lot about prostates, poisons and perjury."

"That makes a change from the three Ps we'll be talking about when we explain how the toilets work on the ship," Mary remarked.

As she spoke, Max's mobile phone emitted a noise which sounded like an electronic concertina. Max's face lit up as he prodded his screen.

"It's Betcha," he explained.

"Good news?" Mary inquired.

"Absolutely," Max replied, "Canada 2 South Korea 1 and USA 0 Saudi Arabia 2. I got both of them right. Ka-ching!"

Those guests wishing to tour with their friends, such as those who became known to Mary and Max as the Porterhouse Octet, were all down in the

Ballroom before nine o'clock and attached themselves to one of Tomáš, Pavel or Ion, holding, respectively, lollipop 1, lollipop 2 and lollipop 3. Others drifted down and chose a lollipop at random or based on perception of numbers or the look of the lollipop-holder.

Mary elected to go as a sweeper for Tomáš and Max hitched a lift with Pavel.

Mary found herself with many of those guests who had flown with her from Stansted including Lord and Lady Hayter, Lucy Burrage, the Alis, the Billericay Dickies and the Porterhouse Octet. Jane Stanhope also joined Tomáš and Malo and Marigold, the last two guests to come down, were directed towards lollipop 1.

Once his group was assembled - he had a total of twenty-nine guests plus Mary - Tomáš checked that everyone's whisper box was functioning properly on channel one. This ensured a delay of some five minutes whilst the Blackwells and the Smiths returned to their rooms for their boxes. But, once everyone was fully equipped, it appeared as if all of his group had used the devices before.

Leaving the hotel, Tomáš headed away from the Vltava River along the aptly-named Paris Street, home to a number of designer shops including Hermes, Gucci, Dior, Prada, Jimmy Choo, Cartier and Louis Vuitton. The party halted briefly for Tomáš to point out, on the opposite side of the street, the Old-New Synagogue.

"If you join the Jewish Prague tour tomorrow morning, you will be able to visit the Old-New Synagogue. It's one of the oldest synagogues in Europe. You'll also be able to go inside the Pinkas Synagogue and walk through the Old Jewish Cemetery. Let's go."

Within a few minutes, they arrived at the Old Town Square.

"I am probably biased," said Tomáš, "but this must rank among the finest public spaces of any city in Europe."

It was relatively early, so the tourist crowds had not yet overpopulated the square, and he took them over to the monument which stood in its centre.

"This is the Jan Hus Monument. It was erected in 1915 to commemorate the five hundredth anniversary of his burning at the stake. Jan Hus attacked the corrupt practices of the Roman Catholic Church and he assembled a fearsome fighting force known as the Hussites. His execution led to the start of the Hussite Wars." Only Mrs Waterstone, with her master's degree in European history, knew what wars he was talking about; and everyone else was too embarrassed to ask.

"Over to the left," he continued, "is the magnificent Church of Our Lady before Týn. The present Gothic building dates to 1365. If you want to visit the church in your free time, you might be surprised that the inside is Baroque. The church was taken over by the Jesuits in the seventeenth century."

Lady Hayter was not impressed. "One really can't compare it with Bedchester Cathedral, you know." Not that she had ever been inside that building and she probably didn't realise that its noble edifice had been covered in scaffolding and tarpaulins for almost four years while extensive renovation works were being carried out to the stonework.

Tomáš felt that a shrug of the shoulders was perhaps the best response as he had also never been inside Bedchester Cathedral.

Leaving the square, they walked past the Church of St James, and Tomáš spoke to his whisper box. "If you went inside, you would see a mummified forearm hanging in the entrance. Four hundred years ago, a thief tried to steal some jewels from the high altar. The Virgin Mary grabbed his arm and held on to it so tightly that it had to be cut off. And his arm has been hanging there ever since."

"This next building," he continued, before anyone had a chance to go and look for the arm, "is known as the Municipal House. It's the most important Art Nouveau building in Prague and was built between 1906 and 1911 on the site of a former royal palace. Look at the semicircular mosaic on the façade." Most of the group's eyes followed the direction of lollipop 1 which was now pointing at the mosaic.

From there, they made a brief visit to Wenceslas Square to see the bronze statue of St Wenceslas.

"Is he the same person who looked out when it was snowing and sent his poor servant into the cold?" asked Marigold.

"One and the same," replied Tomáš. "He was a tenth century Prince of Bohemia. After his death, he was posthumously declared to be a king and he became the patron saint of our country."

"More recently, this is where Jan Palach burnt himself to death in 1969 in protest against the Soviet-led invasion of 1968 and it was also here, in 1989, that a protest rally against police brutality led to the Velvet Revolution and the overthrow of communism in what was then Czechoslovakia."

From Wenceslas Square, Tomáš led his wearying troops back towards the Old Town Square and the Astronomical Clock.

"When does one get a chance to stop?" complained Lady Hayter. "I'd like to get a cup of coffee if it's not too much to ask."

"We'll be back in the square in just a few minutes," Tomáš replied. "It's now just after ten thirty and, in about twenty-five minutes, the Astronomical Clock will be putting on a show for you."

As they walked on, the lollipop 1 crocodile became ever more extended as its constituent parts began to weary so he gave the House of the Black Madonna little more than a cursory mention as they passed. Mary sweeping behind the crocodile was now some one hundred metres adrift.

"OK, here we are back in the square," Tomáš announced. "So, the Town Hall is in front of us. This dates back to 1338 when a private house was purchased by King John of Luxembourg. The tower was added in 1364. Over the years, several nearby houses have been knocked together and, as you can see, the Town Hall now consists of a colourful row of Gothic and Renaissance buildings.

"The five-sided building to the right of the tower is called the Oriel Chapel. Its original stained-glass windows were destroyed in the Second World War but they have now been replaced.

"Right, the Astronomical Clock. When the clock strikes the hour, mechanical figures of the apostles will appear through those two blue doors above the upper section of the clock. You can see the signs of the zodiac in the upper section. The lower section is a calendar.

"You have time, if you want, to climb the tower and you can get a great view of the city from the top. You will need a ticket which costs three hundred of our Czech crowns or *korunas*. That's about ten pounds. There are, I believe, one hundred and thirty-eight steps to the viewing gallery.

"OK, that's enough from me. I would suggest that you now find yourself a nice café and sit down and enjoy some refreshments. Or you can climb the tower. Let's all meet back here after the clock has struck 11.00 am and we will make our way to the Charles Bridge."

As his guests gradually regrouped in front of the Town Hall to await the arrival of the apostles, Jane, Lucy and Marigold found themselves standing next to one another.

"Hello," said Jane, "I'm Jane."

"Oh, I'm Lucy," said Lucy, "pleased to meet you both."

"And I'm Marigold," said Marigold. "I'm here with my husband, Clarence," looking over in the general direction of where Malo was also waiting for the eleven o'clock show.

The ladies chatted for a while and, after Jane and Lucy had identified themselves as a merry widow and a rich widow respectively, Marigold said, "Well, I teach a bit of astronomy to older people."

"How interesting," said Lucy, "so what does the future hold in store for me? I'm Cancer."

"So am I," replied Marigold, "but I'm an astronomer, not an astrologer. But I guess the answer to your question would be 'a fabulous holiday'."

They talked a bit more about astronomy and Marigold told them about an app called AstroWatch which she had helped to develop.

By this time, the temperature was approaching thirty-two degrees (or, as Lady Hayter would have it, ninety degrees) and the tourist population of the square was increasing exponentially. Lollipops 2 and 3 had also made it there from different directions and shade and somewhere to sit were both becoming something of a rarity.

Some of the more adventurous of Mary's guests had gone back to look for one of the numerous shops selling *trdelník*. Tomáš had explained, as they were walking, that what these shops were offering was a local speciality known as a spindle cake. Thin dough was rolled over a spindle and glazed with caramelised sugar, cinnamon and crushed nuts. The dough was cooked over open coals and then the warm cylinder was filled with anything from ice cream to fresh fruit and from chocolate to caramel. "You eat a *trdelník* very much like you would eat an ice cream cone but you'll be eating a lot more calories!" he added.

"They remind me a bit of a cerith shell with its sculpted whorls, only bigger," said Mrs Smith, the marine biologist. Sadly, no one else knew what she was talking about.

Suitably refreshed, or replete with *trdelnik*, most of Tomáš's group were well-positioned in front of the Astronomical Clock as the apostles finally put in an appearance and smartphones and a couple of cameras went into overdrive.

Once the apostles had disappeared again, Tomáš led his guests to the Charles Bridge. The bridge was already supporting a large number of tour groups, distinguishable by the waving by tour guides of colourful umbrellas, lollipops of numerous hues, letters and numbers and, in one case, a larger-than-life plastic *trdelnik*.

"So," said Tomáš, as they passed under the Staré Město Bridge Tower and onto the bridge itself, "this is Prague's most recognisable monument and probably its busiest tourist attraction. The Gothic tower we have just passed through was an integral part of the Old Town's fornications.

"Sorry, did I just say fornications? I meant fortifications, of course."

With a somewhat reddened face, Tomáš continued, "The bridge connects the Old Town with an area called Malá Strana or the Little Quarter. The bridge was built for Charles the Fourth in 1357. As you can see, there are statues on both sides of the bridge. There are thirty of them in total but, for centuries, the Crucifix, which we will come to in a few minutes, stood all by itself. Sadly, only a few of the statues you can see are actually originals."

By the time they had reached the Crucifix, they had made nodding acquaintance with St Bernard, St Barbara, St Elizabeth, St Margaret, St Dominic, St Thomas and the Madonna.

"As I said, the Crucifix stood alone on the bridge for two hundred years. This gilded Christ dates to 1629 and, can you see these words here?" He pointed with his lollipop. "These are the Hebrew words for 'Holy, Holy, Holy Lord' and were paid for by a Jew as punishment for blasphemy."

About ten saints later, they came to the statue of St John Nepomuk.

"This statue depicts the martyrdom of St John Nepomuk and has been here since 1683. You can see that he has been polished to a shine with people touching his image for good luck."

Most of the group went up to the statue to touch it and add to its shine, and to be photographed doing so, but Lord Hayter was stopped in his tracks as he approached the burnished saint. "Don't be such an idiot, Marmaduke," Lady Hayter shouted, "it's all poppycock and nonsense. The only thing you'll get from touching that statue is something nasty from the person who touched it before you."

The person who touched it before him, and still in hearing distance, was Mrs Ali.

As they arrived at the middle of the bridge, Tomáš informed them that, in 1648, it was the exact spot where the truce to end the Thirty Years' War was signed with the Swedish Army. Once again, only Mrs Waterstone, with her master's degree in European history, knew what war he was talking about. And everyone else was still too embarrassed to ask.

A few more saints were passed by and they arrived at St Luitgard.

"This," Tomáš explained, "is the statue of St Luitgard. It dates to 1710 and it shows the crucified Christ appearing to a blind Cistercian nun."

There were another half dozen saints to meet before they came to the last one on the bridge (or the first one if you were coming from Malá Strana). "And here is our old friend, St Wenceslas."

As they passed under the Malá Strana Bridge Tower, Tomáš announced that the tour was over.

"You have several choices. You can walk slowly back to the hotel with me along the banks of the river or you can continue to explore or maybe have lunch in one of the local restaurants. For those of you who might be interested, John Lennon Wall is just a five-minute walk from here.

"Another option would be to stroll through the Waldstein Gardens. If you take the exit from the gardens to the Malostranská metro station, you can cross over the bridge and then, if you walk along the embankment, your hotel will be one bridge down on your right."

Lady Hayter, perhaps not surprisingly, suggested that it was totally unacceptable that the excursion ended so far away from their hotel, that she had no intention of getting food poisoning from a foreign restaurant and that she would catch a taxi back to the hotel and look to be reimbursed by Sovereign. Tomáš insisted that it was hardly more than five hundred metres to walk back to the hotel and that it was probably three hundred metres to the nearest taxi stand at the bottom of Paris Street.

"Let's walk, dear," said Lord Hayter, trying to appease his wife, "and maybe we can look in one or two of the shops along the way."

"You are really quite pathetic! I have no idea why I'm still married to you," said Lady Hayter in a loud voice which could have been heard by the lollipop 2 group which by this time was almost halfway across the bridge.

Lord Hayter thought to himself, "Maybe the title," but felt it more tactful to say nothing. However, he did agree with her assessment that he was pathetic.

Malo and Marigold made straight for John Lennon Wall. And, after numerous selfies, they retired to the nearby Wall Pub where they enjoyed a somewhat liquid and lengthy lunch. They were not intending to go on the excursion to Prague Castle in the afternoon, which was fortunate given that they only made it back to the hotel at 8.00 pm and proceeded to sleep in a very limited state of undress until dehydration took its toll at three o'clock the next morning.

There were no takers for the Waldstein Gardens and most of the group headed back to the hotel with Tomáš and Mary although the Billericay Dickies, who were also having the afternoon off, decided, notwithstanding Lady Hayter's dire predictions, to risk food poisoning by having lunch in one of the local restaurants. They were, of course, fine and had a great meal.

A taxi transporting the Hayters pulled up outside the entrance to the hotel moments after the last few remnants of lollipop 3 had disappeared through its revolving doors.

They were never reimbursed for the taxi fare.

14

Day 2 – Afternoon and evening
Prague

Mary joined Max, Tomáš, Pavel and Ion for lunch in a small café about a two-minute walk from the hotel. The café overlooked the river.

"So, how was your morning?" Max asked Mary.

"Well, Tomáš was brilliant and Prague is really, really interesting. I think almost everyone enjoyed the tour, even if it was a bit tiring," Mary replied.

"I expect by 'almost everyone' you mean that her Ladyship didn't," said Max. He'd already received a fusillade of complaints after breakfast, while they were waiting to start the tour, about the lack of a teapot, Earl Grey tea and thick-cut marmalade and, for which Max had some sympathy, the temperature of the toast.

Mary's silence told all.

"Anyway," he continued, "you were lucky. Pavel and me had those Americans with the MAGA baseball caps..."

"Mr and Mrs Harris," suggested Mary.

"Yes, them," Max confirmed, "and the Nixons, one of them is wearing a 'Bernie Sanders for President' T-shirt."

"I know who you mean," Mary replied.

Max continued with his complaint. "Mr Harris and Mrs Nixon spent the whole morning arguing with one another. At one point, when we were in Wenceslas Square, I thought Mrs Nixon was going to start hitting Mr Harris. I think Mr Harris called Mrs Nixon a 'commie murderer' when Pavel told us about Jan Palach and Mrs Nixon called Mr Harris an 'effing racist'."

"That's right," Pavel agreed.

"Well," said Ion, "I didn't have it all plain sailing, you know. I had that Sir Claude chap. He spent the whole tour trying to wind up what's-his-name, umm… Mr Mortimer, that's it."

"That's right, he's a famous lawyer, I believe," said Max.

"Anyway," Ion continued, "Sir Claude kept referring to the lady he was with as his daughter and asking how his wife was. He got very excited when we passed an Italian restaurant. For some reason, he suggested that they should go in and see if Mr Mortimer's wife was serving one of the waiters, whatever that meant. I won't repeat what Mr Mortimer said to him."

"By the way, Tomáš, where's the nearest vape shop?" asked Mary. "Much to my surprise, Lord Hayter is a vaper, if that's the right word, and he asked me if I could buy him a refill. I've got a photo of what he wants."

Mary opened her phone to show the photograph of a bottle of Nic Stick Flavourless Vape Juice Nic Salt 20mg (50VG/50PG).

"What does that all mean?" she asked.

"It means Lord Hayter rather likes his nicotine," said Ion, "because that's the strongest vape juice you can buy. Mind you, not many people like a flavourless one." Ion was himself a vaper.

"There's one down the next street," Tomáš replied to Mary's question. "I'll come with you if you like. I don't know how good their English will be, so you might have some difficulty getting exactly what he wants."

"I'll do it for you, Mary," Max volunteered, "I've got nothing on this afternoon and I'm guessing you will be going on the Prague Castle tour."

Mary raised an eyebrow.

Lunch over, Max headed off to the vape shop while the other four made their way back to the hotel to prepare for the afternoon excursion. Numbers had gone down since the morning, so there was going to be plenty of space on the coach.

Ion was the guide for the tour and was wielding lollipop 1. Whether or not jet lag might have been playing a part, none of Mary's transatlantic guests had made it through to the afternoon. But all her Porterhouse alumnae and their spouses decided to go, as did the Eagles, the Alis and Sir Claude and Lady Liz. And Mrs Stanhope, of course.

With another cathedral in the offing, Jane was first on the coach and she claimed her favourite seat immediately behind the central door.

Viktoria was at the wheel.

Once heads had been counted and the presence of whisper boxes confirmed, Ion took to the microphone. "Good afternoon, everyone. I hope you all had an enjoyable morning and a good lunch.

"So, this afternoon, we are going to visit Prague Castle. To do it justice, you would need to spend a week there, but we only have a couple of hours. So we will mostly be looking at the exteriors of the important buildings.

"The castle was founded around 880 by Prince Bořivoj. According to the Guinness Book of World

Records, Prague Castle is the largest castle complex in the world, with an area of almost seventy thousand square metres. It's a UNESCO world heritage site and it consists of an array of palaces and ecclesiastical buildings of various architectural styles, from the Romanesque of the tenth century through to late Gothic, Baroque and Neo-Classical modifications and additions."

Viktoria dropped her passengers off near Hradčany Square and, with whisper boxes live, Ion led his group towards the castle and began to talk. "As you can see, this square is lined with a number of imposing palaces. They date from the sixteenth century and were built by noblemen eager to live close to the court of the Habsburgs. The building on our left is the Schwarzenberg Palace. As you can see, it has been decorated with *sgraffito* which makes its façade look like Italianesque diamond-point stonework. The building opposite with the pink and white Rococo façade is the Archbishop's Palace.

"Come, let's go and look inside the castle."

They passed through a first courtyard and, as they crossed the second courtyard, Ion informed them that they were facing the office of the President of Czechia.

They entered the third courtyard.

"And here we have the Gothic St Vitus's Cathedral. Work began on the cathedral in 1344 but it took another six hundred years before the building was completed. St Vitus's Cathedral is one of Prague's most famous and identifiable landmarks.

"Where we are standing is the West Front, which is now the main entrance to the cathedral. Have a look at the Rose Window above the portals. It depicts scenes from the story of Creation. The window was installed about one hundred years ago.

"Also, you can see that the gutter spouts are disguised as gargoyles."

Walking round to the south side of the building, Ion stopped in front of a beautiful entrance.

"This is known as the Golden Portal and, until the nineteenth century, it was the main entrance to the cathedral. Look at the mosaic of the Last Judgment above the entrance. This dates to the fourteenth century and it was made by craftsmen brought here from Venice.

"Now look up at the Renaissance bell tower. You can see that the tower is wearing a Baroque helmet.

"If we were to go inside, we would be able to see the Chapel of St Wenceslas. The chapel is encrusted with precious jewels and it's where you will find the tomb of the Good King.

"The building behind us is the Old Royal Palace. From the eleventh century, this became the seat of a long line of Bohemian kings. Under the Habsburgs, the palace housed government offices, courts and the old Bohemian parliament. This is also where the famous 'Defenestration of Prague' occurred in 1618 when some Protestant Czech nobles threw three Catholic officials out of the window for rescinding their religious freedoms.

"On the top floor is the massive Gothic Vladislav Hall. There is a flight of steps off the hall known as the Rider's Staircase. The knights used to ride their horses all the way up to the top."

Leaving the palace behind, they crossed to St George's Basilica. Directing his lollipop towards the south portal of the Romanesque church, Ion told them to have a look at the relief depicting St George and the Dragon.

Another point of the lollipop and he said, "And this is the former Benedictine nunnery. It was founded in 973. The building now holds the National Gallery's collection of nineteenth-century Czech paintings.

"Follow me."

They did, and turned left from the main thoroughfare into a lane replete with picturesque, brightly painted cottages.

"This is Golden Lane. The cottages you can see were built originally in the late sixteenth century to house the King's palace guards. They are actually built into the arches of the castle walls. A century later, the goldsmiths moved in. That's why it's called Golden Lane.

"But, by the nineteenth century, the area had become a slum. After the Second World War, the area was cleared and renovated. As you can see, most of the buildings have now become shops selling books and Bohemian glass to us tourists.

"Franz Kafka lived here during the First World War and a very famous Czech writer and poet, Jaroslav Seifert, who won the 1984 Nobel Prize in Literature, was also a one-time resident.

"Right, it's now four o'clock. I'm going to give you thirty minutes of free time. You can visit some of these shops or you could have another look at the buildings we have seen. Please meet back here at 4.30 pm. We'll be leaving through a different gate to pick up the coach. We should have you back at the hotel by 5.00 pm. I'm going to grab a cup of coffee."

Mary decided to stay at the designated meeting place to make it easier for her guests to locate and, indeed, by 4.25 pm, all of them were waiting for Ion to finish his Americano.

The lollipop soon came into view and, after a brisk five-minute walk and a speedy journey in the coach downhill and over the river, Mary was back at the Sovereign counter in the hotel checking for messages.

There were thirty-four takers, including Lord and Lady Hayter and Mr and Mrs Nixon, for what was billed as 'Feasting and Dancing in a Bohemian Court'. The party animals would be travelling by coach to the village of Cicovice, approximately thirty minutes away from the hotel.

Tomáš took the microphone as the coach edged its way into the evening rush hour traffic with Viktor at the wheel. "Good evening, everyone. Tonight, you are going to have a unique opportunity to experience first-hand the traditions which have shaped our Czech identity over the centuries. The gala evening will be held in the court of the village of Cicovice. This is the place where villagers used to gather for harvests, marriages and other important occasions. Take a seat in the rustic country hall as a lively ensemble of dancers, singers and musicians in traditional dress regale you with songs that have endured for generations. Enjoy the strains of violins, a dulcimer and other instruments as you feast on a typical Czech meal served family style. This uplifting evening of carefree entertainment captures the spirit of Bohemia and Moravia."

It was pretty obvious that he was reading from a prepared publicity pamphlet.

He continued, "Be warned: drink too much wine and you might find yourself trying out a few dance steps yourself."

"No way," said Lady Hayter.

"No way," said Mrs Nixon.

This would be one of only two occasions that evening when Lady Hayter and Mrs Nixon agreed on something.

Tomáš switched off the microphone and settled down in the seat next to Mary.

"Sounds like fun," she said but, with Czechia scheduled to play England in Philadelphia in a couple of days, the discussion at the front of the coach turned to football.

"Look, we've got Bellingham, Saka, Palmer, Foden, and Kane, of course, loads of world-class players. We're going to thump you, three or four-nil, you wait and see," Mary confidently predicted.

"I don't know," Tomáš replied less confidently, "I still reckon Souček is good for a goal or two."

"Dream on," was all he managed to elicit from Mary by way of a response.

In little more than twenty-five minutes, the coach arrived at Cicovice. Unfortunately, Mr and Mrs Nixon and Lord and Lady Hayter were the last two couples off the coach, the Hayters emerging from the front door and the Nixons from the middle. As the other five tables of six were already fully occupied, the Hayters and the Nixons had no choice but to sit together on the same table along with Mary and Tomáš.

Immigration, abortion rights, taxation, healthcare, the NHS, climate change, environmental issues, Trump, Farage, Corbyn, Truss, Le Pen, Obama, Musk – all featured in what could politely be referred to as a robust exchange of diametrically opposite views between Lady Gertrude Hayter and Mrs Sarah Nixon. Apart from their views about the United Kingdom's shortest-serving Prime Minister.

All the food was eaten and all the wine was drunk. Neither Mary nor Tomáš drank the wine because the carafe never made it to their end of the table. But neither Lady Hayter nor Mrs Nixon paid any attention to the music, the songs or the dancing and there were numerous requests for them to be quiet, or to keep the noise down, from the other tables – all ignored – as the evening progressed. The Amazonian antagonists probably didn't even notice that, to the delight of the other guests, Mary showed some moves which bore a passing resemblance to the moves of the local ladies dressed in their Bohemian finery.

Lord Hayter and Mr Donald Nixon, however, spent the evening discussing the differences between baseball and cricket and rugby league and American football. But, once the food had been cleared away, Lord Hayter excused himself and went outside to enjoy a few minutes of vaping. Donald, once upon a time a twenty-a-day Marlboro Man, and still missing his nicotine highs, expressed some interest in giving vaping a go. He said that he would discuss it with Sarah, the reformed vaper still nursing her vape pen and nic salt vape juice in her handbag.

Fortunately, Lady Hayter commandeered the seats behind Viktor on the journey back to the hotel while the Nixons opted for the seats at the rear of the coach, so they returned in an atmosphere of relative peace and calm. Most of those on board slept in any event.

Once they had reached the hotel, all the guests made a beeline for the lifts, but Mary and Tomáš checked in at the Sovereign counter. Max was still there.

"Hi Max," said Mary, "still at it! How was your evening?"

"Once I'd given dinner suggestions to about forty guests, it was actually pretty quiet. I gave them all the name of the same restaurant," he said with a smile, "so I'd better go and collect my commission in the morning! Ion is back, by the way. He had, I think he said, six guests sign up for the pub crawl and he thought they all seemed to enjoy it."

"Sounds like you both had a more interesting evening than Tomáš and me. We had to listen to Lady Hayter and Mrs Nixon going on about immigration for two hours. Anyway, gents, I think I'm off to bed," said Mary. Tomáš didn't mention Mary's dancing.

As she left, Mary wished Tomáš and Max a good night and said, "See you tomorrow. Let's hope everything goes smoothly and we can get all our guests safely on board the ship without any more arguments."

Perhaps Mary should have been a fly on the wall in room 406.

Once they were back in their room (406), Lady Hayter complained that the room was too hot, complained that some of the other rooms had better views of Prague Castle lit up at night and complained that the two people from the cruise company who sat at her table didn't have much to say for themselves. Her outburst concluded with, "They should have got that awful commie woman to move to another table."

"Well, dear, I think Mary and Tomáš wanted to watch the dancing and listen to the music. I actually enjoyed talking to that awful commie woman's husband. I will turn the air conditioning up for you but I am afraid you'll have to make do with the view as you've closed the curtains anyway."

"You really are useless… gutless, you know," was all she could say.

Lord Hayter was silent for a moment or two, composing himself. Then he spoke, and what he said took some guts despite what she had said. "You know, dear, we really are well-named. You hate everything which isn't espoused by all your right-wing chums. Anything which hints at being fair-minded, or liberal, or altruistic. Anything which might involve thinking about someone else. And you find fault with everything and everybody. Especially me.

"And as for me, I hate you." These last three words were shouted at the top of his voice.

Lord Hayter avoided much of the tirade of vitriol which followed as he immediately left the room and went for a long walk along the river.

"She's right, you know," he thought to himself, "some rooms do have a better view of the castle."

15

Day 3 – Morning
Prague

With coaches for Děčín scheduled to depart at 1.00 pm, the enthusiasm for the one organised tour on Sunday morning was limited, particularly as hotel rooms had to be vacated by 10.00 am. Many couples opted for a leisurely breakfast and a liberal interpretation of ten o'clock. Others wandered back towards the Old Town Square and some of them had brunch in one of the restaurants around the square. One or two even bought themselves another *trdelnik* to eat.

However, twenty-two guests signed up for the Jewish Prague walking tour. Two of the American couples joining the tour were Jewish: the Streisands from New York and the Topols from Miami. Bill and Hill Harris, resplendent in their red MAGA baseball caps, Mr and Mrs Zieff from Texas and Mr and Mrs Montgomery from Montgomery in Wales had also signed up. Mary tagged along.

Tomáš had organised a young lady called Rebeccah to act as the guide. She was to be found in the Ballroom at 8.45 am with lollipop 1 and her whisper box.

Once she had counted to twenty-two, she began. "Good morning. We are on channel one. Can everyone hear me?"

She received twenty-three positive responses.

"Welcome to Prague, and apologies for such an early start, but once you have seen the queues for the Old-New Synagogue, you will understand why it's good to get there before the crowds. Please follow me. I need to pick up our tickets from the Jewish Cultural Centre. It's just a three-minute walk from here."

The Old-New Synagogue was little more than a hundred metres from the hotel, so she invited her guests to linger outside the building while she collected the tickets. She was back in no time, which was just enough time for Mr Harris to have upset Mrs Topol with a crass remark about Jewish people always being on the fiddle.

Before they entered the synagogue – they would be the first visitors of the day as the Prague clocks began to chime nine o'clock – Rebeccah asked all the men in her party to wear something on their heads. If they weren't wearing a hat or a cap, they were given a *kippah* as they entered. Red MAGA baseball caps were acceptable.

As they made their way around the ancient building, Mary's first time inside a synagogue, Rebeccah explained that it had been built around 1270 and was one of the oldest synagogues in Europe. It was also one of the earliest Gothic buildings to be built in Prague.

"Over the centuries," she continued, "it has survived fires, slum clearances and pogroms and it is used as a place of worship to this day."

On leaving the Old-New Synagogue, Mr and Mrs Topol were still sufficiently upset to break away from the tour and head back to the hotel while the diminished party made its way to the Pinkas Synagogue.

As they walked, Rebeccah told them that the synagogue now served as a memorial to all the Jewish Czechoslovakian citizens who were interned in the Terezin concentration camp and later deported to various Nazi extermination camps.

"The names of almost eighty thousand Czech Jews who went missing during the Holocaust are inscribed on the walls," she explained as they entered.

She invited everyone to wander around by themselves.

Mary was visibly moved by the haunting display of children's drawings from the Terezin camp.

"You should have a memorial for all those fine American boys who gave their lives to save you European guys," suggested Bill Harris, obviously less moved than Mary.

"There are," retorted Mr Montgomery, "in fact, quite a number of American war memorials in Europe." Mr Montgomery, 'Monty' to his friends, was a veteran of the Second Gulf War and had seen dozens of his comrades killed fighting for what many observers still considered to be an American President's vanity project.

That didn't shut Bill up, and a robust exchange of views about American foreign policy followed, involving almost all the remaining members of the tour group. Even Mary found herself contributing to the discussion.

"Please, everyone," an exasperated Rebeccah interjected, "let's get back to Jewish Prague. We are now going to take a walk through the Old Jewish Cemetery before finishing our tour at the Maisel Synagogue."

As they wound their way among and between the gravestones of the cemetery, Rebeccah continued her discourse. "The cemetery was founded in 1478 and, for three centuries, this was the only burial ground in Prague which the Jews were allowed to use. We believe that upwards of one hundred thousand bodies have been buried here on top of one another, sometimes twelve deep. There are over twelve thousand gravestones.

"This is the most visited grave in the cemetery," she announced as they reached the last resting place of Rabbi Löw. "Look at the pebbles on his grave. These have been left by visitors as a mark of respect."

A few minutes later, they were entering the Maisel Synagogue.

"The original synagogue on this site," Rebeccah explained, "was built in the late sixteenth century but the building was destroyed by fire in 1689. The present Gothic building dates from the early twentieth century. The synagogue now houses a magnificent collection of Jewish silver, some of it dating back to the Renaissance. The collection includes a significant number of Torah crowns, finials and pointers. Ironically, many of these treasures were brought to Prague by the Nazis from synagogues all over Bohemia and Moravia. Please wander about. Don't hesitate to ask me if you have any questions."

After a few minutes of wandering and five questions, Rebeccah announced, "OK, ladies and gentlemen, I am afraid that's the end of our tour this morning. I do hope you found it interesting and that you've now got some better idea about the history of the Jews in Prague.

"If you are headed back to the hotel, you just need to turn left at the end of the street. You will be back on Paris Street and you'll be able to see your hotel. It's only a few minutes' walk. I'm headed that way.

"Some of you have asked about kosher restaurants for a quick brunch. This one here" – it was just a few metres from the entrance to the Maisel Synagogue – "is called Golem and it's very popular." She would have offered up some alternatives but, as the restaurant seemed to have a number of seats available, all those wanting kosher food decided to eat there.

"If you have five minutes, let me tell you about the legend of the golem."

She only lost Mr and Mrs Harris, who started back towards the hotel.

"Right," she began, "the golem was an artificial being formed out of clay from the banks of the Vltava. That's the river in front of your hotel. During the reign of Rudolf II, Rabbi Judah Löw, we saw his grave in the cemetery, the one with the stones, created a golem to protect the Jewish quarter of the city and also to defend the Jews against pogroms. There is a Cabalistic concept that a person who is faithful and learned enough to know the exact sequence of the twenty-seven letters of God's name can create a golem and give it life by placing a parchment with this sequence of numbers into its head.

"Before each Shabbat, that's the Jewish day of rest, the Rabbi would remove the parchment from its head to make sure that the golem also observed it. One day, however, he forgot and the energy concentrated in the golem started to look for a way out. With no one giving it orders, the golem tried to set the ghetto on fire.

"The Rabbi realised his mistake, found the golem, removed the parchment and saved the ghetto. The Rabbi resolved not to bring it back to life again. Instead, after Shabbat, he hid the golem in the attic of the Old-New Synagogue.

"It's probably still there," she ended with a smile.

16

Day 3 – Afternoon
Prague/Děčín/MV Baron von Habsburg

By 12.30 pm, the first few of Mary's eighty-eight guests had begun to assemble in the Ballroom on the ground floor of the hotel. It was a very sunny day, with the temperature hovering around thirty-one degrees centigrade. Many of her guests were by now rather hot and sweaty, particularly those who had vacated their rooms by the designated time.

In one corner of the Ballroom were eighty-eight suitcases, almost all of them now adorned with the black and gold leather luggage tags provided by Sovereign River Cruises and with an additional red or yellow paper label indicating the owner's prospective cabin on board the Baron von Habsburg.

The journey to Děčín would take approximately ninety minutes. Tomáš and Pavel would each be accompanying one of the coaches and would be providing a commentary about some of the places they would pass and a bit of information about Czech history, language and culture and the Czech economy. Tomáš felt somewhat deflated when he realised that, as commentator to the red coach, he would be enjoying the close and confined company of Lady Hayter.

Mr and Mrs Eagle, who were also on the red coach, failed to put their watches on an hour when they arrived in Prague and were surprised at being greeted by a degree of hostility, particularly from Lady Hayter, when they returned to the hotel at 1.35 pm with smiles on their faces and two shopping bags. They had only managed to make the walking tour the previous day because they thought that it started an hour earlier than the actual scheduled time.

Also, two couples, the Streisands and the Alis, had dropped off to sleep in the hotel lobby but, fortunately, they had been identified by a hotel receptionist and were therefore only a few minutes late. They were both on the yellow coach and would have only delayed its departure by ten minutes if not for the fact that Mr and Mrs Zieff realised, as the coach started up, that they had forgotten to empty their safe.

"Sorry. Memory like a sieve," said Mr Zieff as he sheepishly returned to the coach with passports and valuables in hand.

Once the Eagles had landed, Tomáš was able to invite the second tranche of guests to board the red coach. By this time, Pavel's yellow coach with Viktoria at the wheel was well on its way through the Prague Sunday traffic and out towards the motorway heading north.

Entry through the front door of the red coach appeared to have ground to a halt so Tomáš excused himself past those hovering in the heat on the pavement and climbed aboard. He found Lady Hayter standing in the aisle, glaring at Mr and Mrs Rook, who were the oldest guests on the tour, each of them in their late eighties. They both used a walking stick. The Rooks were, for the moment, nesting in the two seats immediately behind Viktor.

Lady Hayter was all but shouting at the aged couple. "Can't you see that I have difficulty walking? And I get travel sickness. I insist that you get out of these seats. Tomáš, or whatever your name is, I simply must sit behind the driver or I will be ill. Tell these people to sit somewhere else."

The coach was clearly going nowhere until Lady Hayter had her way so, without the need for Tomáš to do any telling, the Rooks took flight and limped their way to the back of the coach.

Once she had ousted the two octogenarians from their seats, Lady Hayter cajoled Lord Hayter into taking the window seat and, as soon as he was seated, she removed the white handkerchief adorning his breast pocket, spread it on the seat newly-vacated by Mr Rook and lowered her considerable bulk down onto it. Whether the handkerchief was intended to protect the seat from Lady Hayter, or to protect Lady Hayter's tweed skirt from the thousands of germs which she felt must inevitably be lurking to greet her monumental rear, was not clear.

"You've never been travel sick in your life, my dear," whispered Lord Hayter, so quietly that he probably did not intend his wife to hear what he had said.

Max and Mary had reserved the seats immediately behind where Tomáš would be sitting at the front of the coach and across the aisle from the newly-installed Lord and Lady Hayter. The front seats, however, were temporarily occupied by two cooler boxes filled with bottles of water. The bottles, a local brand called CV (presumably from *čistá voda* – pure water), claimed that they had been made from recycled plastic. Whether or not this was the case, the plastic felt quite brittle and regularly collapsed whenever someone tried to break the jaws of the plastic ring anchoring the cap to the bottle. Once the cap was finally separated from the ring, there was a tendency for a quantity of water to announce its release by spilling over the person opening the bottle and their immediate neighbours. Sovereign, therefore, always asked the hotel staff to break the seals on the bottles before they loaded the cooler boxes.

As soon as all the red label guests were on board, Viktor started the engine which, in turn, set the air conditioning in motion, much to the relief of, and with begrudging applause from, many of the guests. Anticipating some bitter barb about the (lack of) air conditioning from Lady Hayter, Tomáš tapped the microphone a couple of times and explained that it was illegal in Czechia to idle the engine.

Once Tomáš, counting in Czech, and Max, counting in English, had agreed that there were indeed forty-four guests on board the coach, Max took to the microphone.

"Good afternoon, everybody. Right, we are almost ready to go. It's going to take about ninety minutes to get to Děčín, so you should be aboard the Baron von Habsburg by around three thirty. We aren't intending to stop on the way but there is a toilet by the central door if you need one. Tomáš will be giving you some information about Czechia during the journey but he won't be offended if you choose to sleep. It's going to be a hot afternoon.

"Mary and I are now going to come down the coach to hand out bottles of water. Once we get going, you will need to stay in your seats and wear your seatbelts unless you need to use the onboard facilities." To utilise these onboard facilities required extraordinary feats of dexterity and balance and Max was confident that the toilet would remain unoccupied throughout the journey. He also explained, for the benefit of those who had not previously been inundated with CV water celebrating its freedom, why they had asked the hotel staff to break the seals on the bottles.

Lady Hayter was clearly not interested in learning anything further about Czech history, language or culture, or its economy, or, indeed, taking in any of the scenery as she somewhat obviously removed a pair of earplugs and a blackout sleep mask from her handbag. She carefully placed the sleep mask over her forehead in readiness for shutting out all views of urban and rural Czechia. She then tilted her seat back as far as it would go and advised her husband that, notwithstanding Max's exhortations, there was no way she was going to put her seatbelt on.

Lord Hayter did not acknowledge the receipt of this advice but he found the mental image of Gertrude flying through the windscreen as the coach stopped suddenly supremely satisfying. "If only," he thought. And then he thought some more.

Mary was delighted when Max suggested that she should start at the rear of the coach with the bottles of water, leaving him to deal with her Ladyship. Before she settled down and shut off aural and optical contact with the outside world, Lady Hayter did accept a bottle from Max, albeit somewhat ungraciously. And, notwithstanding the noise of the engine and Tomáš's commentary, there could not have been that many people on board the coach who did not hear her take a couple of noisy gulps of water before producing an almighty belch.

Lord Hayter, with an enlarged prostate to consider, determined not to take a bottle, given what Max had said about the lack of stops.

Mary had decided that she really liked Lady Liz's glasses. They made a bold statement in translucent olive green and she had detected an Oakley logo on each arm. Lady Liz was one of those short-sighted people who would take their glasses off when they were reading a book, or the papers, or doing any other activity which did not require the use of their glasses. The majority of short-sighted people whom

Mary knew would simply push their glasses over their forehead or, sometimes, have them dangling on a chain.

As the coach was leaving the outskirts of Prague and heading towards the E55, Viktor was forced to brake aggressively when the lorry in front of the coach made a last-second decision to turn left. Lady Liz was catching up with some messages on her mobile phone at the time and she had placed her glasses, somewhat precariously, on the retractable armrest of her seat. Her Oakleys shot forward, sliding along the aisle and coming to rest by Mary's left foot. Mary recognised them immediately, looked back down the aisle, and gave a thumbs up to a squinting Lady Liz. She unbuckled her belt and returned the glasses to their owner.

"Poor thing," she said to Max as she returned to her seat, "she says she's as blind as a bat without her specs." Mary, fortunately, still had perfect vision.

Tomáš pointed out the town of Terezin for those guests who had visited the Pinkas Synagogue in the morning. "Terezin is the town which the Germans converted into a concentration camp during the Second World War. Remember when you were in the synagogue, you could see some of the drawings made by the children who had been interned in the camp."

About seventy minutes into the journey, Tomáš decided that those of his guests who were still awake had probably heard enough about Czechia. Even Mary and Max had dozed off. Notwithstanding Max's confidence that the toilet facilities would remain unutilised, Mrs Nixon, one of the few guests still awake, who was sitting immediately behind the Bearskin-Greens, was able to demonstrate the requisite dexterity and balance to make use of them. Flushed with success, she made her way to the front of the coach and asked Tomáš if there were any more bottles of water going spare in the cooler boxes; and she headed back to her seat with the last two.

The red coach finally arrived at Děčín about twenty-five minutes after the yellow coach. As it drew to a stop, Mary was able to see the Baron von Habsburg moored perhaps one hundred and fifty metres along the riverbank from the coach parking area. The last three or four couples from the yellow coach were already making their way onto the 'Floating Palace'.

Mary got down from the coach and walked with Max along the path to the ship where Captain Zimmerman, the First Officer and the Second Officer were waiting to greet the arriving guests at the foot of the gangway. Viktor began to unload the cases from the underbelly of the red coach, and a number of the crew members, including the sailors and most of the waiters, began to bring the cases to the ship. Once on board, the galley crew took the cases to the appropriate cabins.

Max introduced Mary to Captain Zimmermann and First Officer Stich. Mary, of course, already knew Second Officer Rosov but her attempted hug was awkwardly declined and all she received was a cursory handshake and a "Hello, Miss Mead." Max then boarded the ship while Mary made her way back to the parking area to deliver an envelope containing a goodly number of euros to Viktor. She had sorted out his wife before the yellow coach had left the hotel.

The fastest of her red guests, walking side by side towards the ship once they had emerged from the coach, were already nearing the gangway as she passed them in the opposite direction. Tomáš was continuing to help some of the less leporine of them off the coach, and point them towards their destination if, for some reason, they couldn't see a ship with the words 'Baron von Habsburg' on its bow waiting for them.

Once each pair of guests had shaken hands with Captain Zimmermann, Boris and Mike, like the animals entering the ark being greeted by Noah and his family, and climbed the gangway onto the ship, they were ushered towards Reception. There they found Blume and the Hotel Manager waiting to collect passports and take photographs with what looked like a large, plastic eye on a stalk connected by a cable to an item of technology on the Reception counter, usually called the thingamabob. The thingamabob had the capacity to spit out plastic cards known as shore passes bearing the name of the ship, the name of the guest and an emergency telephone number. These plastic cards, black with an obverse golden three-pointed crown, also acted as electronic keys for the cabins. Once a couple, or a solo traveller, was equipped with the means to enter their cabin and leave the ship, they were ushered away by one of the cabin attendants or the butlers to their bedroom for the next five nights and a reunion with their luggage.

Lord Hayter, tired after his early-morning walk along the banks of the Vltava, had slept for almost the entire journey and only woke up as the other guests began to leave the coach. He hadn't tried to speak to Lady Hayter even when he was awake and she was ear-plugged and blinkered in any event. As she still seemed to be asleep, he decided to wait until everyone else had gone before waking his wife. He picked up her all-but-empty bottle of water, which had fallen to the floor, and placed it in the netting bag in front of her seat. Then, with a certain degree of trepidation, he began to shake her right shoulder gently. She seemed reluctant to wake up and it dawned upon his olfactory senses that she might have evacuated herself. Rather more significantly, it then occurred to him that she was probably dead.

"Oh dear! Mary. Tomáš. Please come. Quickly!" he shouted.

As Mary climbed back on board the coach, Lord Hayter looked up at her and mouthed, "It's Gertrude. I think she's dead."

This would be Mary's fourth dead body with Sovereign River Cruises and she had little doubt that Lord Hayter's diagnosis was entirely accurate. "She'd been a heart attack waiting to happen," she thought, as if such a sentiment in some way made her death less tragic.

Mary turned her attention to the living while Tomáš focussed on the corpse. She persuaded Lord Hayter to squeeze past his dead wife and leave the coach and then sat him down on a conveniently located bench. Mary began to get the impression that Lord Hayter was not particularly upset that his wife was no longer among the living.

Mary next rang Max to explain what had happened. Tomáš was already calling the local hospital and arranging for a doctor to inspect the body. He then telephoned the police.

Dr Ivana Lendl was on the list of doctors retained by Sovereign River Cruises to handle any minor medical issues which might arise as they cruised the Elbe – there was no one on board with any formal medical training beyond basic first aid – and she arrived within about ten minutes of receiving the call from Tomáš. Dr Lendl explained that, given the circumstances of the death, a postmortem would need to be carried out but she confirmed that she was more than happy to certify that Lady Hayter had indeed shuffled off her mortal coil. She said that, most probably, in layman's terms, Lady Hayter had died of a heart attack.

An ambulance from Děčín Hospital arrived a few minutes later. Lady Hayter's body was, with some considerable effort and much grunting, manhandled into a body bag, removed from the coach and transported to the local mortuary.

With the coach now emptied of both living and dead, Viktor took the opportunity to clean the coach's interior as was his normal practice. He was relieved to find that the now-abandoned handkerchief, when working in tandem with Lady Hayter's tweed skirt, had effectively protected the coach seat from the release of any bodily fluids.

Viktor put on a pair of rubber gloves and went through the coach with a large, white plastic bag to collect the abandoned water bottles, a few tissues, one banana skin, two invoices from the hotel, one torn in half and the other screwed into a ball, and several other scraps of paper, all of which had been left behind by the coach's erstwhile occupants. The handkerchief also ended up in the plastic bag, and the plastic bag ended up in a nearby skip, which was also used by the ship for its rubbish.

The cleaning had been completed by the time a young, fresh-faced officer from the local *Městská Policie* arrived. Tomáš explained what had happened to him in Czech. The officer, whose name was Petr Korda, spoke very little English.

Mary had picked up Lady Hayter's handbag from the coach floor to facilitate Lord Hayter's escape and had also taken her tweed jacket from the luggage rack above the seats. She now handed these to the police officer. Officer Korda checked the contents of the handbag and made a list of what it contained: a Google Pixel 8 mobile phone, her blue covered UK passport, a red leather Chanel wallet containing four hundred and seventy euros and two credit cards, a small box for her ear plugs and a silk bag, presumably for her blackout sleep mask. There was nothing in the pockets of her jacket. He returned the handbag and its contents to Mary but he kept the passport, the mask and the jacket.

"It must be cold in the mortuary," Mary thought before scolding herself for her flippancy.

Officer Korda then sat down on the bench next to Lord Hayter. With the help of Tomáš as interpreter and Mary as hand-holder, Lord Hayter was able to answer the few questions which Petr felt it necessary to ask.

Meanwhile, Max had contacted the Sovereign River Cruises head office in Manchester and had spoken to the Chief Operating Officer, Charles Cromwell.

"Not Mary again," said Charles in exasperation.

Exasperated or not, the company contacted the British Embassy in Prague to arrange whatever formalities were required to repatriate Lady Hayter's body and Charles authorised Max to book accommodation for Lord Hayter in Děčín.

It was generally assumed that he would want to fly back to the United Kingdom with his late wife's body.

17

Day 3 – Late afternoon and early evening
MV Baron von Habsburg

With these arrangements in place, Max returned from the ship to explain what had been organised. Both Max and Mary were, therefore, somewhat surprised when Lord Hayter indicated that he would continue with his holiday.

"There's not much point in me hanging around in some place I've never heard of, and certainly can't spell, waiting for the postmortem. I'm sure the British Embassy can manage the repatriation of Gertrude's body, so I might as well enjoy myself. I would be surprised if I'm not back in the UK before she is. I doubt if they'll have a ready-made coffin to fit her!"

Once Officer Korda had departed with Lady Hayter's passport and jacket, and the ship's itinerary, Mary, Max, Tomáš and Lord Hayter all made their way to the Baron von Habsburg. By this time, all the other guests from both coaches had been photographed and had been issued with their shore passes. And all items of luggage had found their way to the correct cabins.

Lord Hayter was duly processed by Blume and exchanged his passport for a black plastic shore pass.

"We'd better keep your wife's passport, sir," said the Hotel Manager.

"The police took it," Mary explained.

"This is Josh, your butler," said Blume, introducing the young man hovering immaculately in a black suit with the Sovereign logo on the breast pocket of the jacket, a white shirt and gold tie. Josh hailed from Latvia and was extremely tall.

"Please follow me, sir," said Josh. "I am very sorry for your loss."

"Thank you," said Lord Hayter. "You know, you're very tall."

Josh thought, "This must be the British stiff upper lip which I've been told about." He replied, "Nearly two metres, sir."

The cabin was no more than a few paces from Reception.

"Just tap your shore pass here, sir," Josh continued, indicating the lock.

The door opened and they entered the cabin. Josh asked if he should remove Lady Hayter's case.

"Why not," Lord Hayter replied, "there's nothing of mine in it. It's the bigger one."

Josh then took Lord Hayter on a quick tour of the cabin's amenities.

With Lord Hayter finally on board, Mary went in search of her own cabin. As a Cruise Director, she would normally expect to have a cabin all to herself but, since Max was still on the ship, she would be sharing with Blume until they got to Wittenberg. She quickly unpacked and rinsed her face before heading back up to Reception. She had agreed with Max on the way to the ship how they would share responsibilities for the first couple of days, so she was going to have first dibs on the public address system.

"Good afternoon, everybody. Welcome aboard your Floating Palace, the Baron von Habsburg. There are still some sandwiches and cakes available in the Portcullis Lounge but could you all please note that, at five thirty this afternoon, there will be a compulsory safety briefing for everyone in the lounge. Unless the Captain is satisfied that all of you have attended the briefing, she is not even allowed to start the engines." Mary had no idea whether this was true or not but the formula generally seemed to work.

"After the safety briefing, Max will let you have some information about tomorrow's schedule and the excursion to Saxon Switzerland. Don't worry. It's just a name. We are still heading for Germany! Then, at seven o'clock tonight, Captain Zimmermann is inviting you all for a welcome drink in the lounge before we go down to dinner at seven thirty.

"Also, as some of you may already be aware, Lady Gertude Hayter sadly passed away during the coach journey from Prague this afternoon. Lord Hayter has, however, decided to stay with us. I am sure you will all join me in expressing our condolences.

"Thank you. And we will see you all at 5.30 pm."

She saw all but four of her guests by 5.35 pm. She had received a "present" or a "here" and even a "yes, Miss Mead" from the eighty-three obedient guests but there was no sign of either Mr and Mrs Streisand, who were found sleeping (again) on two of the sun loungers on the Sun Deck, or Mr and Mrs Ali, who had in fact gone off the ship (without tapping their shore passes) and, having forgotten all about the briefing, were on the bank of the river taking photographs of the Baron von Habsburg.

Once the miscreants had been rounded up, Mary took hold of a microphone and began. The art of fitting a life jacket was admirably demonstrated by

Marina and Pearl and, on receiving her cue from Mary via a walkie-talkie, the Captain in the wheelhouse blasted out the signals for an emergency and 'abandon ship'. Mary pointed out where the assembly point was (they were standing in it).

"Please don't throw cigarettes over the side of the ship. Smoking is only permitted in the open area at the rear of Buckingham Deck.

"And a special request from the Chief Engineer. Please make sure that only the three Ps go down the toilet. Anything else will block the system and that means for everybody."

Notwithstanding the exhortation, it would be an exception rather than the rule that Ivor's plumbing skills were not called upon at some stage during the cruise.

"Thank you for your attention. Over to you, Max, about Saxon Switzerland."

That strange English custom of clapping someone for no obvious artistic reason meant that Mary's safety briefing was deemed worthy of a gentle round of applause.

Max took the microphone from Mary and pressed a button on the remote control which he was holding. Screens conveniently located around the lounge emerged from their hiding places and flickered into life.

He cleared his throat and began, "Right. Tomorrow we will be leaving Děčín at around 6.30 am, so if you are planning an early morning run, please make sure you're back on board before six fifteen. And don't forget, whenever you go on shore, you must tap your shore pass before you leave and then tap yourself back in when you return to the ship. There's a piece of kit at the top of the gangway which looks like an oversized contactless card reader. Your name and photograph will appear each time you tap your shore pass on the screen.

"Early Risers breakfast will be available at the front of the Portcullis Lounge from six thirty and breakfast will be served in the Coronation Restaurant from seven o'clock until nine.

"We expect to moor at Bad Schandau by 9.00 am. There will be a very short coach ride which will take you to some of the most spectacular views anywhere in Europe." To demonstrate this assertion, he pressed his remote a few times to show on the screens what, indeed, were some spectacular views.

"We have arranged three coaches and you will be split up into three similar-sized groups. There will be a local guide with each group. We should be back on board by 12.30 pm."

"I would now like to introduce you to the ship's Second Officer."

A young man – Mary's diffident friend – entered the lounge as if on cue. He was actually the same age as Mary but looked no more than two-thirds of that. He was wearing the white short-sleeved shirt, white belt, white trousers and white shoes of a ship's officer and he had just the one gold bar on his shoulder. Short, spiky black hair and thick-rimmed glasses added to what might have been considered a nerdy look.

Max introduced the nerd. "This is Mike Rosov. Mike was originally from Ukraine and was studying computer science in Lisbon when the Russians invaded in 2022. He is now a Portuguese citizen and he's in charge of all matters involving IT on the ship. So, if you can't connect to the Wi-Fi, or you want to download some photographs, or share them with another guest, Mike's your man.

"He is also the person who will sort out your whisper boxes. I think you all managed to use them when we were in Prague but Mike is the expert if you do have problems. By the way, make sure you put them on charge before you go to bed tonight. You will find the charging units in your cabins. Mike speaks fluent English, French and Portuguese, by the way. And Ukrainian, of course.

"Anyway, these are the latest generation devices and you can connect them to your own earbuds or headphones, even a hearing aid, if you want. Mike can show you how if you are interested. You can also download an app to your smartphone which will turn your phone into a whisper box and the app will even act as a guide if you venture off on your own. The app also provides a running commentary as we are cruising along the Elbe, pointing out places of interest as we pass them.

"Mike will be around in the lounge after dinner and you will always be able to find him when a tour is about to leave.

"Anything to add, Mike?"

Mike added, "Only that you will find the app in Google Play or the App Store. It's called SRC Tour Buddy. It works really well but make sure you log on to the Elbe."

"Thanks, Mike," said Max, which triggered more applause as he left the lounge.

"OK," Max continued, "it's now almost six fifteen. Please join Captain Zimmerman for a welcome drink back here in the Portcullis Lounge at seven o'clock.

18

Day 3 – Evening
MV Baron von Habsburg

Captain Zimmerman, resplendent in her best uniform jacket, took up position by the entrance to the Portcullis Lounge at 6.55 pm. Next to her, and similarly attired, were the First Officer and the Chief Engineer. Beyond the first triumvirate, a second one, comprising the Hotel Manager, the Maître d'hôtel and the Executive Chef, lay in wait. And then came Max and Mary, Max in a black Sovereign River Cruises blazer, black trousers and a black polo shirt, and Mary in a black mini dress recently bought from John Lewis and making its debut that evening.

Although arriving guests would have had some difficulty in avoiding a handshake with the senior officers, they were at least rewarded with a glass of Basserman-Jordan N/V Riesling Sekt Brut (also known as German prosecco) before they advanced any further into the lounge.

For the more seasoned cruisers, a Captain's welcome reception would, once upon a time, have been considered a formal evening necessitating the wearing of a black bow tie for the men and the airing of their more expensive items of jewellery for the women. But now ties, and even jackets, were very much in the minority, although at least none of the men were wearing shorts. And, with Lady Hayter's demise, there was hardly a string of pearls or a pair of diamond earrings to be seen.

Once the Portcullis Lounge was sufficiently full to suggest that most, if not all, the guests had put in an appearance, the Captain positioned herself in front of the bar as Max took the microphone and requested, "Ladies and gentlemen, please welcome Captain Suzanne Zimmermann."

Max handed the microphone to Suzanne and, after the enthusiastic applause which greeted his announcement had died down, and she had been given a glass of what looked suspiciously like water, the Captain spoke.

"Welcome, everybody, to the beautiful Baron von Habsburg. She is a wonderful ship and she has a wonderful crew. The weather is set fine for the next week and the recent rain means that the water levels are more than enough for us. You will be having a beautiful holiday along the Elbe.

"Please let me introduce you to my senior members of staff."

The First Officer, the Chief Engineer, the Hotel Manager, the Maître d'hôtel and the Executive Chef were all introduced by name and nationality to polite applause and were then handed a glass of Sekt.

"Bon voyage and happy holidays," toasted the Captain, as she raised her glass and took a sip of her water-like Sekt. Her senior officers were generally less restrained with their consumption and five empty glasses joined the Captain's almost full glass on the bar before they headed out of the lounge.

"Ladies and gentlemen, dinner is served," Mary announced once she had seen Marco-Peer give her a thumbs up as he departed for the galley.

The announcement prompted a general surge through Reception and down the stairs to the Coronation Restaurant. There were a number of tables for two, four and six diners and one table for eight. The Porterhouse Octet had already carried out a reconnaissance of the restaurant and the Smiths had been dispatched, even as the Captain was raising her glass, to ensure that the table for eight was theirs. The Smiths achieved similar success on each subsequent evening until the night of the Captain's Farewell Dinner.

Mary and Max invited Lord Hayter to join them and he was pleased to accept. Although they were sitting at a table which could accommodate six diners, no one else elected to sit with them. However, throughout the meal, guests would, somewhat diffidently, if British, and somewhat brazenly, if from the United States, come up to their table and express their condolences. A sheepish smile and a polite 'thank you' greeted their efforts, diffident and brazen alike.

They were on desserts – apple strudel all round – when Max's phone emitted the electronic concertina sound which she now recognised as an alert from the Betcha website. She realised that Betcha must have news.

"So, who won?" she asked, remembering that she hadn't checked the results from yesterday.

"Not me, sadly," Max replied. "Oh, the results you mean." He looked down at his mobile phone and read out, "Brazil 0 Tunisia 2. Poland 3 Australia 1. Greece 4 Rwanda 0, and Slovenia drew 0 – 0 with South Africa."

"I'd forgotten all about the football," confessed Lord Hayter, "I must get online and catch up with the other results. My money's on Portugal even if

Ronaldo is almost my age." And with that, he stood up, thanked his dining companions for their company and announced that a glass of port in the Portcullis Lounge was calling.

Mary chatted for a while to Max and then she went up to the Portcullis Lounge herself and spent some time speaking to a number of her guests. She could see that Lord Hayter was still there with a glass of port in his hand. He was talking to a couple of the Porterhouse spouses, Professor Blackwell and Mr Waterstone, she thought, so far as she could remember who was married to whom.

Mary made a habit of walking round the ship before she retired for the evening. As she left the lounge, she found Blume in Reception and stopped to have a few words with her.

"Lord Hayter seems to be taking the death of his wife in his stride," Blume remarked.

"Yes, he is, isn't he," agreed Mary but wondered to herself if he wasn't taking her death too much in his stride.

Whenever the ship was moored overnight, one of the sailors would be on duty from 11.00 pm until 6.00 am to make sure no uninvited guests came on board. Jan was the Night Duty Officer for that night and, as he settled down on one of the chairs behind the Reception counter, Blume rose from the other one and wished both Jan and Mary a good night.

Mary then checked out the smoking area on Buckingham Deck. It was located through a fire door at the end of the corridor leading from Reception which provided access to the Royal Suites and the Luxury Balcony Suites, as well as the Captain's and the Hotel Manager's cabins at the far end. The area, which was open to the elements, seemingly had no official name, although the crew generally referred to it as the Smoking Lounge. There was just one person availing herself of the freedom to smoke but, as Mary was leaving, Lord Hayter arrived holding what was probably a second – or even a third – glass of port in one hand and his vape pen in the other. She left the two of them to indulge their ingestion of nicotine and bade them both a good night.

She then made her way up to the Sun Deck.

Mrs Stanhope was sitting at one of the tables, talking to Lady Liz. Jane looked as if she also had a glass of port in her hand and she assumed that Lady Liz was drinking either a Virgin or a Bloody Mary.

Mrs Burrage, much to Mary's surprise, was enjoying a late-night dip in the Spa Pool. Admittedly, it was a balmy evening with just the gentlest of breezes. It looked as if there had been a shortage of available material when her bikini had been manufactured. Mary shuddered. She couldn't help but think of the Duke of Sussex.

Lucy was not alone in the pool. Mary recognised Mrs Waterstone and one of the Mrs Heffers enjoying the warm water. They were both wearing somewhat more modest and, dare she think it, age-appropriate swimwear.

Mr and Mrs Streisand were playing a late-night game of chess. Mary had never mastered the rules of the game so she had no idea that Mrs Streisand was on the point of winning. "Watch closely now," she said to her husband as her knight moved to a vacant square. "Checkmate!"

At the stern of the ship, she found Malo relaxing on one of the sun loungers with a glass of what she imagined would be cognac in his hand. She was aware of what premium drinks had been ordered by her guests. Horace Mortimer and Phyllida were leaning on the stern rail and it looked as if Horace was also partaking of Malo's cognac. Phyllida was holding what looked like a gin and tonic. Or maybe vodka. Or sparkling water.

She managed to say a few words to each of her guests, asking them about their day, before retiring to her cabin.

It had been a difficult twenty-four hours.

19

Day 4 – Morning
MV Baron von Habsburg/the Bastei

The Baron von Habsburg cast off from Děčín at 6.30 am.

Mary no longer felt it necessary to watch each time that the ship moored or sailed away, or to welcome guests making their way into Early Risers breakfast, so she was asleep when Mrs Smith returned from her daily run at 6.10 am and when Boris followed her aboard moments later with a copy of the *Sächsische Zeitung*. She was still asleep when about ten guests made their way to the Sun Deck to watch the ship depart before retiring to the Portcullis Lounge for the Early Risers' coffee and croissants.

But, by 7.30 am, Mary was up and about. Her first task of the morning was to check the result of the England match on the internet.

"England 1 Czechia 2," she read, with, would you believe it, Souček scoring both the Czech goals. Stones had scored for England. She noted down the other scores and wondered how long she would be able to avoid the inevitable smirking from Tomáš and Pavel. And, indeed, from Mr Montgomery as Wales had beaten France.

The answer to that question was 'not long' as both Tomáš and Pavel made a point of coming to speak to her about everything but football.

There was a notice board on the wall opposite the Reception counter, tucked between the sliding glass entrance doors and a small, glass-fronted display case which offered for sale black baseball caps bearing the legend 'MV Baron von Habsburg' in gold, some expensive items of jewellery, three or four designer handbags and a teddy bear wearing a black jumper with a golden, three-pointed crown on the front. And little else. But, as Blume would say, there's always someone who will buy something.

The notice board had mugshots of the principal members of the crew and Max and Mary, but not Tomáš or Pavel, a map of the Elbe with their destinations marked, and the day's lunch and dinner menus. Mary decided that each morning from now on, she would post the overnight results coming in from the World Cup. She got on to this immediately.

With Blume's help with the typing, she pinned up a sheet of paper declaring:

England 1 Czechia 2

Senegal 0 Uruguay 0

France 0 Wales 1

Iraq 3 Jamaica 1

Pleased with her efforts, if not the England score and the smirks, she decided to grab some breakfast before the ship moored at Bad Schandau. Most of her guests had already finished eating and were back in their cabins, gearing up for the Bastei. However, there were still a few remnants of fast breakers in the Coronation Restaurant and Mary noticed that Mrs Burrage was sitting by herself. She asked if she might join her.

"Of course, Mary. Please do."

Mary placed her mobile phone on the table, ordered a coffee from Dietmar and helped herself to a bowl of strawberry yogurt and a banana from the buffet.

Returning to the table, she sat down, unravelled her napkin and, as she started to unpeel her banana, spoke to Lucy, "So, Mrs Burrage, how are you enjoying your holiday so far? Did you like Prague?"

"Oh, very much so. And it's Lucy, please. I was a little bit hesitant at first about cruising after what happened to my nieces on their hen party. But I'm having a lovely time."

The penny finally dropped. "Oh, Burrage. Of course, Ali and Ellie. You're their Auntie Lucy," said Mary.

"That's right," Lucy confirmed.

"Ellie told me you paid for all the girls," said Mary. "That was very generous of you."

"Well," said Lucy, "not really. I'd just won seven million pounds on the National Lottery. It's certainly very nice to be able to buy whatever you want or to treat people. But I'm not sure having all that money has brought me a lot of happiness."

She explained to Mary about the deaths of Ned and Lando.

"Actually," Lucy continued, "with all these people dying, I've just made a will. My solicitor persuaded me to make one so that my money doesn't end up with someone I don't really know."

"Very sensible," Mary replied, although making a will was about the furthest thing from her mind.

Lucy continued, "I used the firm where Ellie works. I never really got on with her but she was ever so helpful with sorting things out when Lando was killed. Silly bugger, driving so fast."

Mary then said, "I remember Ellie posting something on Facebook to say she'd got her old job back. I was very pleased for her. Some very Dickensian-sounding name." A few of Mary's younger guests had added her as a friend to their Facebook pages. At least she still called it Facebook.

"Yes, that's right, Tulkinghorn and Tangle," Lucy confirmed.

Changing the subject, Lucy asked, "And how do you like working with Max?"

"He's lovely. He told me how much he'd been looking forward to having you on board."

"Well, I hope it stays that way. I don't really know him that well. I'd hate to fall out and have him throw me overboard!" Lucy replied.

"Well, if he does, the water's very shallow. You should be able to wade ashore!" Mary said with a grin.

Mary was still holding a half-peeled banana in her hand.

"Oh, sorry, Mary. You need to eat your breakfast. I'll leave you be."

"Have a good day. I'll hopefully see you on the Bastei tour," said Mary as Lucy got up to leave.

And then Mr Montgomery passed by her table and mischievously asked if she had made a mistake with the overnight football scores.

The first stretch of the Elbe from Děčín took little more than two hours and the ship moored alongside Bad Schandau before Mary had even finished her banana.

At 9.00 am, Max was on the public address system inviting everyone who was intending to visit the Bastei to make their way off the ship at 9.15 am and join one of the three coaches which were waiting on the quayside. All the coaches were modern Mercedes vehicles with the same livery as the coaches which had been used in Prague.

"Don't forget your whisper boxes," he reminded those guests going on the excursion.

Only three guests forgot.

The Bastei did indeed provide Mary with some of the most spectacular views which she had ever seen. She decided to join the first coach and to be guided by a man in his late twenties named Fritz who was feverishly waving lollipop 1. Fritz taught English at a local school and spoke the language fluently in what sounded to Mary like a Yorkshire accent. She learnt during the tour that his father had played professional football for Leeds United and that Fritz had gone to school there. Mary thought that she knew who his father might be.

Also in the first coach were Malo and Marigold, Lord Hayter, Jane Stanhope, the Montgomerys, the Billericay Dickies and another twenty-four guests.

"Good morning, ladies and gentlemen," Fritz began, "and welcome to the area of Germany which we call Saxon Switzerland. My name is Fritz and our driver this morning is Sebastien. We have a ten-minute coach ride and then maybe five minutes of walking. And then you will be amazed."

Max joined the second coach, guided by Otto and driven by Ralf. Donald Nixon had a migraine and was missing the tour so Max thought that, if he sat with Sarah Nixon, he might be able to distract her from continuing her acrimonious arguments with Bill Harris. As it happened, Mr Harris had also decided not to go on the tour on the basis that no views could compare with the Grand Canyon or Niagara Falls, both of which were bucket list items which he had already ticked off.

Over the course of the morning excursion, Max learnt about Sarah's childhood in Harlem, about stabbing her friend Michele with a barbecue fork – "I thought she had called me a picaninny but apparently she was asking for the piccalilli" – and about serving time; and, indeed, about serving beers with AOC in New York. He learnt how she had met Donald and about her charity work. By the end of the morning, he even knew the colour of her kitchen.

The third coach, with both Tomáš and Pavel on board, was guided by Eva and driven by Michael, who was Ralf's father.

Fritz was spot-on with his prediction of ten minutes in the coach and, as his group walked from the coach parking lot towards the visitors' area, there was a palpable sense of anticipation.

To start the tour, he led everyone out onto a cantilevered viewing platform and asked them to gather round. He began, "I'm going to provide you with a brief introduction to the Bastei and then I suggest you wander round by yourselves. You can stay in this area but you should try and walk down to the stone bridge which you can see over there."

His lollipop pointed towards the Bastei Bridge which was already accommodating a large number of tourists.

"We are in Saxon Switzerland National Park and these are the Elbe Sandstone Mountains," he continued. "The Bastei is a rock formation rising one hundred and ninety-four metres above the Elbe river and three hundred and five metres above sea level. The jagged rocks which you can see were formed by water erosion over one million years ago.

"The Bastei has been a tourist attraction for over two hundred years. In 1824, a wooden bridge was constructed to link several rocks for the visitors. The wooden bridge was replaced in 1851 by the present Bastei Bridge which is made of sandstone.

"This viewing platform was reopened just three years ago.

"Can you see those small boxes on top of some of the peaks? What do you think they are for? Anybody?"

"Something to do with the weather?" suggested Marigold.

"No, sorry. Anyone else?" replied Fritz.

Nobody else felt brave enough to hazard a guess publicly so he explained, "Well, they're for hikers. If they make it to the peak, they record their details in a book which they will find in the box. You can see hikers all over the place."

Indeed, they could.

"Right, that's enough from me, let's take some photographs and then we will go and have a look at the bridge."

Smartphones and the occasional camera clicked into action. Selfies predominated but most couples called upon Fritz to take a panoramic photograph of them with the Elbe and the mountains in the background.

Once everyone had their photographs, Fritz led those wishing to follow him towards the Bastei Bridge and, although the going was no longer as smooth as it had been on the way to the viewing platform, no one missed out on the opportunity to walk on the bridge.

Mary had to admit to herself that the views, both from the viewing platform and the bridge, were, if anything, even more spectacular than most of her guests could possibly have anticipated, no doubt enhanced by a cloudless sky the colour, she thought, of the Manchester City home shirt and the Elbe glistening in the morning sunshine.

Mary was walking alongside Malo as they made their way back from the bridge.

"You know, Mary, if I'd have been married to that Lady Hayter, I'd have been very tempted to push her off the bridge."

"Mr Harrow, that's a terrible thing to say," Mary replied, although she was pretty sure that she could detect a mischievous glint in his eye.

"With my track record," she thought to herself, "the last thing I need is another guest to be bumped off."

20

Day 4 – Early afternoon
MV Baron von Habsburg

The coaches were back with the Baron von Habsburg by 12.30 pm.

The Coronation Restaurant rapidly filled but a number of guests opted to eat outside the Portcullis Lounge in the bow of the ship, with a ringside view of the Bastei, as the Baron von Habsburg started on its journey downstream towards Dresden at 1.00 pm.

Once lunch was over, many of the guests made their way up to the Sun Deck to enjoy the beautiful weather and the spectacular scenery. Several of them were listening on their smartphones to the commentary provided by the SRC Tour Buddy app.

After she had finished her own lunch, and completed yet more paperwork, Mary went in search of her old friend Jane Stanhope. As soon as Mary had seen the name on the passenger manifest, she had been hoping that it was the same Mrs Stanhope who had helped her on her maiden Douro cruise. She had, therefore, been delighted when she saw that it was indeed her Jane when everyone was gathering in the King Charles Hotel on the first day. Mary had managed a little hug on that occasion but they hadn't really had a chance until now to catch up with news about Vera Marple or about Jane's move from Peterborough to the south coast.

Jane was on the Sun Deck, sitting at a table under the black canvas canopy which provided some shelter from the sun. Max was sitting at an adjacent table with Lucy and they were, by the looks of things, drinking cappuccinos. Next to these tables, but in the sun, there was a sun lounger occupied by Mr Clarence Harrow. Marigold was having a facial in the Golden Crown Spa.

Mary joined Jane at her table.

As most of the waiters were still busy clearing up after lunch, the Hotel Manager was helping to serve drinks on the Sun Deck.

"What would you like, Mary?" she asked. Jane already had a glass of white wine.

"Just a sparkling water, please, Martina," Mary replied.

"And what about you, sir?" she asked Mr Harrow.

He ordered a beer.

Then, out of the blue, Martina looked at Malo again and said, "You're Malo, aren't you?"

"Er, yes, yes, I was, but I haven't used that name in years," Malo replied hesitantly.

"I was at that concert in Prague, you know," Martina continued.

"The Moss Gatherers played Prague several times," he countered but he had a feeling that he knew what was coming.

"I mean, *the* Prague concert," she replied, stressing the word 'the', "Your last one. I'll never forget it. I'm so glad you're on the ship. You don't know how long I've waited for this moment."

As she added his beer and Mary's sparkling water to her list of drinks, Malo was able to read her name badge: 'Martina'. He hadn't really paid any attention to names when the Captain had introduced her senior members of staff.

"Martina," he silently reminded himself, as a feeling of unease began to grow, "that was the name of the sister of the girl who was killed."

He hadn't thought about that night for a long time. Malo had received a letter from Ivana's sister on each anniversary of her death. But, about four or five years ago, the letters had stopped coming.

In any event, Malo got up from his sun lounger and headed down to his cabin.

Mary and Jane and, indeed, Max and Lucy, could not help but overhear the exchange, particularly as they had all stopped talking to listen. Mary had heard of Malo and could name a couple of the Moss Gatherers' hits but she'd had no idea that Mr Harrow was Malo and had even less idea what Martina was talking about. She was obviously wearing a puzzled expression.

"You know who Malo is, don't you?" asked Jane.

"Yes, I think so," Mary answered, "he was the lead singer for the Moss Gatherers. Highway to Hades, wasn't it?"

"That's right," Jane confirmed. "My daughter Scarlett used to buy all their records."

"Anyway," she continued, "I expect you don't know about Prague, do you, dear?"

"No, what is it about Prague?" Mary replied, intrigued.

"This would have been, say, about twenty years ago now. You could hardly have started at nursery school. The Moss Gatherers were on a tour of Europe and they always used to smash up their instruments and throw all sorts of things into the audience at the end of their performance. A young girl was killed when something they threw from the stage pierced her eye. I can't remember what it was. I don't think any charges were brought but, so far as I can remember, the Moss Gatherers never performed in public again."

Mary's curiosity was piqued and, when she returned to her cabin later, she searched Google for more details about the Prague concert and discovered that a fifteen-year-old girl named Ivana Pavlyuchelkova was killed with a broken drumstick which pierced her left eye. She died instantly. Ivana had gone to the concert with her elder sister Martina.

She found an interview with Malo in the New Musical Express dated ten years after the date of the concert. Malo continued to express remorse but also told the interviewer that he had received a letter on each anniversary of the concert, accusing him of being a murderer and threatening 'an eye for an eye'. They were always signed 'Martina'. Mary supposed that Martina would now be about forty years old.

She continued her searching and, apart from the New Musical Express interview and numerous articles around the time of the concert tragedy, she also found a more recent article from a Czech newspaper. Although it was written in Czech, she recognised the words 'Ivana', 'Martina' and 'Moss Gatherers'. She bookmarked the article.

"I'll get Tomáš or Pavel to translate it for me," she decided.

She also mentioned to Max what she had learnt about Malo when they met for the evening briefing.

"Yeah, I went on Google myself," confessed Max. "I was never really into music, too busy playing football. I'd heard of the Moss Gatherers, of course, but this stuff about Prague was all news to me. Martina, eh. What a small world."

She forgot to ask Tomáš or Pavel.

21

Day 4 – Later that afternoon
MV Baron von Habsburg/Dresden

The call came at 3.07 pm.

The caller spoke in heavily-accented English. "Good afternoon, Captain Zimmermann. This is Kapitán Antonin Dvořák from the *Policie České Republiky*. That's the Police of the Czech Republic. I am calling you about the death of your passenger, Lady Gertrude Hayter, in Děčín. I very much regret to tell you that she may have been murdered. The postmortem revealed that she had ingested a large quantity of nicotine. Of course, it may have been suicide. Anyway, as you are now in Germany, I have asked one of my colleagues from the *Bundespolizei* to assist with our investigations.

"I understand from the itinerary which you provided to my officer that you will be arriving in

Dresden this evening. *Kriminalhauptmeister* Willy Beckenbauer will be coming aboard once you have moored. He will call you to confirm these arrangements at 4.00 pm. I think you would call him a Chief Inspector in English. Could I ask you that you say nothing about this call until you have spoken to him."

At 4.00 pm, the Chief Inspector called.

Chief Inspector Beckenbauer and Captain Zimmermann spoke for fifteen minutes and, once the call was over, the Captain asked the Hotel Manager to look for Lord Hayter and bring him to the wheelhouse.

Martina found Lord Hayter in the Portcullis Lounge talking to the Rooks about David Attenborough.

Captain Zimmerman broke the news to him about his wife's death and asked him to stay in the wheelhouse until the police arrived. She then called Mary, Max and Tomáš to explain the situation and to expect a visit from the police.

And at 4.45 pm, the Captain made an announcement over the public address system. "Good afternoon, ladies and gentlemen. This is Captain Zimmermann speaking. We will be arriving in Dresden in about ten minutes. Once we have moored, the German police will be coming on board.

They would like to speak briefly to everyone who was on the coach from Prague on which Lady Hayter died. So I would ask all of you who travelled on what we called the red coach to come to the Portcullis Lounge at 5.00 pm. I am afraid that the lounge will be closed to all other guests but we will be serving Sekt on the Sun Deck and the weather in Dresden is going to be beautiful. We do not expect any of these interviews to take more than two or three minutes and, as soon as you have provided your statement to the police, you can join us on the Sun Deck.

"Unfortunately, no one will be allowed to leave the ship until the police have concluded their interviews. However, we do not expect this will affect our visit to the Classical Concert at the Zwinger this evening and the coach will leave at 8.00 pm as scheduled."

Captain Zimmermann was still speaking when the Baron von Habsburg came alongside its mooring so presumably First Officer Stich was at the wheel.

A group of seven uniformed German police officers, and a tall, dark-haired man with saturnine features and wearing a light brown suit, a white shirt and a red tie, were waiting on the riverbank. Mary assumed that the tall, dark stranger must be Chief Inspector Beckenbauer. He must have been in his early thirties and, she had to admit, he was extremely good-looking.

"I wonder whether he is related to 'der Kaiser'," she thought to herself.

Captain Zimmermann, Mary and Max were in Reception to greet the boarding party. The Chief Inspector led his officers up the gangway and, validating Mary's assumption, introduced himself in German as *Kriminalhauptmeister* Beckenbauer and shook hands with Captain Zimmermann. He then produced some documentation which received no more than a cursory inspection from Suzanne.

Chief Inspector Beckenbauer cleared his throat and, with hardly a trace of an accent, said in flawless English to all four of them, "Please just call me Inspector Beckenbauer, it's easier. I would like to interview Lady Hayter's husband myself and also the members of staff who were on the coach with her. My officers will take statements from all the other passengers who were on the coach. I would imagine that most of them will simply say they saw or heard nothing, which is absolutely fine."

Der Kaiser explained that the poison which killed Lady Hayter was nicotine and, as it would have taken effect almost immediately, the police believed that it must have been ingested when she was on the coach.

He then explained that it was almost certainly the case that she had drunk some water which had been laced with the nicotine. He hoped to have a full forensic report from his Czech colleagues before the end of the day but they believed that they were looking at vape juice as the source of the poison.

So Lady Hayter either committed suicide or someone on the coach must have poisoned her.

Mary introduced herself and Max. "We are Sovereign's Cruise Directors for this trip and we were both on the coach."

"And I work for Sovereign in Prague," said Tomáš, introducing himself, before continuing in what Mary took to be German, given that the Inspector replied in what sounded like the same language and, presumably, included a confirmation from Tomáš that he had been sitting at the front of the coach providing a running commentary.

Once the Germanic exchange came to an end, Mary said, "The only other person on the coach was the driver. His name was, um…"

"Viktor," said the Inspector. "Yes, he has already been interviewed."

"OK," Mary continued, "all the guests who were on the coach are now in the Portcullis Lounge, apart from Lord Hayter, who is in the wheelhouse with the

First Officer. There are forty-three of them. Sorry, I mean forty-two."

"Fine," said Inspector Beckenbauer, speaking to Mary, "please show my officers to the lounge and then," looking at Max and Tomáš, "would all three of you please wait outside the wheelhouse while I interview Lord Hayter."

Once his interview with Lord Hayter had finished, the Inspector asked one of his officers to accompany his Lordship to his cabin and wait with him. Mary was then ushered into the wheelhouse for her interview with the Inspector. He was sitting in the Captain's leather armchair and a female officer, whom he did not introduce, stood in the corner with her notebook in hand.

Mary sat down on a second, far less comfortable chair.

She jumped the gun and started to speak. "I assume that the nicotine must have been in the bottle of water which Lady Hayter drank. So I suppose I should explain about the bottles of water on the coach.

"We have four cooler boxes. We use them to provide bottles of cold water for our guests on the longer coach journeys. We asked the hotel in Prague – we were staying at the King Charles – to provide us with four packs. There are twenty-four bottles in each pack."

She then described in some detail the shortcomings in the opening mechanism of a CV water bottle.

She continued, "So we also asked the hotel to break the seals on the bottles to avoid having our guests getting soaked. I should mention that we make sure the hotel staff wear rubber gloves when they are handling the bottles. Just in case you were looking for fingerprints. The hotel placed the cooler boxes on the front seats of each coach.

"Lady Hayter was on what we called the red coach. Tomáš was sitting up front with the cooler boxes and Max and I were in the two seats behind him. Once Tomáš and Max had checked that everyone was on board, Max and I loaded ourselves up with bottles of water from the cooler boxes and we went down the coach, handing them out to anyone who wanted one. I started at the back of the coach and Max started at the front. Almost everybody takes a bottle, even if they don't end up drinking it. And, of course, some guests bring their own drinks.

"We got underway once we had finished handing out the bottles and many of our guests drifted off to sleep pretty quickly. But I would imagine that anyone who was still awake must have heard Lady Hayter take a couple of loud gulps from her bottle and then deliver a resounding belch. I must admit that I gave her a bit of a stare.

"I tried to ignore her after that but I did look across at some stage and I thought she must have been asleep. I do remember she was wearing her blackout mask over her eyes. I couldn't really see Lord Hayter from where I was sitting. Lady Hayter was in the way!"

The Inspector asked her, "Do you think there is anyone on the ship who might have wanted to murder her?"

Mary thought for a moment and then replied, "Well, to be perfectly honest, and remember I only met Lady Hayter for the first time on Friday, she was not a particularly pleasant person. She was very rude to me and I gather that she insulted a member of the cabin crew on the flight from Stansted. Her behaviour in Prague towards Tomáš on the city tour was totally unacceptable. Then she had a very unpleasant argument with Mrs Nixon when we went for a folk evening. I suppose anyone she met might have thought, 'I could throttle that woman', but I am sure none of us would have actually meant it."

As she said it, in the back of her mind, she recalled what Malo had said to her about pushing Lady Hayter off the Bastei Bridge.

"And what about Lord Hayter?" he asked.

"I really don't think theirs was a happy marriage," Mary answered. "She was always belittling him but he was very phlegmatic. He certainly didn't seem very upset when she died and, of course, he decided to stay with the cruise. We were all a bit surprised about that but he said there was little point in him sitting around in some strange place waiting for her body to be sent back to England."

"I assume you didn't see him put anything in her bottle?" the Inspector continued.

"Absolutely not. As I said, Lady Hayter was blocking my view of her husband. And, as you probably know, I picked up Lady Hayter's handbag from the floor of the coach and went through its contents with the local police officer. I am sure there was nothing in it which could possibly have contained any liquid. And there was nothing in her pockets."

"Mind you," Mary continued, "you mentioned that the source of the nicotine might have been vape juice. Did you know Lord Hayter uses a vape pen? And he also asked me to buy him a bottle of really strong flavourless vape juice when we were in Prague."

The interview over, Mary went down to Reception to get on with organising the Dresden excursions.

Max confirmed that he had handed a bottle of water to Lady Hayter but, so far as he could recall, Lord Hayter had not taken one. Tomáš mentioned that, quite near the end of the journey, when most guests were sleeping, Mrs Harris had collected the last two bottles of water from the cooler boxes.

None of the guests from the red coach had much to contribute. Mrs Rook confirmed that Lady Hayter had asked her to give up the two seats behind the driver and she said that Lady Hayter had been extremely rude. Sir Claude and Lady Liz, who were sitting two rows behind Mary and Max, said that Tomáš was very interesting. They were both rather offended when Lady Hayter belched very loudly without even the suggestion of an 'excuse me'. At least, they thought that it was her. The Dickies, who were sitting behind Lord and Lady Hayter, also remembered what they described as a burp. And Mrs Nixon claimed that she didn't notice anything when she went to get some more water, although she also recalled a large belch.

With all statements signed, the other officers left the ship and Inspector Beckenbauer went in search of Captain Zimmermann. She was in Reception chatting to Mary about the football.

"I would like Lord Hayter to accompany me back to our headquarters in Dresden as I need to ask him some further questions. Perhaps you could fetch him. He should be in his cabin with one of my officers."

Captain Zimmermann went to explain to Lord Hayter what was happening. Five minutes later, Lord Hayter and his escort, together with his passport, left the ship under the watchful gaze of a crowded Sun Deck and many of the balconies on the port side of the ship.

It certainly seemed to the onlookers that the police suspected that Lord Hayter had murdered his wife. But many of those watching felt a great deal of sympathy for him. There was really no one on board who seemed in any way upset that Lady Hayter was dead.

Mary made to leave but the Inspector said, "No, no, please stay, Miss Mead, I believe your insights might prove very helpful. Let's all go back to the wheelhouse." She was to learn later why he had said this.

"So what are your thoughts, Mary?" he asked once they were inside.

"Well," she replied, "I suppose that Lady Hayter must either have committed suicide, which seems most unlikely and for which the police don't have any evidence, or she was murdered by her husband, which would certainly seem a possibility. He'd have had an opportunity to add the poison to the bottle of water when she put her sleep mask on, he had access to nicotine, and you can understand why he might have wanted to murder his wife. And he didn't seem to be very upset. But why now? Did something happen when we were in Prague?

"Or," she continued, "I suppose someone from the hotel staff could have put the nicotine in one of the bottles when they were opening them for us. But then they'd have had no idea who their victim would be. No one else appears to have drunk from a bottle laced with nicotine. But why would someone act in such a random fashion?"

"You're right, Mary," said the Inspector, "but, as you say, if that's what happened, it's difficult to see what the murderer's motive could possibly have been."

Another thought crossed Mary's mind but the Inspector seemed satisfied with his afternoon's work and she let it go.

"Please continue with your cruise. You can tell your passengers that we are treating Lady Hayter's death as suspicious, although I'm sure they must already realise that," said the Inspector. And he was gone. Almost.

As he was about to go onshore, Blume stopped him. "Excuse me, Inspector, this is Mrs Streisand. She would like to have a word."

There were, in fact, quite a number of words to be had and they emerged in a breathless torrent. "I really hope I'm not wasting your time, Inspector, but my husband, Mr Streisand, said it would be wrong not to mention it. We were on the yellow coach, so you didn't want to talk to us. But, you see, when we were in the hotel in Prague, we were in room 404 which was the one next to his Lordship's room. Jacob, that's my husband, and me, I'm Rachel, by the way, well, we are both very light sleepers and, with jet lag and everything, we were waking up to any little noise. It's the way we were.

"Well, that last night in the hotel, it must have been just about midnight, maybe later. His Lordship had this almighty row with his wife. He called her all sorts of things. I didn't really catch everything but he most definitely shouted that he hated her. Then we heard him leave the room. We know it was him because we could still hear her Ladyship screaming and shouting next door. 'That's not a marriage made in heaven,' I said to my Jacob. Anyway, we heard the door open again about an hour or so later so I guess that's when he must have come back."

"Thank you so much, Mrs Streisand. You have been extremely helpful. I am going to need one of my officers to get a written statement from both of you, if that's OK?"

"Of course," she said, "anything we can do to help."

22

Day 4 – Evening
Dresden

Once Inspector Beckenbauer had left the ship, with one of his officers heading in the opposite direction to take a statement from Mr and Mrs Streisand, Mary was straight on to the public address system.

"Good evening, ladies and gentlemen. Apologies again for all the inconvenience this afternoon. To avoid any inappropriate or unfounded rumours circulating, the German police have authorised me to confirm they are treating the death of Lady Hayter as suspicious. But no one has been arrested.

"However, we can now get back to our cruise. The Portcullis Lounge is open again. As previously announced, for those of you going to the concert at the Zwinger this evening, dinner will be served at 6.30 pm. A coach will then take us to the concert at eight o'clock. The programme will start at 8.30 pm and will last for an hour and a quarter. So, you should be back on board by ten fifteen.

"For those not going to the concert, dinner will start at 7.30 pm.

"Max will be in the Portcullis Lounge at six fifteen to give you some information about tomorrow's excursions.

"We will, of course, be moored overnight in Dresden so anyone wishing to walk into the city centre is welcome to do so. Thank you."

Mary was going to attend the concert along with twenty-four guests, including her Porterhouse Octet, Sir Claude and Lady Liz, Mr and Mrs Eagle, Mr and Mrs Montgomery and the Billericay Dickies.

The concert was taking place in the Wall Pavilion of the Zwinger which, according to its own publicity, was regarded as one of the most magnificent exponents of Baroque architecture in Europe. And, apparently, the numerous statues on the Wall Pavilion's façade merged the world of Ancient Greece and the claim to power of Augustus the Strong.

Whatever that meant.

Normally, the private concerts which Sovereign organised were given by the Dresdner Resident Orchestra. However, the orchestra had been invited to the United States to provide a Teutonic contribution to an international festival of arts which was being staged alongside the football. Performers from all forty-eight nations represented at FIFA World Cup 26 were taking part.

Accordingly, in the absence of the orchestra, the concert was to be given by students from the Dresden Zwollenhohen Conservatoire under the guidance of its patron, Baroness Steffi Zwollenhohen-Maugnelotte.

The Zwollenhohen-Maugnelottes, an alliance of noble and ancient Prussian and French families, had at one time been one of the most powerful and wealthy European dynasties but its fortunes had foundered during the nineteenth century against the rock of the Habsburgs. For more than a century, successive generations of Zwollenhohen-Maugnelottes had harboured a deep-seated resentment of the Habsburg dynasty.

The Baroness had arranged for four of her students to provide the evening's entertainment. Those chosen had been selected not so much for their musical ability as their indebtedness, financial and moral, to the Baroness. In other words, all of them had their tuition fees subsidised by a charitable foundation established by the Baroness to encourage students with somewhat limited means – and sometimes somewhat limited musical ability – to study classical music.

The concert was a disaster.

The promised welcoming glass of champagne was no more than a very sweet sparkling German wine which unfortunately had spent the day absorbing the sunshine through the windows of the pavilion rather than enjoying the cooling effects of a refrigerator or even an ice bucket.

There were not enough seats, which meant that Mary and the Eagles had to perch on bar stools.

The programme certainly looked promising. The Impresario Overture by Mozart, the Turkish March from the Ruins of Athens by Beethoven, *Idylle* by Elgar, the *España* Waltz by Waldteufel and, after the interval, Andante from Symphony 9 by Haydn, the Gypsy Dance from Bizet's Carmen and Johann Strauss's Thunder and Lightning Polka.

However, once the concert was underway, it sounded as if the piano hadn't been tuned for some time, the cellist was in the wrong key during the Turkish March and the *Idylle*, the bass player set the wrong tempo for the *España* Walz and the violinist screeched her way through the entire first half of the programme.

Surprisingly, the Baroness did not in any way appear to be perturbed by these disasters and she was not at all upset when only four guests, the Bearskin-Greens and the Montgomerys, reappeared after the interval. The others had wandered off in various directions to explore other areas of the city centre.

With a potential audience of five, it was readily agreed to forgo the second half, and Mary and those guests whom she presumed must be tone deaf followed those more musically attuned out into the setting sun.

Mary almost forgot that she was supposed to make a small donation towards the conservatoire and hastened back to the pavilion. She was somewhat surprised to see the Baroness hugging her musicians and exchanging what certainly looked to be high-fives.

Mary never found out why the Baroness was celebrating the disaster. Was this an example of *schadenfreude* and, if so, was the Baroness taking delight in the misfortunes of her quartet or the audience? It was neither.

She might have found out about the animosity towards the Habsburgs but there was no way that Mary would have discovered that, in her dotage, the Baroness had assumed that the MV Baron von Habsburg was somehow connected with the Habsburg dynasty. She thought that, by ensuring the concert turned into a fiasco, this would in some way cause irreparable damage to the reputation of the dastardly Habsburgs. But there was no connection. And no damage.

Mary decided to return to the meeting point and wait for her guests to return. Sir Claude and Lady Liz were closely following her and she couldn't help but listen to their conversation.

Lady Liz said to her husband, "It was so nice to spend an evening without that horrid man, even if the music was terrible. But maybe you should stop baiting him so much."

"I know, darling," he replied, "but it's very difficult when you know how he deliberately destroyed my reputation. I've never told you this, he actually rang me the night before the trial started. He thought I'd be interested to know that my star witness, the gang member who had photographed the murders, had been persuaded to change his evidence and was going to accuse the police of bribing him and forging the photographs. And swear that I knew all about this.

"He was gloating. He knew exactly what would happen: my integrity would be openly called into question, the public's confidence in the justice system would be shattered, and I would be forced to resign.

"I think, I hope, that the only thing he didn't anticipate was the effect all this would have on my dear Angela. I blame him for her death, you know."

Lady Liz squeezed his hand and asked, "What does that passage from the Bible say? 'Vengeance is mine, said the Lord'."

"Perhaps," she continued somewhat enigmatically, "it should have said 'Lady'."

When Mary arrived at her destination with the Bearskin-Greens and the Montgomerys, she was pleasantly surprised to find that the coach was already there.

"Maybe the driver has been to one of the Baroness's concerts before," she thought to herself. She was even more pleased to find that all the guests who had bailed out at half-time had also found the coach. So the concert party returned to the ship about forty-five minutes before they were expected and a number of them headed straight to the Portcullis Lounge to listen to Bennie!

Mary sent an email to Manchester about the concert and checked arrangements for the next day in Dresden. She then found Max in the Portcullis Lounge talking to Pearl and explained to him what had happened. They agreed to place a bottle of Sekt in each concert guest's cabin together with a suitably worded note of apology. But they would leave it with

Sovereign's head office in Manchester to take the matter further with their Dresden agents.

Max went to bed and Mary started on her rounds. She was not surprised to find Malo and Marigold on the Sun Deck, relaxing on two of the sun loungers with glasses in their hands. Horace was also there with Phyllida Ballard.

As Mary approached, Marigold got up to leave and, as she pecked Malo on the cheek, she whispered, "Night, lover. Don't stay up drinking to all hours. We've got an interesting day ahead of us tomorrow."

Marigold headed towards the stairway and Mary assumed that she would be making a detour to the Smoking Lounge for a cigarette before she went to bed. She was surprised to see Phyllida get up to go as well and even more surprised when Malo said to her, "Enjoy your stargazing, Filly."

Ms Ballard felt that she needed to explain to Mary. "Did you know that Marigold is an astronomer? She's going to point out some stars and planets to me from the Smoking Lounge. I've even downloaded her app on my phone. It's called AstroWatch," and, with a knowing smile on her face, she continued, "Marigold says the Smoking Lounge is the place where you can inhale the wonders of creation without being disturbed."

Mary had actually found Marigold in the Smoking Lounge on the first night of the cruise enjoying a Silk Cut as she gazed up at the heavens.

"Please don't tell Malo, will you," she had implored, "I'm sure he thinks I've given up. But I do like a fag before I go to bed if I've had a couple of drinks."

Mary had thought to herself at the time, "I'm sure he realises you haven't given up." It seemed pretty obvious that the rectangular shape in the breast pocket of her silk blouse was a packet of cigarettes and Mary imagined that the effect of alcohol on Malo did not destroy his sense of smell. Mary recalled that her own foray into teenage smoking had been exposed to her parents by the lingering odour of cigarette smoke. Mints with holes might have helped with her breath but they had very little impact on her hair and clothes.

Mary confirmed her commitment to silence.

23

Day 5 – Morning and afternoon
Dresden

The Dresden sun had already been up and about for an hour or more before the first guests emerged for Early Risers breakfast, Mrs Smith headed out for her run and Boris went in search of a copy of the *Sächsische Zeitung*.

Mary sat in Reception and readied herself for the day ahead. She didn't expect to hear anything back from Manchester about the Zwinger fiasco for a day or two. She was, however, pretty confident that the delights which Dresden promised would more than compensate for last night's disappointments.

She checked the football results and, once again, with Blume's help, she posted the overnight scores on the notice board:

Japan 0 Iceland 1

Honduras 2 Niger 2
Italy 1 Columbia 2
Egypt 2 Germany 2

Four local guides had been booked for the Dresden city tour. Hans would be carrying lollipop 1 with Pavel sweeping. Alexander would be waving lollipop 2 with Max. Manfred would be holding lollipop 3 with Mary. And lollipop 4 with Jurgen would be taking a more sedate approach to the morning. It would be going by coach into the town centre and Tomáš would do the herding.

Max joined her in Reception and she ran through with him what had been organised.

"Looks great," he said. "You're going to love Dresden. It's one of my favourite cities."

As they waited to announce the departure of the tours, Mary and Max chatted about some of their guests.

Max started. "Did you know that Mrs Nixon has done time in prison? She apparently stabbed one of her friends with a barbecue fork."

"No, I certainly didn't know that," Mary confessed, "but I do know that she can't stand Mr Harris. And that the feeling is mutual."

She continued, "Jane was telling me that Mr and Mrs Triste had a daughter who was murdered when she got caught in the crossfire of a couple of South

London gangs. Apparently, they are going to visit their daughter's fiancé in Berlin. He was German."

"I wonder if our learned King's Counsel knew the killers," Max replied, "Sir Claude Bearskin-Green told me that Mr Mortimer is pretty pally with some of those London gangs."

Mary immediately thought about last night's eavesdropping.

There was no time to discuss the apparent demise of teams like Brazil and Italy as Max needed to be on the public address system with the daily exhortations not to block the Reception area and to remember to bring whisper boxes and shore passes.

"Don't forget that those of you who have signed up for the tour which involves less walking will be going with Tomáš on the coach," he added.

By 9.15 am, the Reception area was blocked and three guests had forgotten their whisper boxes. Four of them had left their shore passes in their cabins but,fortunately, their respective spouses were able to provide them with access.

By 9.30 am, the ship had all but emptied itself of guests.

Horace and Phyllida were going with lollipop 2 and, of course, were joined by Sir Claude and Lady Liz, while Mary found herself with Malo and Marigold, Jane, the Billericay Dickies, Mr and Mrs Ali and the Porterhouse Octet. Mr and Mrs Nixon were with Hans and Mr and Mrs Harris were taking the coach with Jurgen.

Mary was hoping for a less frenetic morning.

If it were not for the fact that Mrs Heffer and Mrs Heffer had an almighty row about the legitimacy of fire-bombing Dresden, it would have been a less frenetic morning for her. In any event, Mary considered it to be one of the most interesting tours on which she had ever been.

A later middle-aged man with a bald head and a florid face was brandishing lollipop 3.

"Good morning. *Guten Morgen.* Welcome to the beautiful city of Dresden. My name is Manfred. My father's name was Otto Mann but we didn't come from Türkiye. I was actually born in what was then East Berlin in 1965. Unfortunately, I was born at five forty-three on the second of the first, and that's why my parents decided to call me Manfred."

Fortunately, Malo was able to explain to Marigold and, indeed, Mary, about "54321".

The first thing the group could see as they started to walk towards the town centre looked strangely out of place. "Don't worry," Manfred assured them, "you haven't been transported by Harry Potter's Floo Network overnight. This isn't the

Mississippi but they are indeed paddle steamers. They take tourists on trips up the river as far as the Bastei."

Much to everybody's surprise, Mrs Ali informed Manfred that the Floo Network wasn't intercontinental.

After a short walk along the bank of the Elbe, Manfred led the group up some steps to the Brühlsche Terrasse.

"These terraces used to be known as the balcony of Europe," Manfred explained as his lollipop indicated a parade of beautiful buildings looking out over the Elbe, including the Albertinum which was once a royal arsenal, and which now housed art collections, the Academy of Fine Arts and the Neo-Renaissance Landtag. "That's the parliament building," he added.

Leaving the terraces behind, they found themselves in the area where the coach had stopped the previous evening and Manfred pointed out the Saxon State Opera House, the statue of King John of Saxony and the Hofkirche, a Catholic cathedral in his staunchly Protestant Saxony.

"But now," Manfred continued, "I must show you the most famous building in Dresden," and he led them to the Zwinger.

"The beautiful Baroque structure we can see was commissioned by Augustus the Strong and was built between 1709 and 1732. He was inspired by a visit to Versailles. The vast courtyard in front of us, with its fountains and lawns, is completely surrounded by galleries. And you can also see that there are gates and pavilions inside the galleries. Those of you who went to the concert last night were in the Wall Pavilion which is the building at the far end of the courtyard.

"Right," said Manfred into his whisper box, "it's time for us to go to the Royal Palace. This building houses some of the most beautiful art collections in Germany. We are going to be visiting one of the famous Green Vaults this morning. If you want to visit the ground-floor vault later today, you will need to book before we leave.

"Wasn't there a robbery there a few years ago?" asked Mrs Waterstone.

"Absolutely," Manfred replied, "that was in 2019 when a number of pieces of jewellery were stolen in a break-in. The stolen pieces were officially valued at one hundred and thirteen million euros. But I am pleased to say that we were able to recover most of the exhibits."

The Green Vaults comprised a vast collection of royal jewellery, clocks and table decorations. Many of the pieces – there were hundreds of them – were quite spectacular and, indeed, unique. They were nearing the end of the visit when Manfred declared that he had been saving the best for last. Displayed alone in a darkened alcove was the magnificent Dresden Green, a forty-one-carat green diamond.

Mary was pretty sure that some of her group would have been quite content to stay in the Green Vaults for the rest of the morning but Dresden had more to offer them.

As they reluctantly left the Royal Palace behind, they arrived outside the Langer Gang.

"It's nothing to do with Bernhard Langer's fan club," said Manfred, "it's a long building which connected the Royal Palace to what is now the Museum of Transport. On this wall behind me you can see a frieze which depicts a procession of Saxon rulers from over the centuries. The frieze is one hundred and two metres long. It dates back to the late nineteenth century and was originally created using the *sgraffito* technique but, in 1907, it was replaced by twenty-four thousand Meissen porcelain tiles.

"Right, we have one more place to visit. As we walk, I must explain a little bit about the bombing of Dresden in 1945 to provide some context. We are going to visit the Frauenkirche or, as you would say in English, the Church of Our Lady."

In front of them stood a magnificent Baroque church.

"On the night of 13th February 1945, British and American forces mounted a vast carpet-bombing raid. The church withstood two days and nights of attacks before succumbing to the heat generated by some six hundred and fifty thousand incendiary bombs which were dropped on the city. The temperature surrounding and inside the church eventually reached one thousand degrees.

"The church's most distinctive feature was its unusually high dome, sixty-seven metres above the ground. The dome finally collapsed at 10.00 am on 15th February.

"The ruins were left for nearly half a century as a war memorial but, following the reunification of Germany, it was decided to rebuild the church. The work started in 1994 and it took only eleven years to complete the reconstruction of both the exterior and the interior of the building. As you can see, its shining dome once again dominates our city's skyline.

"Wherever possible, we have used the original limestone blocks to rebuild the church and you can see them in the walls. They are black, the new limestone blocks are white. But, in time, the white blocks will also become black as the chemicals in the limestone react with the air."

"This is Martin Luther," he said, pointing to the bronze statue standing in front of the church with the inscription 'Martin Luther'. "The statue dates to 1885 and it survived the bombing. Let's go inside."

It was not what Mary had been expecting. There was an almost luminescent glow to the interior. White and gold dominated. A magnificent organ rose above the altar. She heard several of her guests using the word 'awesome'.

"Two thousand pieces of the original altar have been incorporated into the new structure," Manfred explained as they moved closer to the chancel.

He then asked, "Does anyone know what a Coventry Cross of Nails is?"

Whether they did or not, nobody answered.

"In Germany," he explained, "we call it a *Nagelkreuz von Coventry*. It's a Christian cross made from iron nails which has become a symbol of peace and reconciliation.

"Coventry Cathedral was severely damaged by German bombs on 14th November 1940 and its roof was destroyed. The original Coventry Cross of Nails was made from some large, hand-forged, medieval carpenters' nails discovered in the ruins of the cathedral on the morning after the bombing. Three of these iron nails were bound together with wire into the shape of a Latin cross with one vertical nail and two nails, head-to-tail, as a cross-piece.

"Several hundred crosses have now been made out of these nails and given as gifts to various organisations, including churches, prisons and schools, and a worldwide ecumenical Community of the Cross of Nails committed to peace and reconciliation was established in 1974.

"The iron cross you can see at the front of the altar is a Coventry Cross of Nails."

Once they were all gathered outside the church, Manfred said, "I am afraid that this is where our tour comes to an end. I do hope you have enjoyed our beautiful city. Please come back and visit her again.

"I will be taking the most direct route back to your ship if you would like to walk with me but, by all means, stay and continue to explore. There are some excellent restaurants where you can have lunch. Please let me know if you would like some recommendations.

"But even if you don't stay in the city for a meal, you should at least try our famous Dresdner *eierschecke*. It's a three-layered cake. The bottom layer is made from yeast dough, the middle layer is a quark-based cheesecake and the top layer is vanilla custard. And it's covered with a glaze made from cream, eggs, sugar and flour."

"What's quark?" asked Mary.

"It's a soft cheese," Manfred replied, "somewhere between cream cheese, yogurt and cottage cheese." And he suggested a couple of cake shops which, in his opinion, sold some of the finest *eierschecke* in Dresden.

In the end, only Mary and Marigold accompanied Manfred back to the ship, but Mary was carrying a brown paper bag containing two slices of *eierschecke*. And Marigold had four slices in hers.

"Thank you so much, Manfred," she said as she exchanged a white envelope for lollipop 3 and his whisper box.

Max was already back on the ship.

"How did it go, Max?" Mary asked.

"Well, of course, Sir Claude and Mr Mortimer were at each other's throats again. Otherwise, what a great city! And Alexander aced it."

A large number of guests headed back into Dresden in the afternoon, although the Porterhouse Octet, with Mrs Heffer and Mrs Heffer having reconciled their differences, went on a guided cycle tour along the Elbe. The tour wasn't organised by Sovereign but Blume had helped them to book it with a local company.

As for Mary and Max, they put their feet up for a couple of hours. Mary decided that it was time for some serious tanning, at least for her legs, and took herself up to the Sun Deck. She found Jane in her usual reclining chair and bagged the nearest sun lounger, the one once occupied by Malo.

"So," Mary asked mischievously, "what have you found out about your fellow travellers?"

"Well, dear," said Jane, without even a hint of embarrassment, "not that much. But I was having breakfast this morning with your nice Mr Hunt and his stepmother and Lady Bearskin-Green asked if she might join us. And we got chatting. Did you know her name really is Liz, it's not short for Elizabeth. She's Sir Claude's second wife. She told me that his first wife died of shame. Very mysterious. I didn't get a chance to ask her what she meant because we had to get ready for the tour."

Mary thought about last night's eavesdropping again.

Jane continued, "Lady Liz's parents were what I think you call champagne socialists. Keep the Red Flag Flying and all that but they sent her to an exclusive public school for girls on the south coast."

Mary thought to herself, "I wonder if that's the one where Mrs Briony Fry-Cox was headmistress." She had met Mrs and Mrs Fry-Cox on the Duke of Sussex.

"Liz was apparently a very talented sportswoman," Jane informed her. "She was captain of the school hockey and lacrosse teams but, better still, she was a national champion at fencing. She went to an Olympics. She did tell me which one, I think it was Barcelona. No medal, unfortunately. And then her eyesight deteriorated and she had to give up the sport."

"I didn't know about the fencing but she did tell me that she was very short-sighted," Mary confirmed.

Jane hadn't finished. "I also had a good old chat yesterday with the Second Officer. He was so helpful with sorting out my Wi-Fi on the Douro cruise.

"Anyway, I didn't think he seemed to be his usual cheery self and – you might have known this already – he told me that he'd been dating Barbie last year. Then Barbie was transferred to this ship and, by the time he had managed to get a transfer to be with her, she had decided to end their relationship. The words he actually used were that she had dumped him."

Mary confirmed that she knew about Barbie and agreed that something definitely seemed to be troubling Mike.

But Jane still hadn't finished. "Did you know that both his grandfather and his great-grandfather came from Ukraine and that they were officers in the Red Army, obviously when all of Ukraine was still part of the Soviet Union?"

"That I didn't know," Mary confessed.

"Apparently," Jane explained, "there are some famous photographs from the Second World War, when the Allied Forces and the Red Army met somewhere near here, including one with Mike's great-grandfather shaking hands with some American general. But the next day, his great-grandfather was found murdered. He told me that there's a castle in Torgau with a moat. They found his body at the bottom of the moat and his throat had been cut. They suspected that it might have been one of the American soldiers because he'd been seen having an argument with two or three of them earlier that day. But nothing was ever proved. There was a war going on after all.

"Anyway, the Red Army troops were moving out and they only had time to bury his body in the moat. Any sort of grave marker would be long gone. Mike now wants to visit the place where his great-grandfather was killed. And buried. Some sort of closure for the family, I suppose."

"How interesting, and how sad," Mary responded. "That probably explains what seems to be troubling him. Nothing to do with Barbie. I wonder if he still has family in Ukraine. He comes from Kharkiv."

Finally, there was something which Jane did not know.

"Anything else I should know?" Mary asked.

"Well, did you realise that Mrs Harrow – that's Marigold – is an astronomer? I'd never met one before but I used to love watching The Sky at Night when that lovely Patrick Moore presented it."

"Before my time, I'm afraid," Mary replied, "but I did know about the astronomy. And Ms Ballard told me that Marigold has introduced her to stargazing."

"The Sky at Night is actually still on BBC4," Jane said, "it's been running for donkey's years."

But Mary had never watched BBC4.

24

Day 5 – Evening
MV Baron von Habsburg

Max was back on his feet at 5.00 pm to summon guests to the Portcullis Lounge for the daily briefing and to remind everyone about the Royal Trivia Night which was scheduled as the evening's entertainment.

After another excellent dinner, eighty-two guests gathered in the Portcullis Lounge, having formed themselves into fourteen teams of between four and eight members.

Donald and Sarah Nixon had united an all-American team with Mr and Mrs Streisand, Mr and Mrs Zieff and Mr and Mrs Topol. The Harrises 'didn't do quizzes'.

The Porterhouse Octet, with a total of eleven honours degrees between them, would undoubtedly have been the odds-on favourite had there been a bookmaker on board. Mr Rook was, in fact, a retired bookbinder but that didn't count.

Malo and Marigold teamed up with Horace and Phyllida, drinking companions and stargazers together.

Sir Claude and Lady Liz had been sitting at the bar waiting for their team members, Mr and Mrs Dickie and Mr and Mrs Ali, to arrive. They finally entered the lounge and sat down at a table very close to the entrance.

"There they are, dear," said Sir Claude, "let's join them. Bring your drink."

Lady Liz was holding an almost full glass of tomato juice – a Virgin Mary to be precise – and as she passed the table where Horace was sitting she jettisoned the contents of her glass over what was, until then, Horace's pristine white shirt.

"You bastard," she hissed and then promptly exited the Portcullis Lounge. Sir Claude was faced with a dilemma: apologise on behalf of his wife, join his quiz team, or follow her Ladyship out. He followed her out.

At the moment of his Virgin Mary baptism, Horace had only just consumed a spicy prawn canapé and was still holding the cocktail stick on which Ernst had delivered the aforesaid prawn.

Marigold had been sitting next to Horace and, unfortunately and involuntarily, ducked her head to avoid the spicy tomato juice. Horace's right hand, in which the cocktail stick was located, unfortunately and involuntarily, jerked upwards. Marigold's cheek and the cocktail stick met midway between their respective starting points.

A cry of pain, and a "What the…" supplemented with a procreational verb, resonated throughout the lounge in harmony.

The Hotel Manager, who had been standing near the entrance, hurried over. "Lucky it wasn't her eye," she said to Malo as she inspected the damage to Marigold's cheek.

Her comment unnerved Malo. He was hoping that Marigold might want to call it a night when he asked her, "What do you want to do, love?"

"We'll stay, lover. It's no worse than an insect bite," Marigold replied as she dabbed the hole in her cheek with a paper serviette to staunch the dribble of blood.

"We'll stay too. I'll just go and change my shirt," said Horace, not giving Phyllida any choice in the matter.

"And your trousers, I think," said Martina, looking down at the large wet patch of red tomato juice on his light blue Peter Christian slacks.

Martina got Ernst to wipe the table but almost the entire contents of Lady Liz's glass had found its mark in any event.

Once Horace had reappeared, resplendent in another white shirt and light brown Peter Christian chinos, Mary was able to start the quiz.

The Royal Trivia Night had a straightforward brief. Twenty questions, with a tie breaker if needed, general knowledge, a geography question, maybe something on history or films, definitely something on literature and two musical questions.

A team of six to eight guests should be expected to answer fourteen or fifteen questions correctly. No more than an hour. Resolve the inevitable disputes diplomatically and don't make fun of a guest who comes up with a ridiculous answer.

She always liked to start with a question about the Greek alphabet.

"There are four letters of the Greek alphabet which end in the letter 'i' when written in English, pi, which is p and i, chi, which is c, h and i, and psi, which is p, s and i. What's the fourth letter that ends in 'i'?"

Mary had broken away from cruising tradition and no longer asked a question about the length of the ship. The answer was always there for all to see, from the moment guests first boarded the Baron von

Habsburg, in bold, black letters on each side of the ship above the entrance to the Reception area.

Bennie's playing now accompanied the two music questions as he belted out the opening bars of Beethoven's Ninth Symphony, followed by The Beatles' Let It Be.

She was surprised that only two teams knew that "W" was the letter in the periodic table for tungsten but even more surprised that five teams knew that the capital of Myanmar was Naypyidaw. Had she known that all of those particular teams had members who had been on cruises on the Irrawaddy within the last six months – not with Sovereign which only cruised European rivers – she would have been tempted to substitute the question for the capital of Kazakhstan.

At the end of the evening, perhaps predictably, the Porterhouse Octet were crowned Trivia Royalty with nineteen points. They had not cruised the Irrawaddy.

Max presented them with two bottles of Moet & Chandon champagne, both of which were opened and emptied in little more than thirty minutes. And, within an hour, the Portcullis Lounge had also all but emptied.

As Mary made her nightly circuit of the ship, she climbed the starboard stairway from Reception and reached the Sun Deck. The first guests she encountered were Jane Stanhope and Lucy Burrage. They had decided to give the quiz a miss. Notwithstanding their differences in age, Jane and Lucy had become good friends over the first few days of the holiday and were sitting near the chess set, chatting away to one another.

"Evenin' Mary," said Lucy.

"Good evening, dear," said Jane.

"Good evening, ladies," she replied, "how did you enjoy Dresden?"

"It were wonderful," Lucy enthused. "What an amazing city after all that destruction."

"Any news about poor Lord Hayter?" Jane asked. "It must be terrible for him to lose his wife and then have the police take you away as if you were a murderer. I can't believe he's guilty."

Mary wasn't so sure but she had no news to impart in any event.

"Anyway, dear, we mustn't keep you. We're just off to bed ourselves," Jane continued.

Both ladies rose from the comfort of their reclining chairs, taking their empty glasses with them, and made their way down the portside stairway before depositing the glasses in the Portcullis Lounge and making their way back through Reception to their cabins, Lucy on the Buckingham Deck and Jane down below on the Sandringham Deck.

They were closely followed by Marigold.

"How's your cheek?" Mary asked solicitously as she passed.

"Oh, it's fine. Just like a pinprick, really. I guess I'm lucky that it missed my eye, though."

And with that, the lure of nicotine became overwhelming and Marigold continued on her downwards path.

She expected to find Malo and Horace in the stern. And she did.

"If you're looking to say goodnight to Phyllida, she went down to the Smoking Lounge to look for Venus," said Horace, before refocusing on his glass.

25

Day 6 – Morning
Meissen

It was yet another beautiful morning as the Baron von Habsburg cast off and started on its sedate journey downstream towards Meissen. It was only 7.00 am but Mrs Smith had managed a very early run to the balcony of Europe and Boris had procured a copy of the *Sächsische Zeitung*.

Meissen was little more than twenty-five kilometres from Dresden and the ship reached its destination shortly after 8.30 am. Mary and Blume already had the results up on the notice board:

Argentina 0 Sweden 1
Ireland 1 Kuwait 0
Croatia 4 Ivory Coast 0
Cuba 3 Jordan 0

Max was almost incredulous when he arrived in Reception and saw the Argentina result. "Are you sure you got that right?" he asked Mary, while waking Betcha with a tap for confirmation.

With the result confirmed, he waited in silence with Mary as the sailors manoeuvred the ship's gangway into place.

The silence was broken when Lady Liz appeared in Reception. "I really must apologise for my behaviour last night," she began, "it was totally unacceptable. Please could you tell that man that I will pay for any laundry or dry cleaning which he needs doing. I'm sure I don't know what got into me. I can't believe it will ever happen again."

Mary detected a lack of sincerity.

"Looks like we're ready," said Max, interrupting Mary's thoughts, as Ilie indicated to him that it was safe to go ashore.

Excusing herself, Mary took to the airwaves. "Good morning, ladies and gentlemen, and welcome to Meissen. Our excursions get underway at nine fifteen this morning. Don't forget your shore passes and your whisper boxes. It's going to be hot in town so put some sunblock on and wear a hat or a cap. And remember, lunch today will be a barbecue on the Sun Deck."

Their local guides this morning were Helmut, Wolfgang and Andrea. Mary decided to join Helmut, who was wielding lollipop 1. The Sovereign coaches had followed them along the Elbe so the familiar faces of Sebastien, Michael and Ralf were waiting for the guests as they left the ship.

Mary saw that she would have the company of Sir Claude and Lady Liz, the entire Porterhouse Octet, Horace and Phyllida, the Tristes, the Montgomerys, the Eagles and Jane and Lucy.

Helmut started to speak as the coach began its short drive to the centre of Meissen. "Good morning, everybody. My name is Helmut and our driver today is Ralf. I think some of you must recognise him. Welcome to Meissen. Our town has a population of almost thirty thousand inhabitants and it is, I believe, one of the most beautiful towns in Germany. We can trace our history back one thousand years and that is why Meissen is sometimes called the Cradle of Saxony.

"We'll be starting with a walking tour which will take about an hour and we will then have a five-minute coach ride to the Meissen Porcelain Manufactory. When we get there, we will visit the demonstration rooms where you can watch some of our local artisans working on pieces of Meissen porcelain at various stages of the manufacturing process.

"You will then have an opportunity to look around the museum area. There are something like two thousand porcelain objects and over three hundred years of porcelain history on display.

"And, unlike Elvis, you will not be able to leave the building until you have passed through the shop.

"As we make our way to the town centre, I'm going to give you some information about porcelain.

"As you may know, porcelain is a white, vitrified, translucent ceramic. Vitrified means, by the way, something has been transformed into a glass-like substance.

"Porcelain has three main ingredients, kaolin, quartz and feldspar. Kaolin is the most important but it accounts for only a small fraction of the finished product. Once the porcelain has been fired at a temperature of one thousand three hundred degrees Celsius, it is glazed and decorated using cobalt, copper and coloured enamels.

"The discovery of porcelain dates back to ancient China. That's why porcelain products are often referred to as china in English-speaking countries. By the eighteenth century, porcelain had become one of the most valued and valuable commodities in Europe. It was still imported from

China at immense cost and it was so sought after that it became known as white gold.

"Europe's rulers realised that, if they were able to discover how to manufacture porcelain, this would not only bring them immense wealth but this wealth could in turn bring them great power. The man who would come to own the secret of porcelain manufacture was Augustus the Strong of Saxony. On his deathbed, he supposedly confessed that "all my life has been one ceaseless sin." Lucky old him. His ambition was to make Saxony the most powerful state in the Holy Roman Empire.

"Ironically, the discovery of this priceless secret was a byproduct of the failed quest for the philosopher's stone, a mythical alchemical substance capable of turning base metals such as mercury into gold or silver. Alchemists also believed that it could be used to make an elixir of life which gave you immortality."

Helmut paused briefly for breath. And then he was off again.

"Augustus had imprisoned a young German alchemist called Johann Frederick Böttger because he believed Böttger would make him a very rich man. Böttger toiled away for years as Augustus's prisoner but, obviously, his attempts to produce the philosopher's stone were not successful. So he turned his attention to porcelain. And, in 1708, after many more years of experimentation, Böttger was finally able to deliver the secret of making white gold to his turnkey."

The coach by now had arrived at a conveniently located coach stop near the centre of Meissen. Helmut led his led his guests the short distance to the town square with its late-Gothic town hall, some beautiful Renaissance houses and the Frauenkirche, a fifteenth-century Church of Our Lady. "The church has the world's oldest porcelain carillon," Helmut proudly announced. "It was hung in 1929, almost one hundred years ago."

It was all uphill from there to the Albrechtsburg, a vast fortified hilltop castle complex. Helmut continued, "This is the place where the State of Saxony has its origins, and it was the residence of the Electors of Saxony for many centuries.

"Construction of the castle started in 1471 and it was built in the Late Gothic style. The tower you can see is known as the Grosse Wendelstein and it has a magnificent external staircase. This was also the site of the first European porcelain factory. It was founded in 1710 and continued in production for one hundred and fifty-three years before moving to its present location.

"And," pointing with his lollipop to the building next to the castle, "this is Meissen Cathedral, the cathedral church of St John the Evangelist and St Donat. It was erected in the thirteenth century in French Gothic style.

"OK," said Helmut, "now it's back down the hill the way we came to look for Ralf and our coach."

As they descended, he asked, "Does anyone know who Christian Friedrich Samuel Hahnemann was?"

"Something to do with alternative medicine?" suggested Professor Blackwell.

Helmut was pleasantly surprised. "That's right, Hahnemann was the founder of homeopathy. He was born in Meissen in 1755. His principle of 'healing like with like' which, if you know your Latin, is *similia similibus curentur*, was the foundation of a new discipline of alternative medicine which is still practised to this day."

Going downhill was a lot easier and, once they had found Ralf, the coach ride to the House of Meissen took less than the predicted five minutes.

The world's largest free-standing porcelain sculpture, Saxonia, was there to welcome them.

"It's known as Saxony's Statue of Liberty," Helmut informed them.

After they had passed through the demonstration rooms and the museum, wallets and credit cards started to groan as they entered the showroom area.

As Mary's guests browsed the ranks of translucent white porcelain, there was one thing which they all could agree upon. Meissen porcelain wasn't cheap.

Whether it was deliberate or not, only Horace would have known, but Sir Claude had found a particular figurine which would complete his collection of Meissen Savannah animals. He already owned the Tiger Savannah, the Rhinoceros Savannah and the Giraffe Savannah but he had been unable to source an Elephant Savannah to complete the series. He had begun to think that the piece must have been taken out of production. And here it was, his for only eight thousand euros.

He placed his elephant on the counter and went in search of Lady Liz to see if she had taken a fancy to anything.

The sound of a porcelain figurine shattering as it hit the floor stopped him and, indeed, almost everyone else in the showroom, in their tracks.

"Oh no, I'm so sorry," said Horace to the nearest assistant as the elephant lay shattered at his feet, a small piece of white gold marked with blue crossed swords providing the only evidence that the pile of broken china on the floor was once a magnificent Meissen masterpiece.

"I'll pay for it, of course," Horace insisted.

It has to be said that Sir Claude's self-control was exemplary.

Although Sir Claude, and Lady Liz, left empty-handed, most of the other guests parted the shop with small packages containing everything from mugs to plates, and from vases to figurines, and, in each case, a considerable amount of bubble wrap and a Meissen carrier bag.

Helmut's coach returned to the ship at noon and Mary went in search of Max. She wanted to let him know about the incident between Sir Claude and Horace Mortimer and to see if he had any thoughts.

The only thoughts he'd had all morning were not particularly nice ones directed towards the Argentinian football team.

She was describing to Max what had happened when Betcha vied again for his attention.

Looking up from his phone, he started to complain that Betcha was only offering odds of two to one on of Spain beating New Zealand.

"Whatever that means," Mary replied. She had never quite got the hang of betting odds.

"About the same sort of odds as Mr Mortimer and Sir Claude Bearskin-Green, or his wife, coming to blows before we get to Wittenberg," Max suggested.

"Well, if they do, let's hope they don't break anything else," Mary replied.

26

Day 6 – Afternoon
MV Baron von Habsburg/Torgau

The Baron von Habsburg departed from Meissen around 12.30 pm on its journey to Torgau. The ship was expected to moor at Torgau before 6.00 pm.

The sun was high in a cloudless sky, perfect weather for the promised barbecue on the Sun Deck. Pricey porcelain purchases were painstakingly put away in padded places by the returning guests, sun cream was applied to potentially bare areas of skin and many of those who had worn trousers and long skirts in Meissen reappeared in shorts and shorter skirts. The Sun Deck was filled with the smell of cooking and with guests queuing to get at the barbecued meats and prawns.

Mary wondered what particular gene it was which was responsible for making an adult male, who might normally have had difficulty in boiling an egg and would certainly struggle to locate where the vegetables were kept at home, believe that he was on a par with any celebrity chef you might care to name when it came to cooking sausages and chicken joints on a barbecue.

As far as she could tell, Benigno was doing an excellent job in producing bratwurst, chicken breasts, beefburgers and prawns which were cooked through but in no way carbonised. However, Max insisted on replacing him and took up position behind the protein barbecue, relegating Benigno to the corns on the cob, the peppers and the jacket potatoes, and with tongs in one hand and fork in the other, set out to cremate the meat and the shellfish. Fortunately, Marco-Peer saw what was happening and insisted that, if Max wanted to show off his culinary expertise, he had to trade places with Benigno.

Mary noted, as Max reluctantly accepted his diminished responsibilities, that the distinction between the corn and the underlying cob was growing ever less obvious and she decided to leave him to it as he wielded his barbequing utensils over the increasingly blackened vegetables.

The rest of the afternoon promised to be a scorcher and, once lunch was over, most guests took the opportunity to soak up some more sun, and an occasional alcoholic drink, on the Sun Deck or in the Spa Pool as the Baron von Habsburg continued its regal progress downstream. Lucy emerged in her little black number again.

Max, back to doing his day job, was on the public address system at 4.00 pm.

"Once we have arrived in Torgau, you might like to join me on a short walking tour of the town. This will only last for about an hour but I promise you that it will seem like an hour well spent."

Max also reminded everyone that the ship would remain in Torgau overnight and anyone wishing to go into town after dinner would find a number of popular bars to visit.

Once the ship was safely moored, a gangway quickly emerged from the side of the ship and about forty guests took Max up on his invitation to join him for the stroll through Torgau. Many of those who did not join him had overdone the sun and the alcohol or, indeed, were now ruing the earlier consumption of Max's vegetables.

Max made sure that everyone had their whisper boxes and delegated the carrying of lollipop 1 to Tomáš. A long crocodile formed itself behind Max and Tomáš as they set off. Mary and Pavel made up the crocodile's tail. There were about one hundred and fifty metres of waste grassland to cross before they reached the outskirts of the town but there was a rough gravel path which they were able to follow.

Max first brought them to a monument which supposedly marked the site where, on 25th April 1945, United States Army forces met with forces of the Soviet Union during the invasion of Germany. "As a matter of fact," Max explained, "the two armies had their first contact near Strehla which is thirty kilometres upstream from Torgau. But, it seems, Torgau was more photogenic for the war photographers. There are a number of press photographs in the archives showing officers from the two forces shaking hands.

"The Allied advance had started one hundred days earlier on the beaches of Normandy and it came to a halt on the western banks of the Elbe, leaving the Red Army troops to advance northwards to Berlin. The Elbe River became the boundary between West Germany and East Germany."

Mary started to think about what Jane had told her and she hoped that Mike would find an opportunity before they left Torgau to pay a visit to the castle.

The inscription on the monument was written in the Cyrillic alphabet but there were two small plaques underneath the Russian, one in German and the other, in English, which read:

HERE ON THE ELBE
ON APRIL 25, 1945
THE FORCES OF THE
FIRST UKRANIAN FRONT
OF THE RED ARMY
LINKED UP
WITH ALLIED FORCES

Bill Harris and Sarah Nixon both had grandparents who were killed on the beaches of Normandy or during the Allied advance. They spent some time standing next to one another in quiet contemplation in front of the monument before catching up with the crocodile's tail. Sarah was wearing a Miami Dolphins sweatshirt and this brief vigil became something of an epiphany for their relationship.

From the monument, Max led his guests to Schloss Hartenfels. The visitors' entrance was at the side of the castle but, once through the entrance, they found themselves in a large courtyard surrounded by late-Gothic and early-Baroque residential wings. On the far side of the courtyard was a beautiful external spiral staircase. The more energetic of Max's guests would feature in countless videos attached to WhatsApp messages which would be sent later that evening, appearing, disappearing and reappearing again, as they made their way up to the top of the staircase and down again.

As they were leaving the castle through its main entrance, Max said, "Make sure that you turn round and look back at the magnificent decoration above the entrance. I think this is one of the most beautiful gateways in Germany." It was certainly worthy of the considerable attention it received from smartphones and cameras and the entrance photographs would be joining the spiral staircase videos on WhatsApp later.

The gateway led straight on to a bridge over the moat which had protected the castle in earlier centuries. Max suggested that they might want to look over the parapet and down into the moat.

"It's a bear," shouted Mr Zieff from one side of the bridge.

"It's a bear," cried Mr Topol from the other side of the bridge.

"No, look, there are two of them," screamed Mrs Blackwell, racing from one side of the bridge to the other.

Max confirmed that there were, in fact, two bears living in the castle moat.

"The first moat-dwelling bears were documented in 1425 and, at one time, when the Electors of Saxony lived in the castle, there'd been a great many of them. But when the Electors relocated to Dresden and the castle began to billet soldiers, the bears disappeared. They all became bearburgers."

"Back in the 1950s," he continued, "the residents of Torgau built an outdoor enclosure in the castle moat and the first two of a new generation of bears arrived as a gift from Leipzig Zoo. The two brown bears which you can now see came to Torgau from North Rhine-Westphalia in 2015 as two-year-olds. Their names are Benno and Bea.

"OK, there is one more place I would like to show you. It's just up the road."

It took some persuading to convince some of his guests to leave the bears behind. It was going to be a busy night with smartphones and the Wi-Fi.

Their final port of call was the late-Gothic Marienkirche, or Church of St Mary, with an extended Romanesque west section.

"Martin Luther's wife, Katharina von Bora, died in Torgau and her tomb is inside the church," Max explained. "You will learn a lot more about her when we arrive in Wittenberg. There is also a famous painting inside by Lucas Cranach the Elder called 'The Fourteen Helpers' and, when we get to Wittenberg, you will no doubt hear more about Cranach and his son."

The bear-watching strollers were back on the ship by 6.00 pm and all guests were summoned to the lounge for the briefing on Wittenberg at 7.15 pm.

Max, as usual, led the briefing given that Mary had never been to any of the places where they were visiting.

"As you may know, Wittenberg is synonymous with Martin Luther and the Reformation and much of what you will see tomorrow is related to Luther. This will include the Castle Church, the monuments in front of the Rathaus or the Town Hall, Luther's House and another Church of St Mary."

Photographs of each of the places which he mentioned appeared in rapid succession on the screens in the lounge.

Max continued, "There will be a disembarkation briefing in the lounge at eleven o'clock tomorrow morning and we do need one person from each cabin to attend.

"The ship will be leaving for Wittenberg at 8.00 am so please make sure you are back on board before a quarter to eight if you are going for an early morning walk.

"Ladies and gentlemen, dinner is served."

27

Day 6 – Late evening
Torgau/MV Baron von Habsburg

It was his thirty-fifth birthday and, with the blessing of the Hotel Manager, Josh and some of the other members of the crew had been given permission to go into Torgau for a couple of drinks once they had finished for the evening. He wouldn't be joining them, but Boris, whose home was not far from Torgau, had suggested that they go to Dejavu.

Max had been invited along and, when Mary had told him that she had never gone ashore after dinner in all the time that she had been cruising with Sovereign, he insisted that she join them.

"OK," she had relented, "just for one drink."

Max and Marian were already in Reception when she arrived there at 9.30 pm. Then Second Officer Rosov put in an appearance.

"Joining us?" Mary asked.

"No," Mike replied, "I'm just going for a walk."

He tapped his shore pass and walked down the gangway. Mary noticed that Mike was carrying one of the heavy-duty rubber torches which the fire crews would use in an emergency. He was heading in determined fashion in the direction of the castle. Mary realised that the light would soon start to fade and thought that taking a torch was not a bad idea. She knew where Mike was going.

As they waited for the other crew members, Mary told Max what Jane had told her about Mike's great-grandfather.

"That's really interesting," Max acknowledged. "You forget sometimes that Ukraine was part of the Soviet Union. I guess, if he's heading over to the castle, we might see him there before we go to the bar."

As they watched his progress, and the progress of the sun towards the horizon, Max said, "Actually, taking a torch is not such a bad idea. Marian, do you think you could go and get a couple for us?"

Over the next few minutes, the rest of the drinking shore party gathered by the gangway. In addition to Max and Marian and the birthday boy, there were Bruno and Carl from the restaurant, all the cabin attendants, Rishi and Barbie, and Rubee from the Golden Crown Spa.

Mary saw Max lift the right earpiece of Barbie's headphones and say something to her exposed ear. She gave him a thumbs up.

Max noticed that Mary was looking questioningly at them so he explained to her that he had told everyone who was going into Torgau to make time to have a look at the entrance to the castle and to see if they could see the bears. "Bruce, as usual, missed everything I'd said," he added.

Marian returned with a couple of the heavy-duty rubber torches and handed one to Max.

"Right, let's go," Max said, and they began to disembark.

"Oh, bugger, my shore pass!" emerged from Bruce's lips.

Mary thought that it must have been the longest sentence that she had ever heard emerge from that source.

Bruce quickly disappeared down the stairs to her cabin and reappeared in little more than a minute with the overlooked item. There were no electronic locks on the cabin doors for the crew. She tapped herself out and hurried after the other crew members.

The earlier, orderly crocodile of the guests had been replaced by groups of two or three members of crew, each making their individual choices as to the most direct route to their destination.

"Right," Mary said to herself, "let's go and have that drink."

Just at that moment, Jane appeared. "If you are going into town, dear, would you mind terribly showing me the way to St Mary's Church. I know it's only the other side of the grass but I can't remember which entrance into the town I should take. I can find my own way back."

"Of course," Mary said. They tapped their shore passes, made their way down the gangway and headed in the direction which Mary was sure would lead them directly to Jane's destination. Mary was reluctant to leave Jane by herself and stayed with her while she took some photographs on her smartphone. But, with photography finished and darkness rapidly falling, Mary volunteered to walk back with Jane to the ship.

"No, dear, you go and join your friends. I'm perfectly all right. You can see the ship from here. Look." And off she went.

The Baron von Habsburg was indeed lit up like a Roman candle.

Mary assumed that anyone who had gone to look for the bears would now be in Dejavu and, with Jane headed back to the ship, she made her way towards the town centre rather than the castle.

"It's about time Max bought me a drink," she said aloud to herself – which surprised her.

Dejavu was easy enough to find and Mary went in. The bar area was heaving and she couldn't see Max at first.

"I'll just pop to the loo," she decided and, when she returned, she spotted Max at the bar ordering a drink.

"Hi, Max," she shouted, "I've made it!"

"Well done! What would you like to drink?" he shouted back to her.

"Oh, thanks, Max," Mary replied without any reduction in volume, "I think I might have a gin and tonic for a change."

Armed with G and T in hand, Mary began to chat to some of the other crew members.

"Did any of you go and see the bears?" she asked no one in particular.

Rishi replied, "I think most of us have seen them before. Anyway, Josh said he was buying so we came straight here. Before he changed his mind. Far more important."

Mary talked with Rishi for a while longer but she was feeling slightly out of place and was ready to return to the ship. She started to look around to say goodnight to Max. "If he wants another drink, then Josh can buy it," she thought to herself with Prague and the Bridge Bar still rankling.

"If you're looking for Max, he's probably outside," said Rishi, interpreting her intentions.

Dejavu also had an outside area which attracted smokers and midges as well as drinkers.

Max was indeed outside, talking to Maggie and Carl. She noticed that both Maggie and Carl were smoking and that a couple of the other crew members also had cigarettes on the go. She had been aware that the ashtrays in the crew area were often quite full but she hadn't really appreciated just how many of the crew must smoke. So she said, "I hadn't really appreciated just how many of the crew must smoke." All three of them just smiled.

Max then asked whether many of the guests on the cruise were smokers. His question was addressed to Maggie who was responsible for cleaning the Smoking Lounge each morning and after she had refreshed her allocated cabins in the evening.

"I think we've just got the one this time. There are always two or three cigarette ends in the ashtray. With lipstick on the filter."

"Mrs Harrow," Mary said knowingly, then immediately regretted her breach of confidence.

"That's right, the lady in the end cabin. I found an empty packet of Silk Cut in her bin yesterday."

Mary was at least able to console herself about her indiscretion. "If Maggie knows," she thought to herself, "then Blume will know. And if Blume and Maggie know, then half the guests and all the crew will probably know."

"Sometimes," Maggie continued, "the Smoking Lounge gets like Piccadilly Circus. You get eight or nine passengers out the back there and the ashtrays are full to bursting. I expect a few dog ends start going over the side."

"Actually," said Mary, anxious to move the conversation away from smoking after her faux pas, "we should probably call it the Royal Observatory. Mrs Harrow is something of an astronomer and she's now got Ms Ballard interested. The two of them are always out there gazing up at the stars. I guess it's because it's so quiet and peaceful."

Max smiled at Mary's attempt at humour but he could see that neither Maggie nor Carl knew what she was talking about.

It was definitely time to go. Mary said, "Right, I must get back. Thanks for the drink, Max. Goodnight, everybody." And she was gone.

Mary made her way somewhat circumspectly along the gravel path which traversed the grassy area.

It was now getting very dark and some of the lights on the ship had been turned off. However, there was still enough illumination to guide her safely home.

She noticed that it was exactly eleven o'clock when she tapped herself back on board.

She made her rounds as usual. There were still a few guests chatting in the lounge, although Bennie had finished for the night and Pearl was clearly not expecting any more business. Marigold was indeed stargazing from the Smoking Lounge – or the Royal Observatory - and enjoying another Silk Cut. Malo and Horace were on the Sun Deck working their way through another bottle of Malo's cognac. Phyllida was on her way to join Marigold.

Before she made her way to her own cabin, Mary thought to check to see if Jane had made it back to the ship safely.

She had.

28

Day 7 – Morning
Torgau/MV Baron von Habsburg/Wittenberg

Torgau was bathed in morning sunshine as the crew prepared for another day of guest-pampering. It would be fair to say that some of the crew were moving rather slower than normal after their late evening celebrations onshore.

Mary was up early and sitting in Reception talking to Blume as three or four couples made their way into the Portcullis Lounge for Early Risers breakfast, Mrs Smith went for her regular morning run and Boris was despatched to buy that morning's *Sächsische Zeitung.*

She had just finished the football scores when she heard a bit of a commotion onshore with what sounded to her like the wailing of a police car or an ambulance in a hurry.

"It's probably a police car and an ambulance," she said to herself as she thought she could distinguish two different wailing noises. She pinned the scores to the notice board:

**Portugal 5 Morocco 0*

Ukraine 5 Chile 2

Austria 1 Cameroon 1

Spain 2 New Zealand 0

And she put a little asterisk beside the Portugal result: * Ronaldo four goals!

Her auditory instincts were vindicated. As Mrs Smith and Boris returned to the ship, they each told Mary that there appeared to be a lot of activity around Schloss Hartenfels and they had both seen at least two police cars and an ambulance. With the ship heading off to Wittenberg at 8.00 am, neither of them had time to investigate further.

Captain Zimmerman checked with Blume in Reception that everyone was back on board. All guests and crew had tapped themselves back in and the Baron von Habsburg cast off and continued its journey northwards.

Mary was having breakfast by herself in the Coronation Restaurant when the Hotel Manager came in and spoke to Leiter and to each of the waiters. She then approached Mary. "Have you seen Barbie this morning? We can't find her anywhere and I need her to get on with today's laundry."

"Have you actually tried her cabin?" Mary asked. "I know she went into town last night so maybe she overdid it and is still asleep."

It was quite clear from the expression on Martina's face that she hadn't thought to look.

"Let's check," said Mary. "I'll come with you."

The two of them went to the crew's quarters and knocked on the door to Barbie's cabin. For the moment, Bruce had a cabin all to herself as she had been sharing with Generosa, the galley slave who had flown back to the Philippines from Prague.

There was no answer so they entered the cabin together. Barbie was nowhere to be seen but her bed had either been made that morning or she had not slept in it.

Mary went to Reception and asked Blume to double-check the computer records. Barbie had tapped her shore pass at 11.56 pm, around the same time as almost all the other crew members who had gone to the bar had returned to the ship.

Mary couldn't actually recall seeing her in Dejavu but she assumed that Barbie must have taken Max up on his suggestion and had gone to look at the bears. No one had seen her near the castle but that was because, according to Rishi, they had all headed straight to the bar.

Mary went to look for Jane to see if she had spotted Barbie when she had been in Torgau. She hadn't. But she had bumped into the Second Officer and they had walked back to the ship together.

But, wherever Bruce had been, she must have returned to the ship. So Mary left Martina to continue the search as she needed to speak to Max about Wittenberg.

At 9.55 am, Martina went to speak to Captain Zimmermann about Barbie.

At 10.00 am, the Captain received a call from Inspector Beckenbauer. They spoke in English.

"Me again, Suzanne. What is it with your ship?"

"Sorry, what do you mean?" she replied.

"You've just left Torgau, haven't you? Well, the body of a young woman was found in the castle moat this morning. An early-morning jogger heard some loud music and when she looked over the parapet, she saw the body lying in some bushes.

"We think that the deceased must have leant too far over the parapet to get a better look at the bears. I really hope she didn't jump. She was wearing a Sovereign River Cruises polo shirt and the badge on her shirt says her name was..."

"Barbie," said the Captain, completing his sentence.

At the same time as the news of Barbie's death was being received in the wheelhouse, Max and Mary were sitting in the Portcullis Lounge discussing arrangements for the tours that afternoon and the disembarkation briefing which was scheduled for 11.00 am.

Mary was surprised when the First Officer came into the lounge and whispered in her ear that the Captain needed to speak to her urgently. Mary apologised to Max and excused herself.

"No worries, Mary," Max replied, "we're all good to go for the tours and I'm happy to do the briefing. I'll do an announcement now to remind everybody."

When Mary arrived in the wheelhouse, the Captain told her about the discovery of Barbie's body.

"Oh my gosh!" exclaimed Mary. "Poor Barbie, she must have fallen over trying to look for the bears."

"Or she jumped," Martina added.

The Hotel Manager and the First Officer were delegated the task of informing the other members of the crew. Martina decided to ask Kemi to take over Barbie's role for the remainder of the cruise. Kemi had previously impressed that she would be interested if there were any opportunities on the ironing front and, once she had stopped crying, she enthusiastically made her way to the laundry room.

Martina was also able to arrange with Manchester to get Suella, a freelance cabin attendant who conveniently lived near Berlin, to join the ship in Wittenberg before it headed back towards Prague. Assuming, of course, that she was ready, willing and able. Which she was.

By this time, Max had arrived in the wheelhouse. He agreed with Mary that the tours to Wittenberg should go ahead as planned. He then headed down to the Portcullis Lounge for the disembarkation briefing.

Mary realised that there was an elephant in the room or, at least, the wheelhouse.

"You know that someone must have been with Barbie when she fell," she said to Suzanne.

"What do you mean?" the Captain asked.

"Someone must have tapped her back in. We left Torgau because everyone was supposed to be on board," Mary posited, "so somebody must have taken her shore pass before she ended up at the bottom of the moat."

The implication was obvious.

Captain Zimmermann called Inspector Beckenbauer.

Inspector Beckenbauer asked to speak to Mary.

He told her, "The police examiner says she was hit on the head with what he believes was a heavy object before her body ended up in the moat. He can't say yet whether the blow simply incapacitated her, or if it actually killed her, but her head injury was definitely not caused by the fall. She actually landed on her face in some bushes."

Mary really liked Second Officer Rosov. But she had seen him leaving the ship by himself and she knew that Barbie had broken off their relationship. Mary remembered that Mike was carrying a heavy-looking torch. She relayed this information to the Inspector.

And she also knew that Mike had intended to visit the moat, so she let the Inspector know what Jane had told her about his great-grandfather and the war. And she reluctantly explained that Second Officer Rosov had not been the cheerful, helpful young man whom she remembered from the Duke of Sussex.

The Inspector asked Mary to get the Captain to check on the torches.

Suzanne asked the First Officer to find out whether all the torches were where they were supposed to be.

Three minutes later, the First Officer returned holding one of the torches and declared, "All four of our torches were with the firefighting equipment but this one appears to have traces of blood on its rim."

This information was relayed to Inspector Beckenbauer, who told the Captain to expect him when the ship reached Wittenberg. "And please make sure nobody leaves the ship until I get there."

In the meantime, Max was in the Portcullis Lounge for the disembarkation briefing.

One occupant from each cabin was required to attend this meeting. In practice, almost everyone attended. He wasted little time in explaining that cases needed to be in the corridor by 8.00 am and that cabins should be vacated by 9.00 am. And he reminded them that any onboard accounts for massages, manicures and Moet should be settled after the Captain's Farewell Dinner.

"You will be travelling by coach to Potsdam and the Sanssouci Palace, and from there we will be heading to the hotel in Berlin. There will be a blue coach and an orange coach. There is a list in Reception so you can see which coach you will be on. Help yourself to the number of blue labels or orange labels which you need for your cases. The blue coach will leave at 9.30 am and the orange coach will leave about ten minutes later.

"All being well, we will be arriving at the Grand Duchess Hotel in Berlin by 5.00 pm.

"I won't be with you, I'm afraid. I'll be heading to the airport first thing tomorrow morning. I'm going to be on holiday for four weeks."

He waited for the expressions of disappointment to die down before giving his standard spiel about tipping.

"As you know, Sovereign River Cruises has taken care of all gratuities for all the members of the crew and for all your local tour guides and the coach drivers. You've probably seen Mary handing out those white envelopes at the end of our excursions.

"Of course, you may want to show your appreciation for some extra-special service which one of the crew members may have provided and you will find envelopes for this purpose in your cabin this evening. There will be a box on the counter in Reception for these envelopes from tonight."

As a matter of practice, the crew shared the contents of any such envelopes equally.

As a matter of company policy, Cruise Directors were no longer allowed to mention the fact that they did not share in the crew's tips but they were allowed to keep anything which they might be given.

Max finished by spending a few minutes describing what they should expect to see in Potsdam and the Sanssouci Palace.

He then went up to the wheelhouse and Mary filled him in with what he had missed.

"So where is Mike anyway?" asked Max.

"I think he must still be in our cabin," the First Officer replied. "He's not on duty until this afternoon but he must have been up most of the night. He told me that, after he got back from Torgau, he was stuck in Reception until gone midnight. I think he was sorting out a problem with the accounts computer. And then he tried to download an update for the SRC Tour Buddy app but there was something wrong with the coding. He'd only just got to bed when I came on duty at six o'clock. I would imagine he's been asleep all morning."

Indeed, he had been. And he was now in the shower, preparing to come on duty. He replayed in his mind the events of last night. What he had done in Torgau was cathartic. He could now move on.

Max announced over the public address system that lunch was now being served and reminded guests that the coaches for the Wittenberg tour would be leaving at 1.30 pm. And that at 7.00 pm, the Captain's

Farewell Dinner would be held in the Coronation Restaurant.

At 12.32 pm, the Baron von Habsburg arrived at Wittenberg. Two police cars were waiting alongside the mooring. Inspector Beckenbauer came on board and accompanied Captain Zimmermann and Mary to Mike's cabin.

"I'm really sorry, Mike, but Barbie has been murdered," Mary began once he had opened the door to their knock. "They found her body in the Schloss Hartenfels moat this morning."

If Inspector Beckenbauer were hoping for a confession, he would have been disappointed. Mike remained silent for a few moments before saying, "Oh, no. Poor Barbie. I was near the moat last night. But I never saw her." There was no emotion in his voice and he appeared to be focussing on something behind his visitors.

Twenty minutes later, the police cars left with a torch in an evidence bag and Second Officer Mike Rosov.

As Inspector Beckenbauer had explained, the police needed to interview him further about his relationship with the deceased and his movements the previous night. And to understand why he never asked them how she had been killed.

"Hopefully, he will be able to return to the ship by tomorrow," Suzanne said to the Inspector.

"I hope so, too," said Inspector Beckenbauer.

Captain Zimmermann discussed the situation with the First Officer and they both felt confident that they could manage without Mike, or at least a Second Officer, until they headed back upstream towards Prague on the next cruise. There was no more sailing to do and Blume was perfectly able to handle any issues with the Wi-Fi and the whisper boxes or, indeed, the shore passes, for the next couple of days.

Likewise, Martina was confident that her cabin attendants and the butlers would be able to cope until Suella arrived and she confirmed that Kemi was more than happy to look after the laundry until a replacement had been recruited. Kemi had every intention of applying for the position in any event. However, Martina did make an announcement over the public address system that, for logistical reasons, they would be unable to accept any last-minute laundry items. Kemi wasn't quite up to speed yet.

Probably no more than a handful of guests had even met Barbie. Many more would have been unaware of her existence. But after Martina's announcement, with some sad faces among the crew, indeed some evidence of crying, and the presence of police cars and the absence of Mike Rosov, the Captain realised that she needed to make some sort of announcement.

Rather than take to the public address system, she decided to leave a note in each cabin while the majority of guests were ashore in Wittenberg, explaining that Barbie had met with a fatal accident in Torgau and suggesting that, if any guest wanted to make a small donation in her memory, she would ensure that this would be given to her family.

She raised three hundred and five euros.

29

Day 7 – Afternoon
Wittenberg/MV Baron von Habsburg

As Mary had decided to stay on the ship in the light of events over the last twenty-four hours, Bennie joined Max, Tomáš and Pavel on the Wittenberg tour.

Mary introduced Bennie to the lady holding lollipop 3 as the guides waited on the towpath by the three coaches. Steffi had been a tour guide in Wittenberg for almost twenty years but, in her younger days, she had been something of a sportswoman.

As her coach made its way from the river, Steffi took hold of the microphone. "Good afternoon, ladies and gentlemen or, as we say in Germany, *Guten Tag, meine Damen und Herren.* My name is Steffi and our wonderful driver today is Ralf." Again.

"I would like to welcome you to my hometown of Wittenberg. It was, of course, also the hometown of Martin Luther. Our coach will be stopping outside the Castle Church where he nailed his theses to its door.

"Once we leave the coach, we will use your whisper boxes. Hopefully, you all remembered to bring them but I do have a few spares. We'll be on channel three."

Only two of the spares were needed and one of those was for a malfunctioning box.

Those with lollipop 3 for the afternoon included Sir Claude and Lady Liz, Mrs Stanhope, Ms Phyllida Ballard, Mr and Mrs Eagle and the entire American contingent. Horace had to take a call from Chambers and missed the tour. London's criminal fraternity were in need of his services again.

Just as Bennie had been boarding the coach, Mary had remembered to ask, "Bennie, please keep an eye on Mr and Mrs Eagle. I'm sure there won't be a problem but I do know they have some strong opinions about Protestantism."

Bennie gave her a somewhat quizzical look, particularly as he didn't know who Mr and Mrs Eagle were in any event. And since he had learnt his English through the medium of lyrics to popular songs, he wasn't too sure about Protestantism either.

Steffi then launched into a brief history of Martin Luther and the Reformation.

"Martin Luther, as I am sure you are aware, is credited with starting the Protestant Reformation. The movement was so named because it quite literally protested against the doctrines of the Roman Catholic Church and created an alternative strand of Christianity.

"Luther was born in 1483 in Eisleben in Germany. He obtained a bachelor's degree and a master's degree and then enrolled in law school. But, after narrowly escaping death when he was nearly hit by lightning, he dropped out and entered a monastery. He became an ordained priest in 1507 and in 1512 he was conferred the degree of Doctor of Divinity by the University of Wittenberg.

"His study of the Bible convinced him that the Church had lost sight of a number of core truths and so, on 17th October 1517, he changed the course of history when he nailed his Ninety-five Theses of Contention to the door of the Castle Church.

"We will be arriving at the church in just a couple of minutes. You won't see the original wooden door but you can now see his ninety-five theses engraved on its replacement.

"In case you are wondering what he was doing nailing something to the door of a church, you must remember that Wittenberg was a university town and Luther taught at the university. If someone wanted to put forward a topic for discussion and debate, its proponent would nail the details to the door of the Castle Church.

"Luther's views were declared heretical but he refused to renounce his beliefs and the Emperor Charles the Fifth ordered his arrest. Luther took refuge with Frederick the Wise of Saxony and devoted himself to translating the Bible into common German.

"Luther's call to the Church to return to the teachings of the Bible resulted in new traditions within Christianity and the Counter-Reformation of the Roman Catholic Church."

With perfect timing, the coach drew up outside the Castle Church alongside the first two coaches.

"By the way," Steffi added, "the official name of this town is Lutherstadt Wittenberg. It's now named after Martin Luther."

As Steffi led lollipop 3 into the Castle Church, she explained that the building behind the church was Schloss Wittenberg or Castle Wittenberg. The castle was built for Frederick the Wise and was completed in 1525.

Once inside, she pointed out the modest tombs of Martin Luther and his closest ally, Philipp

Melanchthon. Slightly less modest was the tomb of Frederick the Wise.

Leaving the Castle Church and its much-photographed doors behind, Steffi brought her group to the pedestrianised Schloss Strasse.

"So, on the right, we have a beautiful early-sixteenth-century Renaissance house which belonged to Lucas Cranach the Elder. His son, Lucas Cranach the Younger, was born in the house. I don't know how much you have learnt about these gentlemen but they were prolific portrait painters and printmakers. Lucas Cranach the Elder was a friend of Martin Luther and he is the artist most closely associated with the Reformation."

A few more metres and they found themselves in the Market Square.

"The building in front of us is the Old Town Hall or the Rathaus. The building dates to the sixteenth century. The monuments in front of the building are from the nineteenth century. That's Martin Luther on the right and Philip Melanchthon on the left."

They walked through the square and entered the Parish Church of St Marien.

"This Gothic church was built between the thirteenth and fifteenth centuries. Luther was married in the church to Katharina von Bora. You probably saw the church where she was buried when you were in Torgau. I'll be telling you a bit more about her later. Luther used to preach here.

"Please have a look at the magnificent Reformation altar. This was the work of the Cranachs, father and son."

They continued walking and passed Philip Melanchthon's house. Their last stop was the Lutherhaus.

"This is where Luther and his family used to live. It's now a museum to the works of Lucas Cranach the Elder and it also contains a large number of documents relating to the Reformation and Luther's translation of the Bible.

"I promised to tell you a bit more about Luther's wife. Katharina von Bora was a Cistercian nun who had been living in a convent from a very early age. She was disillusioned with her monastic life and became interested in the growing Protestant movement. Luther helped to arrange her escape from the convent, along with eleven other nuns, hiding inside herring barrels on a horse-drawn cart. She married Luther in 1525.

"Their marriage was very significant in the history of Protestantism. Luther wasn't the first cleric to marry because of Reformation ideas but he was the most prominent. Melanchthon thought that his marriage would hurt the Reformation by causing a scandal but Luther eventually decided that marrying Katharina von Bora would 'please his father, rile the pope, cause the angels to laugh, and the devils to weep'."

The coach had found its way to the far end of the street and Steffi's group boarded.

Bennie was none the wiser but he thought that 'laughing angels and weeping devils' might make for good lyrics.

30

Day 7 – Late afternoon and early evening
MV Baron von Habsburg

The coaches were back at the ship by 5.30 pm. The Castle Church had not been razed to the ground nor had the door to the church been vandalised by the Eagles.

The Captain's Farewell Dinner would be underway in less than two hours. There was no talk scheduled as Max had covered Potsdam and the Sanssouci Palace in the morning. But there were plenty of showers to be had, hair to be brushed and combed, make-up to be applied and, in some cases, jewellery to be taken out of cabin safes.

And Mary had been thinking.

Two people had died in less than a week.

Lady Hayter had died of nicotine poisoning. How did the nicotine get into her bottle of water? It had to be Lord Hayter, didn't it? But is nicotine really that poisonous?

"I must have a word with Professor Blackwell," she said to herself. As she bumped into Professor Blackwell as they were both going into the Portcullis Lounge shortly before dinner, she was soon able to accomplish the task she had set for herself.

Barbie had been murdered. Someone had hit her on the back of her head with a heavy object. And then taken her shore pass. So, it must have been someone from the ship. She had dumped Mike. And Mike was by himself in Torgau that night. He was carrying a heavy torch when she saw him and a torch with traces of blood on it had been found with the firefighting equipment. And, she had learnt earlier from the Inspector, it had been wiped of fingerprints.

Thankfully, neither Bea nor Benno had contributed to Bruce's demise in any way. Mary thought that Bruce's taste in music might have led them to keep their distance. The lead connecting her new iPhone to her headphones had fallen out and it was the noise of the Moss Gatherers' Highway to Hades playing at full volume which had first alerted a concerned citizen of Torgau to the presence of her body.

"No, no, no," Mary thought to herself as another earworm invaded her head.

We're on a highway to Hades/We're all going to Hell/The Devil's gonna roast us/The Devil's gonna toast us/We're all going to Hell…

Over and over again.

She had also spoken to Charles Cromwell a couple of times during the course of the afternoon. There were no issues with the hotel crew but there was some doubt that a replacement could be found for Mike before the next cruise was due to leave Wittenberg.

There was, in fact, an issue with the hotel crew. The Executive Chef, Marco-Peer, was not happy. He would meticulously clean and sharpen all his knives and his other cooking implements each time they were used. And his barbecue fork, part of a very expensive set from Japan which included tongs and a slice, had disappeared. No one had seen it since that idiot Max had ruined the corns on the cob the previous lunchtime. He blamed Benigno for letting Max anywhere near his equipment. And he also blamed Carmelo, who was supposed to have brought all the equipment used for the barbecue back to the galley for washing and his care and attention.

Max arrived back in Reception after the tour and touched base with Mary. She duly reported her discussions with head office. Max was leaving the ship anyway, so he wasn't overly concerned about the next cruise.

But he was concerned about the football. As he was about to go and change for the evening, Betcha let him know that his account was in need of replenishment if he wanted to continue betting. A mild expletive, addressed primarily towards the Argentinian national team, passed his lips as he took his leave of Mary.

Mary remembered that she needed to get ready herself for the Captain's Farewell Dinner and there was a little red number hanging in her wardrobe waiting for another outing. It had already featured several times on the Seine earlier in the year. And a pair of really nice red shoes which she had picked up in Marks and Sparks wanted to show themselves to the world.

The Captain commandeered the table which seated eight people, much to the chagrin of the Porterhouse Octet.

Traditionally, the guests in the two Royal Suites were invited to join the Captain and the Cruise Director for the Farewell Dinner, or the Welcome Dinner, depending upon the cruise, together with another couple invited by the Cruise Director.

As this was Max's last cruise for a while, Mary had agreed that he should sit at the Captain's Table.

She had also suggested that he might like to invite his stepmother. As Lord Hayter was still "helping the police with their enquiries" or something Teutonically similar, there were no single men to make up the numbers, so Max agreed that it would be nice if Jane Stanhope could also be asked, particularly as she had struck up a friendship with Lucy.

Sir Claude and Lady Liz were in one of the Royal Suites but, as the Hayters had been in the other one, Max and Mary needed to find another couple to replace them. Max suggested, and Mary agreed, that they should ask Mr and Mrs Rook. Not only were they the oldest couple on the cruise but they also happened to have travelled with Sovereign River Cruises more times than anyone else on board.

The table was circular, so Sir Claude was seated on the Captain's right, resplendent in a white jacket and a black bow tie. Lady Hayter would have approved. Jane Stanhope sat to the right of Sir Claude and Max sat next to her. Lady Liz sat on Max's right. Mr and Mrs Rook sat together and completing the circle was Lucy.

Jane and Mrs Rook wore dresses which they considered suitable both for their age and the occasion while both Lady Liz and Lucy Burrage delivered some glamour to the table. Lucy's plunging neckline left little to the imagination, although a beautiful ruby pendant on a gold chain provided an alternative focal point for those more interested in jewellery than the spathic nature of her chest.

Once everyone was seated, Captain Zimmermann welcomed all her guests and summoned Wiener to take their drinks orders.

"To go with your meal tonight, we have a lovely medium dry white Dönnhoff Tonschiefer Riesling Trocken Dry State 2023 or, if you prefer red, a Knipser Spätburgunder Réserve 2017. The Spätburgunder will remind you of a Pinot Noir. If you would prefer something other than wine, please let me know. And maybe a glass of champagne to start with? I think Pearl has a very nice bottle of Moet & Chandon on ice.

The suggestion of champagne was well received and seven flutes of Moet & Chandon arrived in short order. It was fortunate that Pearl had, in fact, three very nice bottles of Moet on ice.

The Maître d'hôtel presented the menus, bound in red leather.

As they perused the offerings, Andreas brought an amuse bouche of asparagus mousse topped with smoked trout and dill and Fritz arrived with a basket of crackers and freshly baked breads, not all made from rye, and a trio of butter.

Once orders had been taken, tentative enquiries regarding the death of Barbie, the departure of the Second Officer and the current whereabouts of Lord Hayter were directed from all points of the compass towards the Captain.

They received in return, with regard to Barbie, "It's very sad," and "I believe her parents live in Malta but the Hotel Manager is dealing with that," and, with regard to Lord Hayter and Mike Rosov, "I expect to see them both back with us tomorrow."

They steadily worked their way through three plates of beef carpaccio with mascarpone truffle cream and five servings of crispy buttermilk calamari, five bowls of chicken consommé and three bowls of borscht, champagne and blood orange sorbet for everybody, four Wiener schnitzels with triple-cooked chips, three filets mignons served with peppercorn sauce and seasonal vegetables and one herb-crusted salmon with asparagus and sweet potato beurre blanc.

The conversation moved on from murder and mayhem to the delights of Dresden and Wittenberg, what to expect in Berlin and the football. And a third bottle of both the Riesling and the Spätburgunder were opened.

The popularity of the wine seemingly necessitated that Sir Claude leave the table temporarily, explaining that he needed to spend a penny. Then Lucy declared that she needed to powder her nose. Sir Claude was away for some time and Max began to wonder if he was all right. "He could have spent a pound at this rate," he thought to himself.

The third bottle of the Riesling was probably responsible for either Max or Lady Liz – they apologised to each other – spilling her glass of water all over the dessert menu. She had only just taken her glasses off to read what Marco-Peer was offering when the menu got a drenching. Max used his napkin to mop up and it was perhaps fortunate that Lady Liz's water glass had become all but redundant over the course of the dinner as she had been concentrating her efforts on the Dönnhoff.

Sir Claude missed the excitement but, no sooner had he returned to the table, Max had to excuse himself, indicating that he needed to turn his bike round.

Needless to say, Captain Zimmermann was confused as to why anyone would need to spend such a small amount of money, apply powder to their nose or go for a bike ride, during the course of a meal.

As Max passed Mary's table, she looked up questioningly.

"Just going to the loo," he explained, putting her mind at rest.

Once all the tables had been served with the dessert options, in the case of the Captain's Table, two Black Forest gateaux, three apple strudels, three passes and a platter of cheese, accompanied by figs and grapes and a basket of biscuits, the Hotel Manager tapped the microphone and began to speak.

"Good evening, ladies and gentlemen. We hope you have enjoyed the Captain's Farewell Dinner and we also hope that you have enjoyed your cruise. I would now like to introduce you to the entire ship's complement.

"Please welcome, from Reception, Blume, from the Portcullis Lounge, Pearl, your waiters Andreas, Bruno, Carl, Dietmar, Ernst and Fritz, your sommelier, Wiener – go Hot Dog – and your Maître d'hôtel, Leiter.

"From the galley, your executive chef Marco-Peer (cue an increased level of clapping decibels) and Alfredo, Benigno, Carmelo, Dario, Emil and Francesca.

"Your butlers, Rishi and Josh and your cabin attendants, Teresa, Kemi, Maggie and Liz."

She nearly read out Barbie's name from her list but managed to swallow the word.

"Rubee from the Golden Crown Spa, Bennie, our king of the keyboards, and our sailors, Ilie, Marian and Jan.

"And let's hear it for our Chief Engineer, Ivor and our First Officer, Boris." Mike went unmentioned.

As each of the members of the crew were introduced, they entered the Coronation Restaurant, turned to the right and circled the tables before disappearing again the same way as they came in. The circumnavigation of the restaurant was accompanied by smiling faces, waving and clapping from the crew, reciprocated by most of the guests. The crew were well aware that decisions regarding tipping would be made over the next few hours.

Martina hadn't quite finished. "And finally, your local guides, Tomáš and Pavel and your Cruise Directors, Mary and Max."

They were all, of course, seated at various tables so each of them stood up when their name was mentioned and gave a polite wave of acknowledgement.

Once they had left the restaurant (or returned to it, in the case of the waiters), the crew dispersed to various parts of the ship. For many of them, it would be some time before they would get to bed.

And tomorrow would be a long day.

Very, very long, as it turned out.

31

Day 8 – Late evening and early morning
MV Baron von Habsburg

The Captain was particularly fond of cheese but, once she had demolished her third helping of the compté, Suzanne decided it was time to finish the book she was reading. It was a murder mystery which took place during a river cruise on the Douro.

Suzanne stood up. "Thank you for joining me, ladies and gentlemen. I must wish you a good night. I do hope you have enjoyed this evening."

"Thank you so much, Captain," said Sir Claude, "I've had a lovely time and it's been a wonderful cruise." The culling of his elephant didn't seem to have put a dampener on his overall enjoyment.

"Absolutely," said Lady Liz in confirmation.

"We couldn't agree more," said Mr Rook, obviously able to make an assumption about his wife's concurrence after sixty-two years of marriage.

Mrs Stanhope smiled but remained silent. They had certainly visited some lovely places, and she had seen some spectacular ecclesiastical buildings, but she wasn't sure that two more deaths for poor Mary to have to deal with made for a wonderful holiday. Indeed, she wondered whether it might have been more appropriate for Sovereign to have cancelled the cruise and fly everyone home. The police obviously thought that Lady Hayter had been murdered by her husband and, presumably, they suspected that Mike was responsible for Barbie's death. It was all rather upsetting and she rather felt that she shouldn't still be enjoying herself.

Lucy also smiled but she was thinking about her nieces.

The Captain departed for her cabin and Death on the Douro. Sir Claude and Lady Liz retired to their cabin to finish packing. Mr and Mrs Rook had all but finished packing several hours ago but, at their age, they were ready to call it a night.

"One for the road, mum," suggested Max.

"You mean the river, don't you, darling?" Lucy replied.

"That's the first time he's actually called me 'mum'," thought Lucy.

"That's the first time she's said 'darling'," thought Max.

They went arm-in-arm up the staircase outside the Coronation Restaurant and through Reception into the Portcullis Lounge.

Mary and Tomáš had been the last diners into the restaurant and had found themselves seated between Bill and Hill and Donald and Sarah. They were anticipating a fraught evening but, much to their surprise, Hill and Donald had very little to say and Bill and Sarah spent a very enjoyable couple of hours discussing the admittedly remote possibility of the Miami Dolphins adding Super Bowl 61 to their list of triumphs.

Bill and Sarah had discovered that each of them was a died-in-the-wool, lifelong fan of the Miami Dolphins as they stood side-by-side in quiet contemplation at the monument in Torgau. Since then, they had hardly stopped exchanging memories of Super Bowl triumphs and failures, not that they were old enough to have been in Los Angeles in 1972 or in Houston in 1973 when the Dolphins won nor, indeed, in 1984, with Dan Marino facing off in Palo Alto against the San Francisco 49ers, when they didn't. And they'd had nothing really positive to talk about when it came to the last forty-one years. But they could always talk Dan Marino records.

Sarah also complained during the dinner that it was very difficult, and very expensive, for her to get to many games at the Hard Rock Stadium. "Hon, I sure wish we lived in Miami," she had said to Donald, giving him a doe-eyed look.

"Mary, Tomáš, we have enjoyed your company," said Bill as he rose after finishing his coffee. "Please come and join us for a nightcap."

"Of course, I'd be delighted," Mary answered, still surprised at the change which had come over Mr Harris.

"And what about you, Tomáš?" Sarah asked.

"Sure," said Tomáš, "that's very kind."

So Mary and Tomáš spent a further thirty minutes chatting to the erstwhile enemies and their spouses while the two of them sipped on glasses of sparkling water with ice and lemon.

"We'd better go and finish packing," said Bill after one final reminisce of a particular Dan Marino touchdown pass.

"Yes, we need to finish off too, don't we hon," Sarah concurred.

Mary stood up as both couples left and Tomáš also decided to call it a night.

There were a few guests remaining in the lounge finishing their drinks, although Pearl was clearing things away and she didn't look like she expected, or indeed wanted, any more custom. Bennie was still encouraging some old favourites out of his piano.

Max was also still there, sitting with Lucy, but she got up as Mary went over to talk to them.

"Hi, Mary, good evening," Lucy said, "I'm not being rude but I think it's time for my beauty sleep. I'm going to call it a night. I can't believe Max wants me out of my cabin by nine o'clock. Over my dead body, I told him!"

Max smiled and said, jokingly, "Maybe you can get a late check-out. Anyway, let me see you to your cabin."

Mary wished them both goodnight and Lucy took Max's arm as she tottered out of the lounge on her three-inch heels and headed towards cabin 234. Mary checked her phone to see if there had been any updates from head office and then began her evening rounds for the last time on the cruise. She found Blume in Reception. She had just finished dealing with a couple of queries, including a manicure wrongly charged to 108, which she would need to sort out with Rubee. There were also three or four cabins, including 234 and 236, which would have to settle their bills in the morning.

"Who's on duty tonight?" Mary asked.

"Tonight, it's Marian," Blume replied, passing knowing looks with Mary. Even Mary knew that, after about 2.00 am, when everyone else on board had gone to bed, Marian would forward any calls made to Reception through to the telephone on the bar counter. There was a particularly comfortable sofa within a couple of quick steps of that telephone, certainly more comfortable for spending the night than on a chair behind the counter in Reception. He always brought with him a laminated card to leave on the counter which read 'Night Duty Officer in Portcullis Lounge'.

Right on cue, Marian arrived and Blume headed off to bed. "OK, I'll be down in a while. I'll try not to disturb you," said Mary.

She headed along the corridor towards the stern. Mary smiled to herself as she watched Max struggling to open the door to Lucy's cabin without letting her topple over. She had a quick look in at the Smoking Lounge. No sign of Marigold yet. Or Phyllida, for that matter.

But there was still some life on the Sun Deck.

The Spa Pool was empty. Literally. It had been drained for cleaning.

As she reached the stern, she found Horace and Malo. Horace was in no mood to retire early. He was feeling rather smug. He had routed Sir Claude once again. Since the destruction of the elephant, there had been no more snide remarks about daughters and Italian waiters. He knew that Claude knew that he was a beaten man.

But had Mary arrived five minutes earlier, she would have witnessed Phyllida storming off. Phyllida, she would be the first to admit, had probably drunk more than usual at dinner and that probably explained why she said what she had said. Horace had just made the mistake of confessing to her that the destruction of the figurine was, in fact, not an accident.

"You really are an absolute sodding bastard, Mr Mortimer," Phyllida all but spat out.

"It was his fault," he countered, "he's been trying to wind me up ever since we got on the plane at Heathrow."

"We're finished, you horrible, nasty little man."

Horace assumed that she didn't really mean it. "Look, you go to the cabin and finish packing. I'll be down in half an hour or so."

She went.

Mary had started to round up a few stray glasses and coffee cups when Marigold appeared with what was presumably the most recently arrived bottle of cognac from the Harrows' cabin. It was about two-thirds full by the look of things.

"Here you are, lover. Don't stay up all night drinking with this dreadful man, will you. I'm off to bed."

Mary assumed that the 'dreadful man' remark was playful. In any event, she knew, and she assumed that Malo also knew, that she was more likely to be on her way to have a cigarette or two in the Smoking Lounge than going to bed.

It was, in fact, more than the prospect of inhaling tobacco smoke which was drawing Marigold to the Smoking Lounge. Around midnight, comet Atlas was due to make an appearance in the northern hemisphere. Atlas had been voted 'Comet of the Year 2024', but this was likely to be its farewell appearance. There was, in fact, a possibility that it might have 'died' since its last visit but Marigold was hopeful of seeing her old friend one last time. She had been sad to learn about Barbie's accident – she hoped it wasn't suicide and she didn't believe for one minute that the Second Officer had anything to do with her death, and she really couldn't care less about Lady Hayter's demise, but she would be devastated if Atlas were no longer wandering the universe. That really would be one death too many.

As Marigold made her way down the stairway for her tryst with Atlas, Mary wished her a good night and then put the rounded-up glasses and coffee cups on a table ready for collection in the morning.

"OK, goodnight gentlemen, please don't forget to put your suitcases out," she said to Horace and Malo and headed off to her cabin.

32

Day 8 – Before 6.00 am
MV Baron von Habsburg

The emptying of Malo's bottle of cognac (his fourth of the cruise) took its toll and Horace fell asleep with a half-full glass in his hand.

It was almost six o'clock before the early morning chill, and a wet patch on his trousers caused by the now-empty glass in his hand, roused Horace from his alcohol-induced slumber. He checked his gold Rolex Oyster Perpetual Daytona watch.

"Bloody hell," he swore to himself, "we've got to be out of our cabin in a couple of hours."

Whilst he recalled that, after last night, his relationship with Phyllida was perhaps no longer all that it might be, he fully expected that they would patch things up for a couple more days – or nights to be precise – so he thought that he should show willing and at least help with the cases.

He made his way unsteadily down the stairway to his cabin, was delighted to find his shore pass in his pocket, and opened the door.

The bed had not been slept in, there was a half-packed suitcase on the floor, several items of clothing destined for the suitcase were still on the bed, and the bathroom was empty and showed no obvious signs of use since the cabin attendant's refreshing visit the previous evening.

A quick check behind the curtains. There was no one on the balcony either.

He hurried from the cabin to Reception where Blume was readying herself for the last few unpaid bills and for requests to change fifty-euro notes into five tens. As such an exchange indicated the likelihood of tipping, she was normally well-prepared for these requests.

"It's Phyllida," he shouted, "she's missing. She's not been in our cabin all night."

Blume immediately telephoned the Captain and Mary.

As for Malo, he had called it a night shortly after one o'clock when he realised that the noise emanating from Horace was snoring rather than an answer to his question about Horace's favourite murderess.

Malo was so drunk that he hardly made it onto the bed. And he failed to notice that Marigold was not in the bed with him as he passed out fully clothed and still wearing his cowboy boots.

33

Day 8 – 6.00 am to 8.00 am
MV Baron von Habsburg

Her body was actually found by a fisherman at 6.00 am, floating face-down in the Elbe about one kilometre downstream from where the Baron von Habsburg was moored. Whether she had drowned, or had died as a result of the obvious wounds to her back, was perhaps irrelevant at that stage in that she was most definitely dead.

The fisherman, whose name was Klaus Fischer, telephoned the police on his mobile phone. A patrol car arrived within a few minutes and its occupants helped Klaus retrieve the body from the Elbe and lay it on the bank of the river.

Whilst one of the officers called in what had all the appearances of a murder to her superior, the other officer searched the pockets of the corpse's designer jeans. He found a rectangular black plastic card which provided both the corpse's name and an emergency phone number for the Baron von Habsburg. He passed the information to his colleague who was still speaking to her superior. Within little more than twenty minutes after the discovery of the body, Inspector Beckenbauer had been informed of the third fatality.

"What, another one!" the Inspector shouted irritably, realising that the call meant that he would soon need to leave the warm embrace of a particularly buxom young police officer named Camille.

Seven very rude words, including two in English, followed.

Swearing done, the Inspector was on the telephone to Captain Zimmermann at about the same time as the hunt for the missing person ended. His instructions were precise. "Do not let anyone leave the ship until I arrive. That's an order. And please don't tell anyone about the body. No, you can tell Miss Mead. But tell her not to tell anyone else. And that's also an order!"

The First Officer was in the wheelhouse with Suzanne when the call came through and she delegated to him the responsibity for ensuring that the Inspector's first order was duly carried out. Boris raced down to Reception and ensconced himself at the top of the gangway leading to the riverbank. Mrs Smith had already returned from her run and Boris had obviously come back from buying a copy of the paper.

Mary was in Reception at the time. She had just posted the overnight scores:

Mexico 0 Italy 3

Niger 0 Iraq 1

Canada 2 Slovenia 1

South Korea 3 South Africa 3

Boris explained to Mary what he was doing but told her that he had no idea why he had been ordered to do it.

Max joined Mary in Reception just after 7.30 am carrying his suitcase. He was due to be leaving at 7.45 am for Berlin Brandenburg Airport to catch a British Airways flight to Heathrow at 10.50 am. It was something like eighty kilometres to the airport but Sovereign had agreed to pay for a taxi. Max had his four weeks' leave to look forward to before joining the MV Emperor Franz Joseph on the Danube. The prospect of wall-to-wall World Cup football on television, and visits to the pub, and success on Betcha, beckoned. Mind you, only one of the results which Mary had just posted was a scoreline which his detailed research had promised.

Mary thanked him for all his help and agreed to get in touch when she was back in Bury St Edmunds. It was less than thirty miles between Mary's parents' house and where Max lived. "Maybe we can go and watch a game at Portman Road sometime," Max suggested.

"Love to," Mary replied and then belatedly thought to ask, "Have you seen your stepmother to say goodbye? She's such a lovely lady, such good fun."

"I said goodbye to Mum last night. I don't expect she'll be awake yet, she's not an early riser. But I'll be seeing her in Southend in a couple of weeks. Anyway, I'd better see if my taxi is on the way."

"Sorry, Max," said Boris when he heard this, "the Captain says no one is allowed to leave the ship until Inspector Beckenbauer arrives."

Max looked at his watch. "What's it this time?" he asked himself. "I've got a flight to catch." He had, however, built some leeway into his travel time to the airport, so he went and sat in the Portcullis Lounge, decided that the taxi would just have to wait – it was Sovereign's money after all – and took out his mobile phone to see what Betcha might have to offer him.

He was feeling lucky.

34

Day 7 – 8.00 am to 9.00 am
MV Baron von Habsburg

After her somewhat dramatic departure from the Sun Deck a few hours earlier, Phyllida realised when she arrived outside the door to cabin 203 that her shore pass was inside, probably under the pile of clothes on the bed which hadn't yet made it into a case. Returning to the Sun Deck was not an option. To go back and ask Horace if she could borrow his shore pass would have involved a loss of face of a magnitude which Phyllida was unwilling to endure.

However, there were two problems facing Phyllida. First, her bladder was fit to bursting. And, secondly, she couldn't see anybody in Reception to ask to let her into her cabin.

Marian had hardly had time to sit himself down in Reception – it was far too early to be thinking about the sofa – when he received a call from Mr Zieff in cabin 103 to say that he had forgotten the combination to his cabin safe and needed to get his wallet out. And Mrs Zieff had also forgotten it. "Memories like a sieve, both of us," he confessed.

Marian called Martina in her cabin and Martina instructed him how to open Mr Zieff's safe by keying in a particular sequence of numbers. The numbers changed every fifteen minutes, so he checked on the phone that the Zieffs were respectable, got the sequence of numbers from Martina and then hurried down to their cabin and freed Mr Zieff's wallet. He was away for less than five minutes. But the wrong five minutes for Phyllida.

Unable to gain access to her cabin, she sat herself down in the ladies' toilet in Reception, relieved herself and nodded off.

She had woken with a start and a sore head, a dry throat, a very stiff back and her Marks and Sparks white knickers down by her ankles. If she looked hard enough – which was something of an effort – she felt confident that she might become reunited with her rather expensive Jimmy Choo left shoe, the whereabouts of which was not immediately apparent.

It was in the basin. Quickly rectifying the low-flying knickers problem, she emerged, two-shoed, as nonchalantly as possible, from the toilet only to find that half the ship seemed to have been looking for her.

She located a dishevelled Horace in the Portcullis Lounge and straightaway realised that he was also still in the clothes which he had been wearing when she bade her fond farewells a few hours earlier. But the wet patch around the crotch of his trousers hadn't been there when she left him. He was certainly working his way through his wardrobe.

No words were exchanged but the two of them repaired somewhat sheepishly to their cabin to shower (both of them), shave (Horace) and finish packing (mostly Phyllida).

Maggie would normally start her end-of-cruise deep cleaning with cabin 202 and work her way down the starboard side of the corridor to cabin 236. But, with Kemi newly-installed in the laundry, the Hotel Manager was concerned to get the sheets and towels into the wash as soon as possible so she asked all the cabin attendants to strip each cabin the moment its occupants had left for breakfast. She was therefore somewhat frustrated that there was a 'Privacy Please' notice hanging from the door handle of cabin 234. She had already stripped from 202 to 232.

At least the lady had put her suitcase out. It was the first case which she saw Ilie collect as she was coming on duty at 6.30 am. Which is more than you could say for her neighbours in cabin 236, although it was now nearly 8.00 am. She realised that Mrs Burrage was related to Max but she really needed to get the bedding down to the laundry.

"Sod it," she muttered to herself and gave a healthy rap on Lucy's door.

"Mrs Burrage, it's Maggie, may I come in. Maggie, your cabin attendant."

There was no answer and no one came to open the door. She couldn't hear any noises from inside the cabin – certainly no sound of anyone in the shower – so she decided to let herself in using her cabin pass.

Mrs Burrage was lying on her back on the bed. She wouldn't be leaving for Potsdam on the Sovereign River Cruises coach.

There was what looked like a barbecue fork sticking out of her chest, one tine below each breast and its green handle pointing towards the ceiling.

Lucy was wearing a silky red negligée which had been purchased from Ann Summers just days before the start of the cruise. "You never know when you might need to look your best," she had thought to herself at the time. Her murder was probably not what she had in mind.

Blood had seeped from the two wounds, darkening the red silk and finding its way onto what were once crisp white sheets.

Maggie screamed.

Mary was still in Reception speculating with Blume as to why no one was allowed to leave the ship. Maggie's screams brought both of them running. Fortunately, the erstwhile occupants of all the adjacent cabins along Buckingham Deck were either finishing breakfast or waiting on the Sun Deck to disembark or, in the case of cabin 236, either dead or comatose.

As soon as Mary had taken in the scene in Lucy's cabin, she ordered Blume to sit Maggie down in Reception and wait for her there. She told both of them not to say anything to anyone, at least until she had a chance to speak to Max. Whatever conclusions the police might have reached regarding the death of Lady Hayter, there could have been no doubt about the cause of Lucy's death.

She closed the door to the cabin from the inside and called Captain Zimmerman. It had hardly been ten minutes since Suzanne had spoken to the Inspector and now she had another death, another murder, to deal with.

Captain Zimmermann came down from the wheelhouse and knocked on the door of cabin 234. Mary let her in. Suzanne seldom swore but today, when she saw Lucy's body, she made an exception.

And then she told Mary about Marigold. And about Inspector Beckenbauer's order not to tell anybody.

35

Day 8 – 9.00 am to 9.30 am
MV Baron von Habsburg

Mary took control of the situation.

She insisted that the Captain should ignore the Inspector's orders and inform Mr Harrow that Marigold's body had been found in the river. Malo was only next door in cabin 236 and was still blissfully unaware that Marigold had not slept in their cabin. And now he was about to learn that she had been murdered. Mary also asked her to stay with Malo until she could find someone to sit with him.

"OK, I suppose that makes sense. Just keep me informed," Suzanne replied and went to break the news about his wife's death to Malo as he himself was stirring into life.

Next, she had to inform Max about his stepmother. She closed the door to Lucy's cabin and went to look for him. Max was still in the Portcullis Lounge and was talking to Tomáš.

Mary asked if she could have a quiet word but, before she had managed to tell him about Lucy, Betcha commanded his attention and, by the look on his face, the information he received was probably almost as unwelcome as the news she was about to impart.

"I am very sorry, Max, but your stepmother has been found dead in her cabin. I am afraid that she was murdered," Mary said as gently as possible.

With a voice choking with emotion, all Max could do was ask questions. "What? How? What happened? Who did it? Why?"

"It looks as if someone stabbed her with that barbecue fork which went missing," Mary answered. She wasn't sure that she should have told him about the murder weapon but she knew that, with Maggie and Blume on the case, he would find out soon enough.

After his initial anguished outburst, Max appeared to have gathered himself. "I'm obviously devastated but I didn't really know her, you know," he continued. "We only met a few months ago. Can I see her?"

"I think the police will want to seal off her cabin until their forensic people have had a chance to dust for fingerprints and take some photographs," Mary answered, demonstrating her extensive knowledge of police procedures garnered through watching murder mysteries.

"Of course," Max acknowledged. "I can always see her body later. But I can't believe we've had another murder on the ship."

"Actually, we've had two," Mary thought, but she accepted that she was not supposed to mention Marigold's death to anyone.

Mrs Stanhope came into the lounge at that moment and went straight over to Max.

"I'm so terribly sorry," she said, and gently squeezed his hand.

Mary realised that Jane must have spoken to Blume or Maggie. "So much for 'don't say anything to anyone'," she thought to herself.

Then Phyllida entered the lounge without Horace. Mary knew that Phyllida had been getting on well with Marigold, decided to ignore another one of the Inspector's orders, and took Phyllida into her confidence about Marigold's death. She then asked Phyllida if she would sit with Malo for a while.

Phyllida was only too willing to be with anyone other than Horace, so Mary took her to Malo's cabin to relieve the Captain. This had been, perhaps not surprisingly, the first time that Suzanne had needed to tell a guest that his wife had been murdered and she very much hoped that it would be the last. Once Malo had opened the door to the cabin, after much knocking and calling, she had been confronted with an unshaven, dishevelled figure stinking of alcohol. She blurted out the news of his wife's death and was met with complete silence. Malo sat down on Marigold's unused side of the bed and began to cry. He took his mobile phone from his pocket and turned it on. Captain Zimmermann could see that his screensaver was a picture of Marigold. She stood and watched him and said nothing.

He was still crying and staring at Marigold's photograph when Phyllida arrived. Suzanne couldn't get out of the cabin quick enough and went to look for Mary. Phyllida, however, managed to persuade Malo to have a shower and a shave and helped him to pack Marigold's case. She made him a cup of coffee. And then helped him to pack his own case.

"I guess we missed the eight o'clock deadline, then. I hope they don't throw us off the ship," Malo said, trying to assuage his grief with humour.

Captain Zimmermann found Mary in Reception and was on the point of going to see Max in the Portcullis Lounge – Suzanne wanted to give him her condolences – when her mobile rang.

"It's Inspector Beckenbauer," she said, "he would like a word with you. Use my phone."

The Inspector filled Mary in with the details about the discovery of Marigold's body. And Mary made his day by telling him that there had been another murder. She provided the Inspector with the gory details of what was almost certainly the barbecue fork which had been reported missing earlier protruding from Mrs Burrage's torso.

"I guess that's what made the holes in Mrs Harrow's back," Mary suggested.

"So it's perhaps safe to assume that we have only got ourselves one more murderer," said the Inspector with a hint of ironic understatement.

"I also think I know where Marigold must have been killed," Mary continued.

She explained how Marigold liked to have a cigarette in the Smoking Lounge before she went to bed. Her cabin was at the end of the corridor on Buckingham Deck. And Mrs Burrage's cabin was next door to Marigold's.

The Inspector seemed convinced that Mrs Burrage must have seen or heard something which could incriminate Marigold's murderer and, realising that there had been a witness, they had killed her to ensure her silence.

Captain Zimmermann had suitably condoled Max and had been hovering, waiting for the return of her phone. Realising what Mary was talking about to the Inspector, she said that she had not heard anything. The book she had been reading had sent her to sleep and she had still been asleep when her alarm went off at five o'clock.

The Captain and the Inspector then spoke for some minutes and agreed on logistics. The Inspector was fully cognisant of the fact that there were almost one hundred foreigners waiting to leave the ship, visit Berlin tomorrow and fly home, and that about the same number of foreigners were expecting to check out of their hotel in Berlin and board the ship in a little over thirty hours' time.

While they spoke, Mary, with considerable trepidation, called the Chief Operating Officer and, after a somewhat fraught, but informative, exchange, it was agreed that Charles would fly to Berlin later in the day.

The Inspector told Suzanne that he would be at Wittenberg within the next fifteen minutes. The sailors would be allowed to offload the cases from the ship and help the drivers put them on the coaches. No other members of the crew would be allowed to go ashore until further notice. The First Officer was still manning his post. They could continue with cleaning the ship, although Mrs Burrage's cabin and the Smoking Lounge should be locked. The ship could be refuelled and its water tanks replenished. Supplies could be brought on board but any rubbish or recycling should, for the time being, be left on the Sun Deck.

The Inspector would speak to the victims' husband and stepson, respectively, as soon as he arrived.

All the surviving passengers would be taken by coach, with a police escort, to Potsdam, and the visit to Schloss Cecilienhof would go ahead, but with Tomáš and Pavel acting as guides. The visit to the Sanssouci Palace would, however, have to be postponed. From Potsdam, all the passengers would be taken direct to the hotel in Berlin where they would be interviewed during the course of the afternoon.

Mrs Stanhope sat with Max in the lounge.

Phyllida sat with Malo in the Harrows' cabin.

Horace sat by himself on the Sun Deck next to a growing pile of black rubbish bags.

Max spoke to Manchester and got the travel department to book him on a later flight from Berlin. And got Blume to book another taxi.

As soon as the first of what turned out to be five police cars arrived, the First Officer was replaced by a uniformed officer and Boris was despatched to ensure that the restrictions on their movements were relayed to all the members of the crew.

Mary met the Inspector in Reception and took him first to the Smoking Lounge, then to cabin 234, and finally to the wheelhouse. He brought Mary up to speed with what had been agreed with Captain Zimmermann and then asked her if she would fetch Malo for him. Mary told the Inspector that, at her insistence, the Captain had informed Malo that Marigold's body had been recovered from the river. She also told the Inspector that she had explained to Phyllida in strictest confidence that Marigold had been murdered and that Ms Ballard was now sitting with him in his cabin. The Inspector accepted what Mary had done and he also agreed that she could make an announcement over the public address system before she went to fetch Malo.

Mary then remembered that she had another confession to make. "I also told Max that his stepmother had been killed with a barbecue fork."

"That's fine," replied Inspector Zimmermann, "but please don't say anything about Mrs Harrow being murdered when you make your announcement. You can still let people know that she is dead. And once you have fetched Mr Harrow, could you please ask Max to come to the wheelhouse."

Mary assumed that, thanks to Maggie and Blume, most of her guests would, by now, be aware that Lucy had been found dead with a barbecue fork sticking out of her chest. But, apart from her and Mr Harrow, the only other people on board the ship who were aware that Marigold had been murdered were Captain Zimmermann and Phyllida. And the murderer, of course. But there were also rumours beginning to circulate that neither Malo nor Marigold had been seen that morning. She decided what to say.

"Good morning, everybody. This is Mary, your Cruise Director. As some of you may be aware, both Mrs Lucy Burrage and Mrs Marigold Harrow died during the night. I am sure that you will all join me in expressing our condolences to Mr Harrow and to your Cruise Director, Max Hunt. Mrs Burrage was Max's stepmother.

"As you might expect in these circumstances, the German police have become involved. They have agreed that you can leave the ship this morning as planned and our coaches will be taking you direct to Potsdam for the tour of Schloss Cecilienhof. Tomáš will act as tour guide for the blue coach and Pavel will do the same for the orange coach.

"Unfortunately, we need to postpone the visit to the Sanssouci Palace, although I am hoping that we can arrange a replacement tour there tomorrow afternoon.

"The coaches will be taking you from Potsdam to our lovely hotel in Berlin, the Grand Duchess. Once you arrive, you will be asked to wait in a conference room where you will be given your room keys. The police will speak briefly to each of you and, once you have been interviewed, your passports will be returned and you will be free to go to your room or to explore Berlin at your leisure. You will find your cases in your hotel room.

"Please remember to bring your whisper boxes with you. You can keep your shore passes if you want. There is no need to tap them when you leave the ship.

"I will see you all in Berlin. Thank you."

Once Mary had finished, she brought Malo and Phyllida to the wheelhouse. Malo was looking both distraught and hungover which did not make for a pretty sight. But he had at least showered and shaved and changed his clothes. Phyllida waited outside as Malo went in.

"I am very sorry for your loss, Mr Harrow," the Inspector began, beckoning Malo to have a seat.

"Is that right about Lucy, what I just heard?" Malo asked as he sat down.

The Inspector answered him. "That's right, Mr Harrow, I am afraid that Mrs Burrage is also dead."

"So," he continued, "what can you tell me about last night? Anything you can remember is going to help catch your wife's murderer."

"Not a lot, sir," Malo mumbled, "I was really pissed, you see. I was drinking with that lawyer chap, Horace is his name. We must have polished off a lot of cognac last night.

"My lovely, lovely wife even went and fetched a bottle from our cabin to keep us going but then she said she was off to bed.

"I knew she was going for a smoke. I used to pretend I didn't know she'd started smoking again but I'm sure she knew that I did. She loved going to that space at the back of the ship. She's a bit of an astronomer – I mean, she was – and she liked to stare up at the stars in the night sky from there. That's how I first met her, astronomy. She'd even helped design an app for your phone which tells you what stars you can see. Look, here's the app."

He took out his mobile phone, pressed the AstroWatch icon and showed it to the Inspector.

"Anyway," Malo continued, "me and Horace kept drinking brandy but he fell asleep halfway through a conversation about women murderers he'd got off. I looked at my watch. Bloody hell, I thought, it's nearly one o'clock, Marigold will be apeshit. I haven't packed me bag yet.

"So I went back to our cabin and, as quiet as a mouse, I opened the door. I didn't put the light on and I simply lay down on the bed. Didn't even take off me boots."

He swore that he hadn't noticed that she was not in bed. But he added that she would sometimes spend hours at night looking at the stars so her absence wouldn't have immediately caused him any concern even if he had been sober.

"And the next thing I know, it's morning and Marigold is nowhere to be seen. There's a knock on my door, the Captain comes in and tells me that Marigold has been murdered. Found her body in the river."

He was silent for a few moments, seemingly collecting his thoughts, and then he spoke in a very hushed voice, "Martina did it, you know."

"Martina?" the Inspector queried.

"Yeah, the Hotel Manager lady. She blamed me for killing her sister."

Malo explained about the Moss Gatherers' concert in Prague, the death of Ivana Pavlyuchelkova, and the letters he had received, always threatening 'an eye for an eye'.

"We was on the Sun Deck and Martina was taking drinks orders. She calls me 'Malo' and makes a big point about mentioning the concert and how long she's been waiting to meet me. She's Ivana's sister."

Max was waiting outside the door to the wheelhouse as Malo left. As they passed each other, Max said to Malo, "I am so sorry to hear about your wife, Mr Harrow. What on earth happened to her?"

"You, too, mate, your stepmum," Malo replied. "Yeah, the police reckon she was murdered. Found her in the river this morning. Drowned, I guess. It must have been that Martina, the Hotel Manager. Revenge for her sister. Probably knocked her out and pushed her in when she was having a smoke at the back."

Max, of course, realised what he was talking about.

Phyllida was waiting by the bow rail for Malo and they went back down to his cabin. She didn't know, and didn't care, where Horace was.

Inspector Beckenbauer was annoyed with himself that he had allowed Malo and Max to have spoken to one another. He was quite brusque when he questioned Max.

Brusque or not, Max readily answered the Inspector's questions about his stepmother's movements, and his own, the previous evening.

"I sat with my mother at the Captain's Table for dinner and then we went to the Portcullis Lounge for a couple of drinks. I think she probably drank a bit more than she usually does. The Captain was very generous with the wine at dinner. She was a bit unsteady, particularly with those high heels which she always wore.

"Anyway, my mother needed to finish packing and I walked her back to her cabin. There were still a couple of guests in the Reception area as we left the lounge, querying bills and the like. I can't recall anyone in particular.

"I used her shore pass to open the door. I noticed that her large case was already closed and she asked me to put it outside her door in case she overslept in the morning. Cases have to be out by 8.00 am, you see. But I said to her that it was too early and that it would only get in the way. I told her to put it out in the morning after she got up. But she didn't look convinced. She must have got up during the night to put her case in the corridor.

"About the last thing she said to me was, 'I must wear my naughty nightie. You never know who might come knocking at my door.' She was obviously joking. Anyway, we said goodnight and that's the last time I ever saw her alive."

"Did you see anyone else in the corridor?" the Inspector asked.

"Not that I can recall. But, as I said, there were still a couple of people in Reception."

"And did you go outside to the stern of the ship?" he asked.

"No," replied Max, "after I left my mother's cabin, I went back to my own."

"You know, Mr Harrow must be right," Max said as he got up to leave, "it must have been Martina. Our Hotel Manager. She must have murdered Mrs Harrow and then killed my mother."

Max explained to the Inspector how he knew about the Moss Gatherers' concert in Prague, the death of Ivana Pavlyuchelkova and the letters which Malo had received from her sister Martina threatening revenge.

"My mother must have seen her after she had killed Mrs Harrow - I guess coming in from the Smoking Lounge with that barbecue fork. It must have been when Lucy was putting her case out. Martina has a master pass to all the cabins. She must have let herself into my mother's cabin and murdered her."

Phyllida travelled with Malo to Berlin in one of the police cars. Their cases, including Marigold's, went on one of the coaches.

Max was taken to Berlin in another police car but he kept hold of his suitcase ready for a quick dash to the airport.

Surprisingly, things had moved at such a pace that morning that the blue and orange coaches, with Tomáš and Pavel on board, had departed for Potsdam little more than an hour behind schedule. But, before the coaches had left, Mary had a quick word with Tomáš and sent him a link to open on the internet.

Captain Zimmermann, the Hotel Manager and a number of other members of the crew were also asked to accompany the police to Berlin and a plain-clothed people carrier appeared for this purpose. Inspector Zimmermann assured the Captain that all the crew members would be back on the ship before it got dark "unless, of course, I arrest one of them."

The First Officer was left in charge in Wittenberg. He had two crime scenes and a dead body to worry about.

Mary assumed that she would be travelling in the people carrier. She had packed an overnight bag (her Sovereign River Cruises backpack) as she would be back in Wittenberg the next day with a new shipload of guests and a cabin all to herself.

"Perhaps you would like to come with me, Mary. I would be interested in what you think," the Inspector said as she was saying goodbye to Boris.

She sat in the back of a police Mercedes E-Class Saloon with the Inspector. The driver and another police officer sat in the front.

"I met an old friend of yours at a Europol conference in Paris in May," the Inspector began, "Superintendent Carlos Colombo of the Portuguese *Polícia Judiçiaria*. He told me how you had helped him solve some murders when you were cruising the Douro last year. In fact, he actually said that you solved them for him. I was hoping that you might help me clear my thoughts.

"First, though, let me tell you about my interviews with Mr Harrow and your colleague, Mr Hunt. They are both convinced that the Hotel Manager killed Mrs Harrow in revenge for the death of her sister at a pop concert in Prague over twenty years ago. I gather Mr Harrow used to be some sort of pop singer. And Mr Hunt thinks that his stepmother must have seen the Hotel Manager with the murder weapon as she was putting her case out which is why the Hotel Manager then murdered her."

Mary realised that the Inspector's musical tastes probably didn't encompass heavy metal. And something else was bothering her.

"So, Mary, what do you think?" the Inspector asked.

"What I think is that you think that you have three murderers and that you know the who, the how and the why for all four murders.

"And I think that I have probably watched too many murder mysteries. I still can't believe that all these murders aren't connected in some way.

As the car made its way into the centre of Berlin, Mary thought long and hard about what she had seen and what she had heard, and indeed what Jane had seen and heard, and what Charles Cromwell had told her that morning. And what Max had said. And her conversation with Professor Blackwell. She called Tomáš. He had been online. She then focussed on what the Inspector had just told her.

"That had to be it, obfuscation." She liked that word.

She spoke to the Inspector again. "What I think, Inspector, is that you have the wrong murderer and the wrong motive for each murder."

"So do you know who committed each of our murders?" asked the Inspector.

"Do you know, I believe I do," said Mary, mentally apologising to Detective Inspector Neville Parker.

36

Day 8 – Afternoon
Grand Duchess Hotel, Berlin

As the Mercedes E-Class Saloon made its way through Berlin's south-west suburbs, Mary explained. And the Inspector was convinced. As they neared the hotel, the Inspector placed a call to Tulkinghorn and Tangle in England. Mary still had Ellie's work number on Facebook.

By 1.00 pm, a visit had been made to the solicitors and this visit had led to a number of further calls being made. The police in Wittenberg also paid another visit to the ship and left with one piece of evidence and without another piece of evidence.

The police cars bringing Max, and Malo and Phyllida, arrived together at the Grand Duchess Hotel in the centre of Berlin near Potsdamer Platz. Their respective journeys had taken place in silence, although Betcha interrupted Max's thoughts on a couple of occasions.

The people carrier arrived shortly afterwards and two minutes later the car bringing Mary and the Inspector pulled up outside the hotel.

The police had asked the hotel to arrange lunch in one of its meeting rooms for the crew members and for Max, Malo and Phyllida. A table had also been reserved for the police who had escorted them from Wittenberg.

"Making sure we don't make a run for it," Max quipped when he saw that the police were joining them for lunch, although he realised that he might have to make a run for it at some stage if he wanted to catch the last British Airways flight at 7.50 pm. At least the airport was a lot closer. And there was a later Lufthansa flight around nine o'clock.

However, Suzanne was asked to join the Inspector in the hotel restaurant, the Brandenburg.

Mary checked into her room and also went for lunch in the Brandenburg. She ended up sitting at the next table to where the Captain and the Inspector were sitting. The Inspector had no intention of discussing the murders with Suzanne but he wanted to confirm what would happen once the Potsdam coaches arrived, and also to discuss the timing for taking her and the rest of her crew members back to Wittenberg.

Mary contacted Jensen Norris, the new Assistant Cruise Director. He had flown out from Heathrow the previous day and had been on the Berlin city tour with the Berlin-to-Prague guests in the morning. Jensen had already eaten lunch but happily joined her for a coffee in the restaurant. He was about the same age as Mary, hailed from Brixton, wore a pair of expensive-looking diamond ear studs and sported very short curly hair which he had dyed blue. He was in his full Sovereign River Cruises black regalia. This was his second tour of duty, having previously spent six weeks on the Danube on the MV Empress Elisabeth.

Jensen had a very infectious smile which undoubtedly helped to cheer Mary up a bit.

A drinks reception and a buffet meal had been arranged for the new guests in one of the hotel's larger conference rooms for 7.30 pm. Mary asked Jensen to make sure that he was there to welcome them as they arrived as she expected she might be running a bit late.

Jensen confirmed that the coaches taking the new guests to Wittenberg via the Sanssouci Palace and Potsdam would be leaving between 9.30 am and 9.45 am, with the red coach scheduled to depart first.

The coaches arrived from Potsdam at approximately 2.00 pm. All the surviving Prague-to-Berlin guests were ushered into another one of the hotel's conference rooms with their cases following not far behind.

Once they were all seated and settled, the Inspector made his entrance. "Good afternoon, ladies and gentlemen. My name is *Kriminalhauptmeister* Willy Beckenbauer. I am sure many of you will recognise me from the ship over the last few days.

"Once again, apologies for all the inconvenience, especially at the end of your holiday. But, as you will appreciate, we have had four deaths to consider.

"While you are waiting to be interviewed, the hotel staff will check you in and give you your keys. You should then identify your luggage and it will be taken to your room. Please help yourself to refreshments."

He pointed to two tables loaded with tea, coffee, orange juice and water and plates of assorted sandwiches. Mary had agreed that Sovereign would foot the cost of the refreshments and the lunches.

"As soon as you have been interviewed by one of my officers, you are free to leave the hotel and enjoy the beautiful city of Berlin. We will return your passports at the same time. However, we might ask some of you to wait until all the interviews have been completed.

"We would hope to be finished in a couple of hours and I have been asked by Sovereign River Cruises to let you know that you should reconvene in this room at 7.00 pm for an update about tomorrow's tours and your flights home.

Hotel staff went from guest to guest, completing registration forms and handing out keys. Cases were identified and taken to rooms.

All the interviews followed similar lines. "Did you see anything unusual last night?" and most guests had nothing to add to the overall picture which had emerged. Mrs Montgomery did, however, come up with some new information.

Anyone in the hotel lobby at 4.00 pm would have also seen Lord Hayter and Second Officer Mike Rosov arriving at the hotel accompanied by four police officers.

Charles Cromwell landed at 4.50 pm and was immediately on the phone to Mary, to Max and to Tomáš. The result of all these calls was that the morning tour of Berlin for the diminished number of Prague-to-Berlin guests would go ahead as scheduled, but the afternoon tours would be replaced by the tour of the Sanssouci Palace which had been postponed from that morning. And the flight arrangements for the next day would remain the same.

Charles would arrange for the airlines to be contacted regarding the actual numbers travelling.

He hoped that they would not be going down any further.

37

Day 8 – 5.04 pm to 5.30 pm
Grand Duchess Hotel, Berlin

It was just like Death in Paradise.

Inspector Beckenbauer sent his officers scurrying off in all directions to summon his persons of interest, his witnesses and his experts to the Tiergarten Room, one of the smaller meeting rooms in the hotel.

There was a table at the far end of the room. The three seats behind the table were occupied by Chief Inspector Willy Beckenbauer, Captain Suzanne Zimmermann and Cruise Director Mary Mead. There was a microphone and a couple of marker pens on the table and a whiteboard stood to the side.

Facing the table were three rows of chairs.

Cruise Director Max Hunt, Tomáš and Pavel sat with the Hotel Manager, Miss Martina Pavlyucheklova, Maggie, Blume, Rishi and Marian on the front row.

Behind them sat Sir Claude and Lady Liz Bearskin-Green, Ms Phyllida Ballard, Professor Barry Blackwell, Mrs Brenda Blackwell, Mr Clarence Harrow, Mr Monty Montgomery, Mrs Winnie Montgomery, Mrs Birdie Rook, Mr Brian Rook and Mrs Jane Stanhope.

On the third row, there was Mr Horace Mortimer KC, Mr Bill Harris, Mrs Hill Harris, Mr Donald Nixon, Mrs Sarah Nixon, Mr Jacob Streisand, Mrs Rachel Streisand, Mr Beau Dickie and Mrs Trixie Dickie.

There were twelve chairs along the sides of the room, six on each side. Eight of them were occupied by uniformed police officers.

Once everyone was seated, Baron Hayter of Bedchester and Second Officer Mike Rosov entered in the company of two more police officers. Neither of them was being restrained in any way. The new arrivals sat down on the unoccupied chairs along the sides of the room.

It was exactly 5.04 pm when the Inspector began.

"Good afternoon, ladies and gentlemen.

"Over the last five days, a member of the British upper classes, a laundry worker from Malta, an astronomer married to a former pop singer and a rich widow from Southend-on-Sea have all been murdered. And whoever murdered each of them was on the Baron von Habsburg. And is now in this room."

His opening remarks caused quite a stir.

"First, we had the death of Lady Hayter on the coach from Prague. Mary, could you please remind everyone what happened on the coach?"

Mary stood up and started to speak. "Lord and Lady Hayter were in the seats immediately behind the driver and Mr and Mrs Dickie were sitting behind them. Tomáš was in the front seat across from Viktor and Max and I were sitting immediately behind Tomáš. I had the seat across the aisle from Lady Hayter. The seats immediately behind Max and me were empty. Sir Claude and Lady Liz Bearskin-Green were sitting in the next row. And Mr and Mrs Nixon were behind them. All of them are here today.

"Just before the coach left the hotel, Max and I handed out bottles of water. These are supplied by the hotel and we always get the hotel to break the seals on the bottles to make it easier for our guests to open them. We took them from the cooler boxes which were on the front seat. I started from the rear of the coach. Max started at the front.

"That's right," Max confirmed, "I gave Lady Hayter a bottle and you'd have thought she expected a crystal glass with ice and lemon, the way she looked at it. But I don't remember now if Lord Hayter also took one."

Mary continued, "Once the coach got underway, Lady Hayter took a couple of long, and very noisy, gulps of water from her bottle. These gulps were followed by a loud belch. Half the coach must have heard her. I definitely didn't see either Lord Hayter or Lady Hayter put anything into her bottle.

"With Tomáš talking about the history of Czechia and the noise of the engine, quite a number of our guests fell asleep. I do remember when I looked over at some stage that Lady Hayter was wearing her sleep mask and she seemed to have dozed off. I couldn't really see Lord Hayter. Obviously, I now know that Lady Hayter wasn't asleep.

"Unfortunately, I must have also nodded off for a while because I didn't realise, until Tomáš told me, that Mrs Nixon had come to the front of the coach and taken the last two bottles of water."

Inspector Beckenbauer took over. "Somewhat fortuitously, the Czech police were able to recover the bottle of water from which Lady Hayter had taken those gulps -the rubbish skip hadn't been empied for a couple of days. They were able to identify fingerprints belonging to Max, to Lord Hayter and to Lady Hayter on the bottle. They were also able to identify the actual source of the nicotine. A particularly strong and flavourless vape juice.

"There can only be three possibilities, that Lady Hayter added the nicotine to the water, intending to kill herself, or that the poison was already in the bottle when it was handed to her, or that Lord Hayter added the nicotine to the bottle with the intention of murdering his wife.

"There was nothing on Lady Hayter's clothing or in her handbag which could have contained the nicotine. And there was nothing found in the coach either. So we really can't see how Lady Hayter could have poisoned herself by adding nicotine to the water in her bottle.

"But if the nicotine was already in the bottle when it was handed to Lady Hayter, then her death must have been random. Anyone could have drunk it. But why on earth would one of the hotel employees have poisoned just a single bottle of water? None of the other bottles which we recovered had been laced with nicotine. And no one else became ill. What possible motive could the poisoner have had, particularly as the amount of nicotine ingested by Lady Hayter would probably not have proved fatal for any reasonably healthy person?

"So that leaves you, Lord Hayter. Your fingerprints were on the bottle. You asked Mary to buy a particular brand of vape juice when you were in Prague and this was the same brand of vape juice which poisoned Lady Hayter.

"We have been told by a number of passengers and crew that Lady Hayter had behaved abominably towards you. And then Mrs Streisand heard you tell your wife that you hated her just a few hours before she died.

"We did. Jacob and me. We were in the hotel room next to you, sir, and we heard you say it," Mrs Streisand confirmed, almost apologetically.

The Inspector was nearly finished. "You had a motive. You despised your wife. I am sorry, Lord Hayter, but that's a fact. And with you wife gone, you decided to stay with the cruise and enjoy your new-found freedom rather than remain with your wife's body in Děčín.

"You had the vape juice which Max purchased for you. And once your wife had pulled her mask over her eyes, you had the opportunity to lace her bottle with nicotine. She then drank some water and she died.

"Motive, means and opportunity."

39

Day 8 – 5.30 pm to 5.45 pm
Grand Duchess Hotel, Berlin

"Let's now turn to the murder of Barbie Mattel," said Inspector Beckenbauer.

Probably only the Hotel Manager had known what Bruce's surname was before that moment.

"Bruce," he continued, "your iron maiden. As you all know, her body was found at the bottom of the moat at Schloss Hartenfels. However, the fall did not kill her. Her postmortem showed that she had been struck on the back of her head with a heavy object, causing catastrophic brain damage. She was dead before her body was thrown over the parapet. As it happens, she actually landed face down in some undergrowth and the fall only caused some minor scratches to her hands and face and a couple of broken ribs.

"I am pleased to say that her body showed no sign of any injuries which might have been caused by the bears.

"In any event, we knew immediately after I had spoken to Mary that she did not simply fall, or indeed jump, because someone had tapped her shore pass to indicate that she had returned to the ship at 11.56 pm.

"A number of crew members had been in Torgau that evening, celebrating one of the butlers' birthdays. Max suggested to everybody who was going for a drink, including Barbie, that they should have a look at the bears before they met up in one of the bars in the town centre. The bar, which unfortunately didn't have CCTV, was packed that evening and nobody can state with any degree of certainty who might have been, or might not have been, in the bar at any particular time. And, therefore, who might have been on the bridge at Schloss Hartenfels with Barbie. But one thing seems almost certain: Barbie did not put in an appearance in the bar. Her postmortem indicated that she hadn't had anything to drink for several hours before her death.

"We then learnt that Second Officer Mike Rosov was seen leaving the ship about fifteen minutes before the other members of the crew.

"Mary, I believe that you were in Reception at the time and you saw that the Second Officer was carrying a large rubber-covered torch and that he went in the direction of the castle rather than the bar."

Mary confirmed that this was the case and that she also thought that Barbie had every intention of going to look for the bears. But Barbie had forgotten her shore pass, so she was some distance behind the other crew members after they had left the ship.

"The only guest who went ashore after dinner was you, Mrs Stanhope, and you had returned before 10.30 pm."

"Yes, that's right," said Jane. "I wanted to take some more photographs of St Mary's Church – sorry, I can't pronounce it in German. We didn't have very much time earlier. Mary very kindly walked with me to the church but I then packed her off to the bar. I had a little wander and I bumped into Mr Rosov near that monument we saw. We walked back to the ship together. I can't believe that he had just murdered someone."

But it seemed as if Inspector Beckenbauer could. He continued, "The First Officer was asked to check on the heavy-duty torches used by the fire crews. None of them were missing but one of the torches clearly had traces of blood on its rim. Forensics have shown that the blood is from Barbie's head wound.

"We learnt that the Second Officer had fallen in love with Barbie when they worked together last year on the Douro. They had started to date. Barbie was then transferred to the Elbe and Mike asked for a transfer to be with her. But, by the time Mike's transfer came through, Barbie had dumped him. His own words.

"We don't think Mike had arranged a rendezvous with Barbie that evening. He went to the moat for personal reasons but he was in a highly emotional state and, when he saw Barbie, something must have snapped. And he killed her.

"Once again we have a motive, we have a means and we have an opportunity."

40

Day 8 – 5.45 pm to 6.05 pm
Grand Duchess Hotel, Berlin

"Now let's look at our last two murders," the Inspector continued.

"First, we have the death of Mrs Marigold Harrow. We know that she was the first person to be murdered last night as we found the weapon which killed Marigold still sticking in Mrs Lucy Burrage. Both of them were stabbed through the heart, one in the back and the other in the chest, stabbed with the barbecue fork which had gone missing a couple of days ago. Forensics have found traces of Mrs Harrow's blood in Mrs Burrage's wounds.

"It became apparent from our interviews that a number of passengers knew Mrs Harrow liked to have a cigarette before she went to bed. The only place on the ship where passengers are allowed to smoke is the open area at the end of the corridor on Buckingham Deck. I am told that you call it the Smoking Lounge. And it also appears from our interviews that Mrs Harrow and Lord Hayter were the only smokers on board.

"Marigold was also an astronomer and she loved to look up at the stars at night. So it would have been very easy for someone to come up behind her as she was stargazing and stab her in the back with the barbecue fork. The pathologist tells me that, when he examined Mrs Harrow's wounds, it looked as if a swordsman had thrust the fork into her back like a rapier and then immediately withdrawn the tines. Death would have been instantaneous. The murderer must then have pushed her dead body over the ship's rail. They no doubt expected that it would have travelled a long way downstream before it was discovered. We also found a packet of Silk Cut, with four cigarettes missing, and a click lighter, on one of the tables in the Smoking Lounge and a burnt-out cigarette butt on the decking. And there were traces of Marigold's blood on the ship's rail.

"So what possible motive could there have been for someone to want to murder Marigold?"

He answered his own question. "Revenge. As many of you will know, Marigold's husband was once known as Malo, the lead singer for a music group called the Moss Gatherers."

Mr Harrow became the focus of people's attention.

"Mary, you found out about a Moss Gatherers' concert in Prague about twenty years ago. A young girl named Ivana Pavlyuchelkova was killed when a broken drumstick thrown from the stage by a member of the group pierced her eye.

"For years, on each anniversary of the date of the Prague concert, Mr Harrow received a threatening letter from Ivana's elder sister, Martina, calling him a murderer and threatening 'an eye for an eye'."

Some of that focus now turned towards the Hotel Manager.

Malo looked up at this point. "How did you know about the letters?" he asked.

Mary replied, "I read about them in an interview you gave to New Musical Express in 2015. Max and I went online to search the Prague concert after Mrs Stanhope told us about the poor girl's death."

Max confirmed that he had also read the article. "That's why I suggested to the Inspector that it must have been Martina who killed Marigold," he added.

"Martina," the Inspector continued, looking towards the Hotel Manager, "Mary and Max, and Mrs

Stanhope, they all heard you pointedly tell Mr Harrow that you were at that concert in Prague when Ivana was killed. You had recognised Malo. He was the person responsible for the death of Ivana. So was this the opportunity for someone who had waited over twenty years for revenge? To kill the person whom Malo loved most in the world. An eye for an eye.

"Your cabin is at the end of the corridor on Buckingham Deck. You realised that, at some stage during the evening, there would be every chance Marigold would be alone at the rear of the ship, smoking a cigarette and staring up at the stars. And, as Hotel Manager, you could access the barbecue equipment. You took the barbecue fork, thrust the fork into Marigold's back, and then threw her dead body into the river.

"So why then murder Mrs Burrage? You already had your revenge.

"At first, we assumed that Mrs Burrage must have seen you with the murder weapon when she put her case out during the middle of the night.

"But there was no sign of a struggle in Mrs Burrage's cabin. She had been murdered in her sleep. She wouldn't have gone back to bed if she'd known at the time that she had just witnessed a murder.

"So we concluded that you must have seen Mrs Burrage's door closing after she had put her case out and that you were worried that she might have seen you. Mrs Burrage would have realised that she had witnessed Mrs Harrow's murderer when the details of her death became known.

"So you needed to make sure that Mrs Burrage never got to learn those details.

"You still had the murder weapon and you have a master pass to all the cabins. You gave Mrs Burrage time to get back to sleep, used your pass to open the door of her cabin, and then stabbed her in the heart. You then wiped any fingerprints there might have been on the handle of the barbecue fork, closed the door to her cabin. And went to bed."

Martina might have said something but the Inspector continued, "But don't we have another suspect, Mary?"

Mary took a sip of water and continued with the denouement. "After the incident with the tomato juice during the Royal Trivia Night, it was obvious to anyone that there was no love lost between Lady Liz Bearskin-Green and Mr Horace Mortimer. Even before that night, when we were in Dresden for that awful concert, I overheard Sir Claude blame Mr Mortimer for the death of his first wife. And then Lady Liz talked about revenge."

All eyes now turned to the Bearskin-Greens and Horace Mortimer KC.

Horace's "nonsense" was ignored.

"Lady Liz mislaid her glasses during the Captain's Farewell Dinner after she took them off to read the dessert menu. She had told me that she was as blind as a bat without them. Max, you thought they must have been cleared away by one of the waiters when he replaced your napkin."

"That's right," said Max, "some water got spilled and I used my napkin to mop it up. We still haven't found her glasses but I guess they will be somewhere at the bottom of a pile of laundry."

Mary continued, looking at Phyllida, "Many of our guests have remarked on the similarity between Mr Mortimer's companion and the late Mrs Harrow. They were of a similar height and build and they had the same colour of hair and hairstyle. And both of them liked to wear colourful silk blouses.

"Phyllida became interested in astronomy after talking to Mrs Harrow and she had been spending time at the rear of the ship looking up at the stars. She had also been using an app which Mrs Harrow downloaded for her.

"Maybe our murderer saw Phyllida leave the Sun Deck last night and hoped that she might find her stargazing alone. I know that Mrs Harrow was still on the Sun Deck after Phyllida had left.

"You will remember what the Inspector said about Mrs Harrow's wounds. That it was as if a swordsman had thrust the barbecue fork into her back like a rapier."

"I learnt from Mrs Stanhope that you were an Olympic fencer," Mary said, turning her attention towards Lady Liz, "and Marian saw you walking round the ship in your black bathrobe sometime after midnight."

Marian stuck his thumb in the air.

The Inspector took over. "Did you decide that tomato juice was not enough, that you wanted revenge for your husband in real blood? Revenge for destroying his career? Revenge for the death of his first wife? Did you steal the barbecue fork and then, without your glasses, mistake Marigold for Phyllida as she was looking up at the stars? And murder her? And then murder Mrs Burrage?"

Sir Claude had heard enough. "Objection," he shouted, rising to his feet in a manner reminiscent of his heyday at the Old Bailey.

"Hush, dear," said Lady Liz to her husband. "Don't worry yourself."

She then turned to the Inspector and Mary and spoke. "I was indeed walking around the ship last night in my black bathrobe. I was looking for the drinks machine because I wanted to make Sir Claude a cup of herbal tea. He was suffering from an upset stomach after the Captain's Farewell Dinner. I think the calamari must have disagreed with him. He nearly didn't make it back to the table after the main course. And I didn't have my glasses so I walked right past the coffee station at first."

"Thank you, Lady Liz," the Inspector continued. "It's all right, Sir Claude. Your wife is not our murderer. Marian also saw your wife go back into your cabin holding a cup. And, of course, there really is no way that she could have murdered Mrs Burrage."

With Lady Liz no longer a person of interest, the Inspector returned to identifying the murderer. "We even have someone on board who spent some time in prison after being convicted of stabbing her friend with a barbecue fork." Sarah looked very sheepish as the Inspector directed his gaze at her.

He continued, "Perhaps that's what gave the murderer the idea of using the fork. Or perhaps they were hoping that we might think we had another suspect, someone with form, a person who had used a barbecue fork to attack someone once before?

"No, Mrs Nixon, it wasn't you. No, it's back to you, Martina. You had a motive. Revenge. And you had the means and the opportunity."

41

Day 8 – 6.05 pm to 6.30 pm
Grand Duchess Hotel, Berlin

The next thing the Inspector said came as something of a surprise, except to Mary and Martina. "Right, Mary, would you now like to explain how the police have got it all wrong?"

Mary stood up, took another sip of water, and began.

"We only have one murderer.

"Our murderer always seemed to be one step ahead of the police. By the time they had discovered that Lady Hayter had been poisoned, we were in a different country. We were no longer in Torgau when Barbie's body was found. It was pure chance that Marigold's body was discovered by a fisherman before everyone, including our murderer, had left the ship. And even Mrs Burrage's body was only found as early as it was because Martina had asked the cabin attendants to strip all the beds.

"But when it came to the murder of Mrs Harrow, our murderer made one 'ell of a mistake. Literally."

Mary had been practising that line in her head, off and on, for the last twenty minutes and she didn't think it sounded too corny once she had delivered it.

She picked up a black marker pen from the table in front of her and went over to the whiteboard.

"We can get very lazy when we are faced with lengthy foreign names. We hardly ever look at them letter by letter or syllable by syllable.

"This is how you spell Ivana's surname."

She wrote on the whiteboard:

P A V L Y U C H E L K O V A

"And this is how you spell our Martina's surname," she said as she wrote:

P A V L Y U C H E K L O V A

It took a few seconds but finally the penny dropped for Mary's entire audience.

"I've never had a sister. And I've always loved the Moss Gatherers. I was ever so excited to meet Malo in person," the Hotel Manager enthusiastically announced. The Inspector had already taken her into his confidence and she had enjoyed being a suspect for a while.

Mary continued, "Our murderer obviously thought that Martina was Ivana's sister and this would have given Martina the perfect motive for revenge. Malo had taken the sister she loved from her and she would take the person he loved from Malo.

"But Ivana's sister could never have murdered Marigold in any event."

There were a few puzzled looks.

"Let me explain," said Mary. "When I went on the internet to find out about the Moss Gatherers' concert in Prague, I found the New Musical Express interview we mentioned but I also searched for information about Ivana and her sister. I found an article from a Czech newspaper dated around July 2020. It was obviously in Czech but I recognised some names. I bookmarked the article and I meant to ask Pavel or Tomáš to translate it for me but I never got round to it. Until this morning.

"I really wish I had remembered."

On cue, Tomáš stood up and read out what he had written down on a sheet of paper. "The article," he began, "appeared in Blesk, that's a daily tabloid paper in Prague, on 4th July 2020. This is what it says:

Another tragedy for local family

Martina Pavlyuchelkova, the elder sister of Ivana Pavlyuchelkova, a young girl who was tragically killed at a Moss Gatherers' pop concert in Prague in 2005, was killed in a traffic accident last week, almost to the day of the anniversary of her sister's death.

She was leaving the post office in Dejvice where, apparently, she had just bought a stamp to post a letter to England when a passing lorry lost control and shed its load of large boulders. Martina was crushed to death as the stones rolled over her.

No action is being taken against the lorry driver."

"That's why the threatening letters stopped coming, Mr Harrow," said Mary.

For a few moments, there was complete silence in the room, broken only when Malo began to sob quietly.

"So," Mary continued, "we knew that Martina was not our avenging angel. And when we were driving here earlier today, the Inspector said something which made me realise that our murderer had made another mistake.

"There was one person on board the ship who had been on the red coach and handled the bottle which contained the nicotine which had poisoned Lady Hayter. One person who was in Torgau on the evening of Barbie's death and was also carrying a torch. One person who had access to the barbecue fork. One person who knew about Mrs Nixon's conviction and about Lady Liz's fencing skills. One person who knew that they might find Mrs Harrow or Ms Ballard alone late at night at the stern of the ship. One person who also knew about the Moss Gatherers' last concert and the threatening letters from Ivana's sister.

"One person who, by their own admission, had access to Lucy Burrage's cabin last night. Who didn't mind that their fingerprints would be found on her shore pass. And who didn't know that Martina Pavlyuchelkova was dead. And then gave themself away when they spoke to Inspector Beckenbauer."

Mary faltered. Max was her colleague and she had really enjoyed his company. And he supported Ipswich Town.

"That person is you, Max," the Inspector took over.

Max said nothing.

With Max now formally accused, Mary was ready to go again. "These weren't random murders. You chose each of your victims because there was another person on board, or so you thought, who had a motive, the means and an opportunity to murder them. You had even identified Phyllida and Lady Liz as another possible victim and suspect. I don't even think it mattered to you if Lady Hayter had actually survived so long as Lord Hayter was suspected of attempted murder.

"Lady Hayter was disliked by almost everyone she met but it was obvious that her husband hated her domineering ways. Maybe enough to murder her.

"You had dinner with Professor Blackwell on our first night in Prague and he told me that you had shown great interest in his work as a toxicologist. He remembers telling you that nicotine poisoning was seldom fatal but if someone were also a potential cardiac arrest victim, like Lady Hayter, a large dose could kill you. And give the appearance that the victim had died from a heart attack."

As everyone turned their attention to Professor Blackwell, he nodded his head in confirmation.

"And then you volunteered to buy Lord Hayter's vape juice for me. I thought this was strange because Tomáš had already said he would come with me to the shop to avoid any language problems. You don't speak a word of Czech."

The Inspector came in. "The Czech police have confirmed from the shop's CCTV that you purchased not one, but two, bottles of twenty milligram flavourless vape juice, the same vape juice which the Czech police found in the bottle of water. One for Lord Hayter and one for you."

Then it was back to Mary. "Ion told me that this was the strongest concentration of nicotine that you can buy. All you had to do was add the vape juice to a bottle of CV – we all had bottles in our hotel rooms – and give it to Lady Hayter as you handed out the bottles from the cooler boxes. You would always be able to explain your fingerprints on the bottle. Of course, you probably never expected that the bottle would be found in the first place but it certainly helped to confirm Lord Hayter's guilt when the Czech police found his fingerprints on the bottle as well. Lord Hayter swore that all he had done was pick up the bottle from the floor of the coach after we arrived in Děčín.

"But the police also found your thumbprint on the cap of the bottle. The only other print on the cap was Lady Hayter's. And I now remember that Lady Hayter had not pulled her mask down over her eyes before she took those noisy gulps of water. And belched. As I mentioned before, I gave her something of a disapproving stare after her eructation.

"There is really no way that Lord Hayter could have added any nicotine to the bottle before Lady Hayter had taken those fatal gulps from it.

"And then we have poor Barbie. I told you, while we were waiting to go ashore, that Mike was going to visit the moat, the place where his great-grandfather had been killed during the war. You saw him carrying a heavy torch and realised that another opportunity had come knocking. You made sure that

Barbie was going to look for the bears. You had a word in her ear – literally – and, as the rest of the crew members made their way to the bar, you followed Barbie to the moat and struck her on the back of her head with your torch. Unfortunately for Barbie, Mike had already left the castle and had headed back to the ship. He'd walked back with Mrs Stanhope. He tapped in at 10.21 pm.

"Barbie was probably looking over the parapet at the bears at the time and, with her earphones in and her music at full blast, she would never have heard you approaching her from behind. You took her shore pass before you pushed her body into the moat and I guess you hoped that the bears would make the cause of death more difficult to identify.

"I didn't see you when I got to the bar. No one remembers when you arrived but I think you must have come in while I was in the washroom.

"I spoke to Rishi before I went back to the ship and he told me that none of the other crew members had any intention of going to visit the bears. They had all seen them before but, more importantly, Josh was going to buy the drinks."

"That's right," said Rishi, validating his presence.

"Once you were back on board, you tapped Barbie's shore pass and then returned the blood-stained torch to the storeroom, carefully wiping your fingerprints. I assume that you then threw the pass overboard.

"I asked the Inspector if he could arrange for the other torches to be examined and they found Mike's fingerprints all over one of them. That must have been the torch which he took with him that night."

She paused for breath and took another sip of water.

"We then come to last night. You expected to find Marigold in the rear of the ship having a cigarette at some stage of the evening. But you also created a scenario where Phyllida could be your next victim when you deliberately spilt a glass of water at dinner. You must have palmed Lady Liz's glasses. How else do you explain the fact that the police found them, broken in half, in the waste bin in your cabin this afternoon?

"You held on to the barbecue fork after the lunch on the Sun Deck and then you hid it in your cabin. You were certainly reluctant to let go of it that lunchtime. When you left the Captain's Farewell Dinner during the meal, you must have gone to your cabin to collect the barbecue fork and leave it in the Smoking Lounge. You wrapped it in your black bathrobe as you walked through the ship. You probably didn't think you would be seen as you expected that everyone would be in the Coronation

Restaurant but Mrs Montgomery had forgotten her tablets and had gone back to her cabin. She told the Inspector that she remembered seeing you on the stairs carrying what she thought were some black pool towels and she assumed that you were helping out one of the cabin attendants.

"That's right, Mary," confirmed Mrs Montgomery, "it was just before the desserts were served."

"You then ensured that your stepmother had more to drink than usual and helped her to her cabin. You opened the door with her shore pass and no doubt you held on to it to use later.

"You would have noticed that I was on my way to the Smoking Lounge as you were opening the door for Lucy so you must have stayed in her cabin until I'd headed up to the Sun Deck and then gone to the rear of the ship to wait for Marigold to come for a cigarette. You stabbed her in the back as she was looking up at the stars. Had it been Phyllida coming to gaze at the heavens, then she would have met a similar fate and we could have been looking at Lady Liz as her murderer.

"You tipped her body over the rail of the ship and into the Elbe. Mr Mortimer recalls hearing a splash while he was sitting at the rear of the Sun Deck, drinking Mr Harrow's cognac. But he has no idea when that might have been and he didn't think anything of it at the time. Mr Harrow does not remember hearing anything which is perhaps a blessing in disguise.

Mr Mortimer's grunt suggested that he agreed with what Mary had just said about him.

"You then checked that there was nobody in the corridor and you returned to your stepmother's cabin. You used her shore pass to enter and then you stabbed her in the heart with the barbecue fork as she lay in a wine-enhanced sleep on her bed.

"You placed your stepmother's case in the corridor to provide us with an explanation for why she would have been outside her cabin when Marigold's murder was taking place. You waited with your stepmother's body until you knew that Marian would be in the Portcullis Lounge, you placed a 'Privacy Please' notice on her door and then you went back to your own cabin, leaving her shore pass behind.

"I have little doubt that you were wearing your black bathrobe when you stabbed both women and that at some point in time a blood-soaked bathrobe will be recovered from the Elbe. It's not in your cabin.

"Mr Harrow was convinced that his wife had been murdered by Martina and then you tried to convince us that Martina had then murdered your stepmother.

The Inspector took over. "Well, thanks to Mary, we knew that Martina was not our murderer and, as both Mrs Harrow and Mrs Burrage had been stabbed by the barbecue fork, we also realised that we were looking at just the one murderer. And then, because of your next mistake, we knew that the murderer had to be you.

"When you spoke to Mr Harrow outside the wheelhouse, he told you that his wife's body had been found in the river and that the police suspected that she had been murdered. He thought that she had been knocked unconscious and drowned. He didn't know that she had been stabbed to death with the same barbecue fork which was used to murder your stepmother.

"Only three people on this ship knew at that time that Mrs Harrow had been stabbed before her body was thrown into the river. And only three people knew that she had been murdered in the Smoking Lounge. Myself. And Miss Mead. And the murderer. But when I interviewed you, you tried to persuade me that your stepmother must have been killed because she had seen Martina with the barbecue fork coming in from the stern of the ship when she put her case out in the corridor.

"And how did you know that your stepmother's case was in the corridor unless you put it there yourself?

"You didn't arrive in Reception until after seven this morning. Your stepmother's case had already been collected by Ilie. Maggie saw him taking it when she came on duty at six thirty. And she swears that she hasn't spoken to you all day."

"That's right, sir," Maggie chirped up.

Mary took over the narrative. "You expected that you would have left the ship before Lucy's body was discovered. And that you would be back in England before Marigold's body was recovered from the river. But," in a very passable Scottish accent which left everyone apart from Sir Claude, Lady Liz and Horace Mortimer scratching their heads, Mary continued, "the best-laid schemes o' mice an' man gang aft agley."

"You were confident that you would never be in the frame for any of the murders because you had provided the police with a different suspect with a different motive for each of them.

Max had remained silent up until now but he finally spoke. "Why on earth would I want to murder any of these people? I didn't like Lady Hayter, I admit, but I'm not going to poison her. And Barbie was a good friend. I hardly even knew Mrs Harrow and I'd only just met my mum."

"Has anyone ever read or watched Agatha Christie's A.B.C. Murders?" said Mary by way of an answer.

She continued, "The initial premise in the A.B.C. Murders was that a serial killer was murdering people with alliterative names. The first victim, for example, was Alice Ascher and she was murdered in Andover. Subsequent murders followed in alphabetical order. The real murderer wanted to kill his brother, Carmichael Clarke from Churston, and he disguised this murder as part of the series. He even managed to frame someone for all the murders and that person was very nearly hanged.

"Well, your stepmother was our Carmichael Clarke. All along, you wanted her dead. Once you had persuaded Lucy to join you on the cruise she had sealed her fate. You just needed to hide her death in a killing spree of innocent victims and suspects."

"And why would I want to murder my stepmother?" Max challenged her again.

"Remember," Mary answered (no one did), "what Hercule Poirot said in Death on the Nile when he was asked what the most usual motives for murder were: 'Most frequent—money'.

"We have looked at revenge, we have looked at love and we have looked at hate. But we have completely ignored money.

"Money is something you need desperately and Lucy had in abundance.

"Max, I spoke to Charles Cromwell this morning before he flew to Berlin. He should be arriving at the hotel very shortly so he can confirm what I am saying. Your wife divorced you because you had gambled away all her savings and your house was repossessed. You were supposed to sign up with Gamblers Anonymous."

Inspector Beckenbauer took over the disclosures from Mary. "Earlier today, and yes, it's been a very busy one, I contacted some of my colleagues in England. We needed to check the contents of Mrs Burrage's will and Mary was able to provide details of Mrs Burrage's law firm. Fortunately, her solicitor, a Mr Tulkinghorn, was in the office and he was not with a client. So an officer from the local police force was able to meet with him almost immediately and he was shown Mrs Burrage's will."

Max interrupted again. "You don't really think my stepmother was going to leave me any money in her will, do you? Why would she? She didn't even know I existed until a few months ago. And I can assure you that she never showed me her will or said anything to me about what was in it."

"She didn't, but your flatmate in Ipswich did," said the Inspector.

Then it was back to Mary. "Your flatmate Eddie services photocopying machines. Earlier this year, he was fixing a paper jam at your stepmother's lawyers, the very morning that she came in to make her will. Mr Tulkinghorn needed two witnesses. Ellie Burrage, who works at the firm, and is also your stepmother's niece, was a beneficiary under the will so she couldn't be a witness.

"Mr Tulkinghorn's secretary signed as one witness and, as there was no one else in the office at the time apart from Ellie, Mr Tulkinghorn asked Eddie to be the other one. He remembers that he then asked Eddie to take some copies of the signed will to demonstrate that the copier was working properly again.

"Apart from a small legacy for Ellie and all her jewellery, which she also left to her niece, your stepmother's entire estate, over six million pounds, goes to you, Max. As you well know.

"The police officer saw that there was a note attached to your stepmother's file which listed your current address next to your name, presumably to enable Lucy's executors to get in touch with you.

Remember that Mr Tulkinghorn had employed a private detective to locate you after Lucy had married your father. The officer was very surprised, and observant enough, to note that this was the same address as Eddie had provided when he witnessed the will.

"The officer obtained the phone number of Eddie's employers from Mr Tulkinghorn and they provided him with Eddie's mobile number."

The Inspector took over again. "I spoke to the officer about an hour or so ago. He told me that, when he called him, Eddie quite happily volunteered that he had seen your name when he was copying the will, so he made an extra copy and showed it to you that very same evening, before you headed off to the football. He seemed to think that he had only done what any mate would do for another mate. He certainly didn't believe he'd done anything wrong.

"You have known for some months that you would be inheriting a fortune. Your only concern must have been that your stepmother might change her mind if she ever found out about your gambling. You needed the money and you needed it now. You certainly couldn't risk her changing her mind."

Mary continued, "I know that you have been betting continuously on the World Cup and, from what you have told me, the results so far haven't really been going your way. Certainly not with Argentina losing."

"The police in Ipswich have also been very busy," the Inspector came in again, "and they spoke to your bank. You have gone over your overdraft limit and your credit cards are maxed out.

"Eddie says that you even owe your flatmates for your share of an Ipswich Town season ticket!"

And for a fan of the Tractor Boys like Mary, that was unforgivable.

42

Day 8 – Evening/Day 9 – Morning
Berlin

Max Hunt was arrested and taken away by the German police in handcuffs. His parting words describing Mary are unprintable. Some of his expletives, however, were directed towards the Argentinian football team and, indeed, Betcha.

Mary started to cry but Tomáš and Pavel both gave her a comforting hug.

Once he had seen that she had managed to compose herself, Inspector Beckenbauer came over to Mary and thanked her for all her asistance. He couldn't help himself and he also gave her a hug. He just hoped that none of his officers had noticed.

A further eighty-six guests had arrived the previous afternoon at Berlin Brandenburg Airport from various United Kingdom and other European airports. They had been met by Hansel and Gretel, two of Sovereign River Cruises' part-time employees in Berlin.

The Berlin city tour that morning for the newly-arrived guests included the Brandenburg Gate, the Holocaust Memorial, Checkpoint Charlie and the East Side Gallery, adorned with the works of more than one hundred artists and with the graffito of Leonid Brezhnev and Erich Honecker kissing one another proving the usual selfie magnet. They were also driven along Unter den Linden and past Berliner Dom and Alexanderplatz. An identical tour for the surviving Prague-to-Berlin guests was scheduled for the next morning.

Most of the newly-arrived guests ventured out on their own in the afternoon, although they were certainly curious to see all the police activity at the hotel and took every opportunity to speak to the Prague-to-Berlin guests as soon as they were set free by the *Polizei*. Museum Island, and in particular, the temporary exhibition by the Pergamonmuseum, comprised of masterpieces from Pergamon and an amazing 360-degree panorama of the ancient city created by Yadegar Asisi, proved a very popular destination.

And, from seven thirty, the Berlin-to-Prague guests were enjoying a drinks reception and buffet as

Mary introduced herself, and Pavel and Tomáš, to the new arrivals. And answered or avoided questions about the cruise which had just ended.

Mary was down in the hotel reception early the next morning, hoping to see as many as possible of her departing guests before they went off on their tour of Berlin and she left for Wittenberg and the Baron von Habsburg with her new arrivals. She managed to get one of the receptionists to lend her a whiteboard and wrote down the scores:

USA 0 Greece 6

Rwanda 2 Saudi Arabia 2

Brazil 0 Australia 0

Tunisia 5 Scotland 0

Malo was the first guest she saw. He came and thanked her for helping to find Marigold's murderer. Phyllida was still with him.

Bill and Sarah both told Mary that they'd had a wonderful holiday. Bill had abandoned his MAGA baseball cap and there were no signs of any communist revolutionaries on Sarah's T-shirt, just Dan.

The Billericay Dickies, as cheerful as ever, scolded her. "We told you, no more murders, Mary. Heaven knows what our insurance will cost next year when we travel with you."

The Porterhouse Octet said to her that they had enjoyed the cruise so much that they had already decided not to wait five more years and were now planning another cruise for 2027. They thought they might try the Rhône.

Sir Claude and Lady Liz came to wish her all the best. Lady Liz's glasses were held together with Sellotape.

There was no sign of Horace – he had apparently booked himself on a flight later that morning back to Heathrow.

She saw Mr and Mrs Triste talking to a tall, blonde, well-dressed man in his early forties and she assumed that this must be their daughter's fiancé. Mary realised that she had not really been emotionally involved with the deaths of any of her guests. She had, of course, been concerned about her mounting death toll from the perspective of being the responsible Cruise Director and Barbie's murder had certainly affected her. But now she could not help but feel empathetic towards the Tristes, who had come on the cruise to celebrate their daughter's life, only to be confronted with a further four murders.

Mrs Stanhope gave her a squeeze and a kiss. She still thought that it might have been more appropriate for Sovereign to have cancelled the cruise after Barbie's murder, the more as so as Max would not then have had the opportunity to murder Marigold and her new friend Lucy. But she was pleased for Mary and she accepted that most of Mary's guests had nonetheless enjoyed wonderful holidays.

Charles arranged for the repatriation of Marigold's and Lucy's bodies. Lady Hayter's body was already back in Bedchester and Barbie was on the way to Malta.

The coaches for Wittenberg arrived and she watched as the hotel staff loaded the cooler boxes. Perhaps *Vorsprung durch Technik* also applied to the manufacture of plastic bottles in Germany because the tops came off the bottles of Saxonia water with ease, but they remained attached to the mother ship and the water remained in the bottle.

Ten days later, Mary was back at Václav Havel Airport awaiting the arrival of EA2217. Two young girls came and sat next to her. They told her that they were from Prague and were going on holiday with their parents to London. One of them was holding a bottle of CV water and was struggling to remove the cap. Her twisting eventually caused the plastic to crack in the neck of the bottle and it started to leak.

"*Strč prst skrz krk*," she suggested.

43

And then
Germany/England/Florida

Sovereign River Cruises, in particular, but the European river cruising industry in general, were extremely concerned about the negative reaction that the four murders might have on their business. Newspaper and television coverage of the events of the previous few days ensured that there were very few members of the cruise companies' target demographic who would not now have become aware of the perils of river cruising.

They expected cancellations and budgeted for a significant fall in passenger numbers (or guests) for the 2027 season. Nothing could have been further from the actuality. The chance to rub shoulders with aging rockers, mob lawyers and mass murderers provided surprisingly alluring and companies reported record bookings.

There were repeats of Death on the Nile on television with Poirot played by Peter Ustinov, David Suchet and Kenneth Branagh respectively.

Death on the Douro by Julia Nevin made it to the lower echelons of Amazon's best-sellers list.

In due course, Max was sentenced to twenty years to life in a German prison with the prospect, rather like an unfortunate Monopoly player drawing the Chance Card which read 'Go Directly to Jail. Do Not Pass Go. Do Not Collect $200', of heading straight to prison in Czechia for the murder of Lady Hayter after his release from Teutonic incarceration.

Mary became known in Manchester, behind her back, as the Grim Reaper. But she had a very successful half-season on the Elbe. Every tour was fully booked and Kemi turned out to be excellent at sorting out dirty laundry and smoothing things over.

Sir Claude instructed his lawyers to sue Horace Mortimer KC for trespass to property but their German correspondents queried whether the porcelain elephant actually belonged to Sir Claude, as he hadn't paid for it before it disintegrated. So Meissen sued him instead on the basis of his promise, witnessed by almost one-third of the tour group, to pay for the shattered elephant.

Horace himself continued with his very successful practice of representing South London's criminal lowlife but he now regularly resorts to the services of GlamorGirlsrUs for company outside of court hours.

Phyllida moved to a new set of Chambers in the Inner Temple and became, in short order, a King's Counsel, Mrs Harrow and the mother of Bona (in the dative).

Within six weeks after the end of the cruise, Mephistopheles had reached number one in the album charts. And Malo was invited to make featured appearances on recordings by artists such as Taylor Swift, Beyoncé and Eminem. At the end of the year, he appeared on Jools Holland's Hootenanny.

Ellie was admitted to Porterhouse College, Cambridge to read law with the promise of a partnership at Tulkinghorn and Tangle once she had qualified. And, with Max barred from benefitting under her will, Ellie had inherited all of Auntie Lucy's millions as well as her jewellery. She was certainly one of the ten wealthiest undergraduates in her matriculation year. A strong endorsement of her application to the college from Professor Clare Downing certainly helped in the absence of three or four A*s.

Bill and Hill divorced. Bill resigned from FUCKU and cashed in all his shares and stock options. It turned out that Donald and Sarah had never actually married. Donald became a ski instructor in the winter and taught yoga during the summer. Both Bill and Sarah moved to Miami. Bill bought a sports bar and moved into the flat above the bar where he is now living with the bar's co-owner and head barperson, Ms Sarah King.

Mr Eagle and Mrs Eagle converted to Protestantism and, in due course, the Reverend Edward Eagle was ordained in Coventry Cathedral.

Lord Hayter was appointed as the Chairman of a public inquiry into the need for public enquiries.

Jane presented, with some reservations, the details of the deaths on the Elbe to the TV Murder Club. Cassandra had Max bang to rights. It was also agreed that, if she would be interested, Mary should be elected as an honorary member of the club.

Mary, however, had other things to think about, including a romantic involvement with Bennie. But when she was appointed as Cruise Director on the MV Sun King for the 2027 'Remarkable Rhône and Lyon' cruising season, she left Bennie behind on the Baron von Habsburg. As Mary said to him at the time, "Breaking up is never easy, I know, but I have to go."

THE END.

Acknowledgements

My heartfelt thanks go to everyone at Woodbridge Publishers, particularly Samuel, Sofie and Kelly, for their tireless efforts in bringing Mary Mead back to life and into print once again.

I'm also grateful to the many authors and their unforgettable creations, as well as to the politicians, musicians, sports personalities and celebrities who have, knowingly or not, inspired my characters or lent their names to them.

And, of course, thanks to my long-suffering wife and our wonderful daughter.

About the Author

Kevin Julian is a retired commercial lawyer. He has a Master's degree in Law from Downing College, Cambridge and a Master's degree in Classical Studies from the Open University. When not travelling, he watches and reads murder mysteries, tries to solve cryptic crossword puzzles and struggles to get his golf handicap down.

Printed in Dunstable, United Kingdom

68766218R00208